Lord of Dust

Erme Lander

Cover image – Panagiotis Lampridis

ISBN 978-1-9997453-8-7

Table of Contents

Preface

The seam popped apart like a joint dislocating, ripping with a silent meatiness. Refusing to allow her disgust to stop her, she forced her terror down and peeled her fingers away to push further in. It gave suddenly and enveloped her, enclosing her body in a viscous rubber, leaving her unable to grasp anything. She flailed in desperation, held tight in the greyness.

She shouldn't be able to do this, she hadn't believed him despite what he'd said. He was asleep in the room behind her, unaware she was pinned here, a world away from her cellar. She'd had to know she could do this on her own, she couldn't allow herself to fail even if his eyes didn't see. He was a nob and a weakling, unable to survive on his own without falling over his own feet. She was strong and quick, nothing could beat her and get away with it. Held in place, she forced her way forwards, muscles twitching impotently. The nothing enclosing her didn't want to give, didn't want to let her move. She gritted her teeth and fought it, snarling in terror.

Blindly she struggled, her world contained into a skin's thickness. The call of the place she wanted to go to was a wispy summoning, the memory of a scent on a breeze. Black spots swam in front of her eyes as she struggled. She had no way of sucking in a breath, no way of even opening her mouth. She imagined opening it and having the nothing pour into her. Filling her in the same way panic filled her now. A shell of skin suspended in the void, forever screaming. She was going to die, held in the grey nothing, never to be found.

A lightening of the pressure brushed a finger and she fought to turn, reaching out towards it. The way out was a tantalising feather's touch away. There was a way through – the knowledge taunted her – she'd come this way before. His arm around her waist, the comfort of another human in this hell and afterwards his intellect making sense of a place that defied any meaning. He'd called it a void, a way of moving between their worlds. The light in his eyes and excitement in his voice catching something inside her, despite her dismissive snort. Another twist and she had two fingers loose with warm air around them. The tight grip peeled away from her hand, her wrist…

Two hands free and she grasped the edges of the exit, pulling herself towards it, wriggling through the channel. The void didn't want to give her up and she struggled to free her body, dizziness hitting as she used up her last few resources. A shoulder through and a vicious triumph filled her.

Her head was struck by sunlight. She squinted, unused to the brightness and gasped at the fresh air streaming down her throat to gurgle through the years of muck in her lungs. A rustle of leaves assaulted her ears. The seam narrowed as she pulled herself through, the convulsions now thrusting her in the direction she wanted to go. The drag on her legs ceased as the rift spat her out as though wanting nothing further to do with her and she was hit by an exhaustion that sent her staggering into the slope.

Chapter 1

Saw the counsellor today. Complete waste of time. Thank goodness no one knows I booked these appointments.

She sits, curled up on the comfy chair beside mine and looks at me. There's not much on the table beside her – a box of tissues, a few bits of paper and pens. Some nice pictures on the walls, an attempt at making the place feel homely when the atmosphere is stiff. I study the landscape picture behind her, it's got open water in the foreground and mountains beyond. I try to work out where it's been painted, the Lake District maybe?

"Daniel." I jump and look at her. "You've come to talk to me. What would you like to talk about?"

I'm paying her to listen. I can't quite believe I'm in this situation, I am actually paying someone to be sympathetic to me. I open my mouth and nothing comes out. The feeling of not being quite part of this world sounds too strange, of feeling like an observer to everyone. She'd probably have an official name for it. One I'd get locked up for. I'm not nuts, just don't feel connected to anything. I'd had the idea I could talk about it. She'd nod, smile and tell me it was normal, that everyone had these feelings and I'd grow out of it.

She smiles encouragingly and waits. My mind goes blank. What do I say? All my thoughts become too big, I can't get them past the blockage in my throat.

There's a white clock on the wall, one of those cheap plastic ones. No tick, nothing to disturb the silence. No sound of cars or the outside world penetrating the room. The silence here is stifling. It presses down, forcing me into a corner.

The pressure builds, why am I here? The words whirl around my brain, shredding into tissues. All those things I'd wanted to say. I'm paying her to listen to me, finally I have the permission to say them. I'd constructed it all in clever well thought out sentences, to show that I'm not strange, not weird. Gone. Nothing left but an empty mouth as silent and cheap as the clock on the wall.

"Shall we start with something easy, if you're having problems deciding?" She smiles again. I nod, mute. "What hobbies do you have?" She wants to know about my hobbies. Inwardly I groan, I can't believe I'm paying to have this conversation.

"Um, I have a dog." I sound stupid.

The stilted conversation continues for the required forty minutes. Her asking questions, me giving short replies. I don't even mention the new receptionist when she asks if I have a girlfriend or if there's anyone I like. It's not working. My anger at the situation is a knot inside me. Unable to unpick or release it, it stays and tightens. I've paid her for the three recommended sessions in advance. The anger tightens further, I can't do this. She looks sympathetic as we come to a close and suggests that I think about a subject to talk about next time. She says it's not easy to open up. Maybe I could write something down over the next week, some people find it easier to write than talk. I nod and leave.

In the car, I stare at people walking past. It gives me no space to relax and to be myself. I let my head sink into my hands resting on the steering wheel and jerk it up again at the thought of being seen.

I'm not going back to work, I'd timed the appointment to end roughly when work should finish and had taken the afternoon off. Clive had poked me verbally about wanting time off, I'd shrugged it off as a doctor's appointment. I decide I'm not going back for another session and refuse to think about the money I'll lose. I cringe at the thought of ringing up and saying I'm a failure at counselling. Closing my eyes, I shut out the world in a less obvious way, take a few deep breaths to control myself and drive off.

The anger builds again at the memory of bumping into Clive on the way out of work. He'd been leaning against the receptionist's desk, chatting up the new temp. I'd thought she was pretty, sympathetic even when I'd first met her. Not now. My anger burns hotter. She'd grinned at him, barely noticing me as I'd signed out. Clive had made a comment in my direction and she'd laughed. I'd walked out feeling the back of my neck going red. The laughter had continued all the way to the door, all fifteen feet of it. I'd walked straight-backed, trying not to notice. I force the feelings down and concentrate on the road.

I count the number of cars not indicating, the numbers not looking as they pull out of junctions, pushing into queues. The impatient masses trying to get home at the same time as me. Let one person out politely and another shoves his nose in. I force a smile at the people not seeing my car at roundabouts and pulling out in front of me. How can people miss a bright red car? I rub my head as I stop in traffic and wave a pedestrian to continue crossing in front of me. A comedian talks frantically on the radio as I turn it on, matching the chaos in the roads.

"There were one too many in the queue for the aeroplane. We all knew who would be the one left sitting on the toilet during take-off..." I switch off. The one left sitting on the toilet, yep that's me, the one too polite to protest. Clive at work now, a year younger, less qualified, cheeky and assertive. He'd get that last seat, smooching his way up to the air hostess. My eyes smart and I rub my face with the back of my hand.

My mind runs back to the previous afternoon when I'd been asked to help downstairs in the morgue. Despite my initial reservations, it was interesting, far more so than the work I'd been paid to do in the office. My mood plummets further, something's definitely wrong with you when you find it more appealing to work with the dead than the living. The soft stream of conversation and the questions with no expectation of a reply. The gentle humour used, made it more like dealing with babies than dead people.

I leave the chaos behind as I turn off the main road to drive down green lanes. High hedges take the place of the busy roads and grey buildings. I open the window to let some fresh air in and the sound of birdsong follows. It's spring, a warm day with a chill still in the air. Not quite warm enough to take a jumper off, but close. I take a deep breath, I'm nearly back.

A clash of gears through the open window alerts me to the final terror before home and I slow in anticipation. A flash in the gap in the hedgerow ahead and a car careers around the corner and squeals to a stop in the middle of the single track lane at the sight of me. The driver flaps her inability to reverse, her face peering over the half-moon of the steering wheel. Mrs Pickles, far too old to be driving in my opinion, she must be at least eighty and has never backed up for anyone. In fact, there's a story going round that once she simply abandoned her car and walked back to her cottage to put the kettle on when the other driver refused.

She also drives far too fast on these roads, she's an accident waiting to happen but no one seems to dare tell her. I sigh and reverse down the lane to the passing place. She inches forwards, pushing her way through. She gives me a cheery wave and a hello as she passes. I smile and wave back through gritted teeth.

I pull into our drive and tuck the car into the hedge, leaving space for everyone else when they arrive tomorrow. Biggles is bouncing against the gate, overexcited and with a silly grin on his fat spaniel face. Here, outside in the spring with a daft dog desperate to greet me, I can finally let go of the afternoon and relax.

I tap on the kitchen window as I pass, wave to Mum and walk through the orchard, Biggles leaping beside me. Buds are forming on the apple trees shading the shed down at the bottom where I've been living since I returned from university, desperate to pay off my debts. Well, I say shed, it's more like a wooden office, several rooms and the shower room Dad and I fitted last summer.

I walk into the room and stop. Biggles shoves at my legs, trying to get past, excited by the smell I've noticed. That fucking cat again. I search the room, staring into the dark corners trying to see it. Biggles' nose pushes frantically against the back of my knees.

Finally I spot it on the stool next to my computer. Black shiny plastic covers the seat and a large elegantly deposited turd on the top.

Swearing, I push Biggles out of the way so I can get in properly and shut the door on him. Mum must have been in here and left the window open. I peer through the room, eventually spotting the cat in the shadows at the top of my bookcase, curled up in a tight ball. Its nose is tucked into its tail, its eyes slitted and it watches me with a malicious intent. Biggles thumps against the door, not understanding, I can barely breathe in here. One turd on a cool spring day…

Choking, I open the rest of the windows and grab the packet of wet wipes kept especially for these occasions. It'll take ages for the smell to disappear. Leaving the door open for Biggles to galumph in, I dump my stool outside and wipe it off.

The cat looks smugly at me on my return. I can't get it out without getting scratched and the books'll get wet if I throw water at it. The breeze helps the smell disperse. Biggles gazes at the cat with a hopeless passion and the cat stares back, its malevolent intentions equally clear.

At dinner I complain about the cat to my parents. It's still in there, trapped by Biggles it can't do anything else. My complaints fall on deaf ears as do the ones about the shed being my personal space. I want a flat or house of my own, but I can't afford to rent. The prices around here are abysmal. Same goes for buying a house. I have to live here, I can't save up if I'm spending out on rent. Sometimes though, the thought of not having a landlady who is your mother going through your rooms looking for dirty washing appeals. I managed at university, finding the cheapest ways to get through by not going out, by trying to work and study at the same time. My sisters had it easy, being ten years older they didn't have to pay tuition fees. They had proper student loans and racked up debts having a good time. House prices were lower then too.

I go back to the shed and find the smell's nearly gone. The coolness of early evening is starting to chill as I shut the windows. I look for the cat. It yawns at me, showing its pink mouth and sharp white teeth. You're fish bait I think savagely, you don't look so different from the rabbit Mum cooks. Just wait, one skinned cat. I let my imagination run wild, stewed cat and the horror of it being served for dinner…

I hear Mum calling, rattling the tin of cat food. I get Biggles to sit with the bribe of a biscuit. His fickle adoration is instantly transferred. The cat lazily stretches and jumps down, sauntering out with its tail waving. I kick the door shut in relief and allow Biggles his biscuit.

Stretching my legs before bedtime, I walk through the woods on the hill above our house. Biggles bounds in front, every so often stopping to gaze back at me with a spaniel smile. I can hear people shouting and laughing in the spring evening. A movement catches my eye in the deep shadows. Yards away, a girl is watching me. She looks about fifteen years old. Her family must be somewhere close by, there's loads of paths around here and it's a popular walking area.

She's leaning against the tree to one side of the path as though she doesn't want to be seen. She looks like she's trying not to laugh. I surreptitiously check myself to make sure everything's in place. Good grief, I'm even feeling paranoid around complete strangers, it must be a trick of the light. I decide to act normally. I wave and turn to join the path leading down the hill. Biggles barrels into me and I stumble, feeling rather than hearing a ripping sound. Flushing, I look back. She's gone.

Chapter 2

The next day I come back from Biggles' late afternoon walk to find the house crowded. Dominic is sitting on the floor, trying to play with his toy train and getting upset when the tracks get kicked. My mum and two sisters are shouting between rooms, talking about children. My older sister is breastfeeding her youngest. Dad is sitting in the corner, trying to stay out the way and mumbling comments about the conversation that everyone ignores. Biggles bounces in to everyone's dismay and I get shouted at to remove him. I drag Biggles out to his bewilderment, his spaniel face not understanding the disgrace.

Dominic bellows at his track being kicked again. Poor kid, he's only four, all big eyes and snotty nose. Samantha swoops down and wipes it, cradling the baby in her other arm. I hunker down to chat to Dominic and he screws his face up as I knock the tracks out of line. The younger of my two sisters mutters about it being in the wrong place, with a look to suggest it's my problem.

I grin at him, "Come on, let's go to my shed. We can make a really good layout there." He considers me with a serious look then nods. I scoop up the track, he grabs his precious train and we escape to the quiet of my shed.

"Want to help me change the lock on my door?"

He follows me to the garage and helps with sorting out screwdrivers to carry back. I show him the new lock I've bought, chat to him about manly things like keeping your mother out of your room when you're a big boy and give him the old lock. He plays with the key and wipes grease over his jeans.

We sprawl out on the floor. He chats quietly away in his own world, happy to have an adult paying attention. We make bridges, level crossings, cows die in droves and the trains are always on time to pick people up. An order in the chaos of reality. A four year olds idea of the adult world. Nothing can go wrong that can't be fixed between the Railway Controller and Uncle Dan. I feel grown up and in control of life.

An hour goes by and he needs a wee. I'd rather not go back into the house and get shouted at, my head twinges with the memory of the stress from yesterday. Dominic's face screws up as I suggest going in the orchard. He's been too well trained by my sister. Mustn't wee outside, it's not nice. I tell him I do it all the time and his eyes grow wider at the thought of an adult weeing outside. I send him out towards the hedge, giving him the chance to be a big boy on his own. I peer through the window after a few minutes and see him looking back at me, confused.

I go out and find he's not been taught to wee standing up. I can't believe it, I know he doesn't live with his Dad but this is ridiculous. I decide it's something I have to teach him. I take him closer to the hedge, talk him through what to do. He's still looking sceptical but Uncle Dan's an adult, so he must know best. A shadow flits over me, a cloud passing the sun. I blink to squint through the light breeze.

"Daniel?"

A girl's voice, there's an edge of fear to it that catches me. It's not one of my sisters, it's from the footpath beyond the hedge and the accent isn't local. I stretch up to look, forgetting Dominic standing beside me. A wetness splatters against my leg and a sharp smell rises. I look down to see Dominic failing at weeing in the hedge. I suppress a swear word at his small face twisting. He knows it's not good. I didn't check the breeze. His trousers are far wetter than the drops on mine.

I sigh, "Come on, let's take them off."

"Mummy's not going to be happy."

I look at his clean shiny face, pressed shirt and damp trousers. This isn't fair on him. He's got to be allowed to get grubby at some point. "I'll sort your trousers out, we'll put them on my heater to dry. Maybe we can dry them before Mummy finds out."

His small hand takes mine with the reassuring comment of, "Mummy finds out everything."

I wrap him in a towel and he settles down again to play with his train set. I dab at the dampness and try to scrub the grease stains out for good measure, setting them close to the heater to dry. The smell coming from them is not good, I hope it'll be better once they've dried.

Wondering who it had been calling my name, I mutter something to Dominic and slide out of the shed to casually walk down the orchard. Neighbourhood watch and all that, there were problems a few months ago with someone breaking into sheds. Mrs Pickles had wanted to organise a vigilante group to walk the lanes. She's a regular one woman army, everyone's terrified of her. I stretch my neck as I walk, trying to peer over the hedge without being seen. A tugging inside pulls briefly and I sway to take a step closer to see a man's figure in the shadow, close to the end of the footpath. I can just see the outline in the deep shade, something about it makes me shiver.

"Daniel!" An indignant yell comes from the shed. I close my eyes, my sister's discovered her son and his jeans. I turn back to see Samantha has Dominic by the hand and is dragging him towards the house. His face is set into a determination not to cry. "Why couldn't you bring him into the house, I can't believe he wouldn't have told you."

I raise my hands to start explaining that I'd been distracted while teaching him something important and stop. My sister's monologue hasn't stopped. Dominic meets my gaze and his face changes into a world-weary air far beyond his years and goes with her, content to be scolded and thrust into the busy kitchen.

I stand alone in the trees and watch Biggles chewing a large stick. I'm left with the feeling of being dislocated from real life stronger than ever. A lump rises in my throat and lodges. This can't be right, maybe normality will hit at some point and I'll get it right for a change. Biggles notices me and brings the stick in the vain hope I'll throw it for him. I ignore him and go to look over the hedge at the footpath. No one to be seen, whoever it was, they've gone.

Mum calls from the window, dinner is ready. I breathe through the lump, trying to disperse it, scrub my face and go inside. Samantha's voice rises in the clatter of the kitchen, telling Dominic to sit still. He's got a clean pair of jeans on and is waiting for his food. Dinner is a continuation of the noise, the baby managing to sleep through in its carry cot to the side.

Sarah, the younger of my two sisters, finds Dominic's adventure hilarious. She leans towards

Dominic, "I remember when your Uncle Daniel did the same thing as you – only he was ten!"

Sarah's face is a mirror of the cat's yesterday. The turd deposited on the stool with smug satisfaction. I remember her laughing at me as I came back into the caravan. She was a lordly nineteen year old, on holiday with us as a break from university. She'd had so many tall boys around her, hanging onto every sharp comment she'd made and glancing with irritation at me hanging around.

The lump rises sharply. I'd needed a wee that evening and rather than walk me to the toilets, someone had suggested the hedge. I hadn't realised the wind had been blowing in the wrong direction. I'd stayed out in the dark for ages, not knowing what to do until Dad had come to find me. Dominic's face is a picture, he doesn't know where to look. Poor kid, only four and already he knows what embarrassment is.

"Got a girlfriend yet?" Sarah again. I grit my teeth, knowing she'll jump at any opportunity to wind me up.

"Leave him alone. He's got plenty of time." Mum glances at me fondly and looks as though she wants to adjust my collar. I shift away. I'm the afterthought of the family or maybe simply the mistake. The baby that happened by accident after the other two were nearly grown. My parents were settling into a quiet middle age when I came along and disrupted it.

The meal carries on at a snail pace with its dissection of family life. Once a month the family descends on us. I'd go out for a meal to the local pub if it wouldn't upset Mum. I allow myself to drift off, imagining the sun, the birds singing in the pub garden and the sour smell of beer.

"How're the stiffs?"

I bite back the comment I want to make, knowing Sarah always manages to outsmart me in any verbal fencing. She finds it hilarious that I work in an undertakers. Jokes about stiffs have been coming thick and fast ever since. The fact that I actually work in the office is beside the point, although I did get an induction into the morgue for the first week.

I must admit, it was fascinating, I wouldn't mind doing more on that side of the business although I'm not sure about children or murders. I think with a longing that dead people are easier than their living relatives. They're cold and quiet, don't talk much do dead people. Having had the extra time there the other day when they were short of staff was nearly enough to make me ask to swap jobs. Still, my degree is in figures on paper, not figures in coffins and at some point I'll make enough to pay for my own place, at which point I'll be the one laughing.

Dessert happens at a desolate pace and the slow clearing of plates afterwards. I manage not to attract any more comments. Samantha gathers up the baby, reaches up to kiss me goodbye and tells me not to mind Sarah. Dominic is looking tired. I carry him to the car and he nestles into my arms, clutching his train. I get a sticky kiss as I buckle him in and I tousle his hair, telling him we'll do more together next time. He sticks his thumb in his mouth and nods with the vacant stare of a child about to fall asleep.

Sarah leaves with her usual sharp remarks and a blast of car fumes. I stifle the urge to mutter something rude at her back. I spend the rest of the day in the usual black mood, thinking up all the retorts I could have said. None of them are ever good enough. I always see Sarah's smirk and imagine her replies shooting back.

Later that evening I go back to the end of the orchard, just a wander down to check everything is fine. Biggles whines next to me, a wistful note as he gazes at the footpath. I peer around the hedge, trying to look casual. No one to be seen, he's probably heard a bird or a cat. The sun is coming down in a glorious sheet of orange sky, pink streaking in the clouds and the deep indigo of night behind.

A pile of something is on the tarmac, it's like someone has emptied a pile of wood ash over the path, completely out of place. I mutter a swear word under my breath, some people will dump anything given a chance. I'd better make sure nothing else has been left otherwise Mrs Pickles will be up in arms again – the footpath runs along the back of her cottage as well.

I hook myself over the hedge by scrambling onto the fence and jumping, nearly falling flat on my face in the process. I stumble, managing to catch myself and hope no one's watching. I stand upright with the familiar burn threatening the back of my neck and nearly walk into the pile of dust. This close I can see it's practically enough to fill a wheelbarrow and is spread out across the tarmac. The nettles that grow in the ditch next to the path have been broken as though someone's fallen in and splattered green sludge everywhere. I nudge the pile with my foot and a fine powder puffs up. I have an instinctive revulsion for it, as strong as the compulsion had been to investigate.

A movement flickers at the edge of my vision. A girl is on the footpath, she's close to the end, near the road that passes on the other side of our property. Her shadow falls over me, the only way I'd have seen her. She is a silhouette against the setting sun, she sees me notice her and freezes.

"Hello?" The sound of my greeting makes her jump and she charges towards me. I automatically step back, out of her way but she still pushes past. My eyes burn from looking into the light and I stagger into the fence, feeling the sting of nettles on the hand I fling out.

"Hey!" My childish exclamation of pain brings the stress of the day back into sharp focus. This wasn't right, no one should do this without reason.

No reply. I blink hard from the dazzle, all I see is the flash of her eyes, wide with fear as she passes. Spots in my vision stop me seeing much. The girl flinches from the cows leaning over the fence and skitters off in a way that makes her look as though she's unused to the surroundings. Not from round here, I bet she dumped that ash over the path.

"Stop!" My shout is ignored. I'm not having this, she can't mess up the footpath and then push people out of the way. What it had been Mrs Pickles? I imagine the wailing of a supine old lady and I give chase without a further thought, I'm going to make her clear up and apologise. I'm going to do something right for once.

Despite her stumbling panic, she is faster. I make a heroic effort, lungs burning and shoot past the corner, feeling rather than hearing the wet ripping sound. My eyes have partly cleared as brakes on, I spin and see her disappearing. The sight stops me in my tracks.

She's halfway through a grey seam. It's hanging in the middle of the air, not connected to anything. It twists the eye, preventing me from focussing on it. Her jeans hang off her skinny backside and her head's missing, like she's stuck it round an invisible corner. I blink and see an elbow hauled through as though sticking to the sides.

Bloody minded and with my lungs gasping from the run, I reach out to grasp the greyness and find my fingers slide straight through it. I pinch them together, not believing what I see. A foot lashes out and thumps me solidly in the stomach. I double up, winded and with eyes watering, see her knee begin to disappear.

The frustration of the family dinner boils through and not thinking, I grab at the girl's waist as she pulls herself further in and nearly shout my disgust at the feel of rubber around my arm. I slide my other arm in and wrap it around her middle. I'm going to pull her out and make her apologise. It becomes a fight of itself, my anger at my family not taking me seriously, the problems at work, of feeling like an outsider, even the superiority of that bloody cat. Everything. Completely irrational.

Rubbery and thick, the seam manages to feel damp without making my skin wet. I feel an instinctive revulsion, wanting to wipe my hands clean. It gives slightly and I jam myself into it, pushing and trying to lever her out. The edge thickens around my arms and I begin to gasp, it's trying to close with me in it. My struggle reverses and I try to get out, this shouldn't be happening. The girl slides further in, dragging me with her. I find I can't unpeel my fingers. A ripple and my feet lift off the ground as it encases me completely and snaps shut like a vice.

A greyness inside, I can't see anything, including the girl I'm holding. She slides through my fingertips, wriggling away and I lunge forwards or try to. A small part of my mind begins to question what I'm doing. This isn't anything natural. What the hell am I doing? I try to draw a breath and find I can't even do that. Terror begins to fill me as I flail, pinned in the void. My lungs are burning, lights flash in front of my eyes. I'm going to die. Nobody's going to know where I went. That pile of dust, that must have been the last poor sod to try and get through, regurgitated onto the path as a pile of ash.

The anger boils up, that girl got through, I can too. I want to know where she came from. I feel a seam at my fingertips, I wriggle my fingers into it, pulling it apart. I shove my hand through further and my fingers brush cool air. Everything turns black and white, inverts and my stomach tries to follow. A smell hits me as my feet touch the ground, it's indescribable. Open sewer, damp and mould, my gorge rises. My stomach is still protesting from being kicked and I wonder vaguely if I'll lose my dinner. It's dark. I can't see much – apart from a few spots jarringly bright against the black and I'm not sure if they are the remnants of the sun blindness. I stagger against a wall, retching and try to catch my breath.

A hand grabs me and I start to explain that I'm alright, that there's nothing to worry about when it slams me backwards. The shock jars through the sickness and my eyes finally focus. The distant lights outline a face seamed with dirt, pushing itself into mine. Breath stinking, crusted eyes gleam with a feral intelligence. I struggle to loosen his grip on my neck and my life narrows down to seconds. Unable to breathe, I frantically elbow him, trying to raise my leg to stamp, to kick him somewhere painful. I catch something soft with my knee, he grunts and his grip loosens. I gasp my relief, thinking I'm winning until I see the flash of metal.

He's got a knife.

Chapter 3

I catch the upraised arm, barely keeping it away from me. My struggles become more frantic, I've never been one for wrestling or rough housing. My muscles are like jelly and a bone weary numbness grips me, making me want to lie down despite this maniac attempting to kill me.

A sharp pain through my temple and I have a moment's outrage before I feel the sickening jar of my head hitting the wall behind. The head butt has left us nose to nose, his foul breath in my face. I lose the battle with my stomach and heave, folding double. He pulls away from the stream of vomit and swears. My fingers slide off his wrist, losing control of his arm and the knife pushes forwards. I twist sideways in desperation and it slides through my jumper to scrape against the wall. I've barely enough breath to stop myself from whimpering. Acid burns my nose and mouth and I spit, wondering if I'll throw up again. I roll to one side and look up from clutching my stomach to see his outline readying itself for another attack.

"Please… I don't have anything on me..." I can't think of anything he'd want. I'd left the shed with nothing in my pockets, no money or phone. My head is spinning, I'm shaking with cold and I'm going to die. The lights in the distance flicker momentarily and I wonder if I'm going mad. This shouldn't be happening, it's a spring evening, the birds are singing and Biggles is on the other side of the fence…

He lurches forwards, knife raised in one hand, the other outstretched to brush aside my own weak defences. His hand reaches out and grabs my collar, pulling me towards the knife flashing down. My knees give way and I clench my backside as other parts of me turn to liquid. I'm aware of every detail in the long moment – the gleam of corrugated skin, the smell of his body, the rasp of his clothes against mine as we struggle. He's strong, with big hands, I've not got a chance. I'm going to die.

A jerk, his breath huffs out of him and he falls against me, face into my shoulder. His fingers slide off my collar and I push him away. Stupid in shock I stare as he falls to the floor in a boneless crumple. My hand is grabbed and I'm dragged into a run. Lights in the distance bob up and down with my spinning head and my stomach lurches again. The air burns through my windpipe, scoured from reflux. The ground is uneven and stony and I stumble into a pothole. The hand holding mine is small but insistent, it pulls me along and I skin my knees as I fall. No mercy is shown, I'm hauled to my feet again and we continue the headlong pace.

More lights and the sharp edges of buildings in the dark. We slow to a more respectable walk. The lights grow larger and resolve the black into an intersection of streets. I'm in a city. My breath wheezes and my feet scuff through unseen debris.

"Hang on." My voice is barely a croak. I resist the hand, still trying to look back and at the floor at the same time. The hand lets go and I nearly fall. The wall I grab for instead is damp with something nasty. I lean on it gasping, not caring about my clothes. I dab at my forehead and it comes away dark. I feel sick. I lean my head back and wince at the other lump throbbing in time with my heart. I finger the lump and wonder if the dampness is blood or from the wall.

Have we outrun my attacker? I feel like a fool blinking and bobbing my head, trying to see through the black. Nothing to be seen to the dark behind us, I can't hear anything beyond the pounding in my ears. I turn to peer through the dim street lights at my rescuer. She is slender, her eyes gleam under tangled hair and she stares at me, waiting in the silence.

"I'm Daniel." No reaction. "What's your name?" Uneasy at her silence, I ask, "Can you speak?" She looks completely unimpressed. "What happened over there? Shouldn't we ring the police or something?"

She's eyeballing me as though I'm something the cat's brought in. My breath frosts the air and I rub my arms gently, not wanting to jar my head further. She doesn't seem to notice the cold despite the goosebumps on her thin arms. Her silence is becoming un-nerving.

I try again, "I won't hurt you." I jump at the unexpected sound of her snorting.

"You, hurt me?" Another knife flashes in the dim light and I skitter away, tripping over my heels. A scornful laugh as I pull myself up. "Nob." I flush at the sting of someone else laughing at me. The knife disappears. "Come on nob."

"My name's Daniel. What do you mean?"

"We need to go somewhere safe." She strides off and I glance around, no one else to be seen. The lights leave trails, smearing my vision. Now my eyes have adjusted and I have the chance to look around, I see tall brick buildings, grey with dust and mould. I shiver, remembering the pile of dust in the lane at home.

Everything is decaying here, this place looks like it has been abandoned for years. Gaps and piles of rubble show where buildings used to be, the street has puddles where cobbles have been taken out. Rats dart through the piles of rubbish. Mist completes the dismal scene and I feel stupid. How the hell did I get myself into this?

"Are you coming?" A mocking voice in the dark. What choice do I have? A tramp trying to kill me several streets back or this skinny girl who saved me. With little other option, I follow.

Lights show at the crossroads otherwise there's nothing. I'm cold and tired, my head swings as I try and keep the girl in sight by her silhouette against the infrequent lights. I stumble against walls and trip over unseen rubble. She waits impatiently and snorts her disdain at my clumsiness.

Another set of lights, I've lost track of the way back. I worry about concussion and can only remember that you shouldn't sleep. "Where are we going?"

"Shush." A movement of her hand warns me to stay back. My attacker? I freeze, glancing about, trying to work out how he's managed to circle us. I'm tense, ready to run again. She slows and I try to see by peering over her shoulder. A flash and a squeak. A dead rat with a knife in it. She picks it up and stows her knife somewhere. I feel sick.

"Here," The rat is waved at me. I stare at her, not understanding. "Aren't you hungry nob?"

She thrusts it into my shrinking palm and I take it, the weight swinging from its tail. The rat is warm and heavy, blood drips from its limp body. She turns around in the light, her face concentrating. The knife snaps out several times, misses once to a muttered swear word.

Each time I'm given the dead rat to carry, her eyes flick to mine in a native contempt.

The girl raises her arm again and then freezes in the act of throwing. Scaly tails rub my palm and I open my mouth to ask what the matter is. A flash of wide eyes is enough to halt any questions. She grabs my arm and points, her nails digging into my flesh. In the shadows in the street ahead are a pair of men. One is a bulky figure, the other is greyer and harder to see. Before I even focus, I somehow recognise the slimmer of the two and the inevitability of what will happen. A lethargy hits me and this too is part of it. I sway, stepping back and lean against the wall. The girl watches, breathing lightly as though not daring to catch their attention. A muffled cry and the larger of the two figures collapses into a heap. My eyes sharpen to peer through the gloom and I watch the grey man straighten and disappear into the shadows.

The lethargy dissipates. The girl hesitates then runs up to the fallen body and I follow to see if I can help. She's crouched over the body of an older man, rummaging through his pockets. I begin to protest and stop at the sight of the face on the pavement. The face is shrivelled, the skin taut across the skull. I've seen a dead body before in the morgue but nothing like this. The man's skin is like parchment. Without thinking I reach down to touch and it crumbles into dust, exposing bone. Dead, nothing left.

"Why…?"

She ignores me, her breathing harsh. The body collapses further as she rummages, a pile of clothes left on the floor, rags of skin and bones. I'm reminded of the chalk marks the police draw around bodies in crime scenes – a man once lay here. Even the skull, peering out from its earthly covering is looking stained and old. I stare at the smudges of dust on my fingers, touching them together in the dim light and hurriedly wipe them on my trousers. This isn't real. It must be a dream, people don't just disintegrate. I can't understand this, I stand shivering in the cold, my head aching. The bundle of rats swing forgotten from my hand and the gloom turns darker.

"Come on." The girl has finished going through the man's pockets, hiding the items she's stolen in a small bag hanging from her shoulder. I cringe back as she grabs for my hand, not wanting to touch a looter of the dead. Uncaring of my feelings, she takes my arm instead and drags me away as other shadows hunch by on business of their own.

More dark streets. Images flicker across my eyes, the orchard, the smell of the blossom drifting, the quiet of the morgue and the silent tick of a white plastic clock. I'm drained from the fight and my head aches in the cold. I follow passively, no longer thinking.

She pushes me into a small street away from the lights and leads me into a building. I fumble my way around the door frame and nearly fall down a set of stairs. The girl snorts and I'm too exhausted to care.

A snapping sound and a flame appears. She's holding an old fashioned lighter and I stare at it, greedy for the light. It throws wavering shadows across the empty room. Black empty windows stare down on us, the lower ones have been boarded up and the floor above is missing. There's a clearer track in the dust from the door to the stairs, the only marker that this place is inhabited.

With my handful of dead animals, I follow her down, grateful for the light. She rummages through a box, lights a single candle and drips the wax to stick it to the floor. I stand in exhaustion and watch as she bustles about, shoving me out of her way. The rats are removed from me, gutted in short order and then spiked to cook over a tiny fire in a metal container. Blue flames flicker through the holes and a rank smell of fish oozes out. It throws more light into the room, making me feel better, despite the smell.

I edge, close as I dare and hold my hands out, trying to warm some feeling into them. "Where am I?"

She shrugs and says, "Somewhere safe." She wipes her hands on a rag and throws it into a corner.

The mocking tone is still there but she now appears more amenable to conversation and I try, "I saw a girl go through the gap."

"What gap?"

How do I describe what I came through – a rift? Complete incomprehension is coming from her and I'm beginning to doubt my memory. How could I have come through something like that? The blow to my head isn't helping, everything seems a dream. "The gap I came through tonight. Didn't you see?"

Her face twists and with narrow eyes she says, "I've been away all day. Didn't see you until you were being killed." I wince at the reminder of my incompetence. The girl begins to cough, a deep wrenching sound that makes my own lungs ache.

I look at her, the girl I'd seen had been dressed normally for my world, this girl's clothes look stained and worn. Her knee pokes out of a hole in her trousers, bony in the flickering light. Stubbornly I keep trying,

"You must have seen her. I chased a girl after I looked at that pile of dust she'd dumped over the footpath. It's the same crap that's all round here. I came through the gap she wriggled through."

An expression passes over her face, wiping away the contempt and it takes a minute to recognise fear. "You saw another grey man?" Grey man? What did that have to do with a pile of dust?

"I saw a man by the orchard."

"Or-chard?" She pronounces the word as though she'd never heard it before.

"Yes, by the trees where I live." Her hair is a tangle down her back. I can't see what colour it is in the gloom. I wonder where the other girl has ended up, if she'd been killed by the same man who'd attacked me.

"You live with the nobs." Her voice is now definite. "I'll get a reward for taking you back."

"I want to go home. Can you take me there?" I wasn't sure we were talking on the same wavelength but if she could get me back...

"Can't now. It's too dangerous. We'll go in the morning." She reaches over to grab a large tin, prises the lid off and shakes a grubby looking loaf out. She saws a chunk off with her knife and offers it. The knife still has blood stains on from the rats and she hasn't washed her hands, I shake my head. She shrugs and chews off a lump. Still chewing, she turns the rats over.

We sit in silence, the rats sizzling on the fire. A good smell starts to rise and without warning my stomach grumbles. She laughs and exposes teeth that have more in common with an adult smoker. She wraps a sleeve around her hand and passes a rat on its metal spike. Roast rat, spread out like a star, its burnt paws and tail hanging down. She takes one and eats hungrily. I sample it, more out of curiosity and politeness. It tastes like chicken. I've only eaten a bit by the time hers is a pile of bones. She takes another, eyeing me as though I might object. I'm reminded of those wildlife programmes, of large cats staking out kills. I nod for her to take the rest, noticing her thin arms and her elbows sticking out of her short sleeves.

A cap is dropped over the tin of oil and the flame goes out, dropping us back into candlelight. The girl sucks on an oily finger. "Talia."

"What?" I jump at her starting a conversation.

"My name, nob." She's smaller than me, she looks fifteen. Her eyes say she's worlds older in experience. I'm left feeling useless.

"Why do you keep calling me nob?"

"Cos you are one."

I fight the anger down, first my sister now this scrawny girl. Knob. Something to be laughed at. "My name's Daniel."

She shakes her head, "Nob. Useless, stay on the hill, employ other people to do the dirty work. Fancied an adventure did you?"

I remember the bloody minded state I'd been in when I'd followed the girl through the rift and shudder. I'd never been one for adventures. Getting through university had been enough of one for me. I shake my head and regret it as I try and follow her train of thought. "What hill? I'm not from the hill. I live in the valley."

"You smell like a nob. Dress like one too." I look down at myself. My jeans are a mess with mud and filth, my jumper destined for a short trip to the bin when I get back. Then I compare myself with Talia and have to agree, her clothes are stiff with unspeakable substances leaving them grey.

"What are you up at the hill?" She talks through the roast rat, her mouth open.

I can't get her to understand that I'm not from here. Her life is encompassed by the city and this unknown hill. I give up, "I work in the office section of the undertakers."

"Undertakers?" She looks confused.

"You know, people who lay out the dead." I mean to carry on, surely she must know this and stop when she flinches away from me.

"You lay out the dead? I need to get you back. You don't belong here."

Too right I don't. "Can't we go now?"

"It's too late, it's not safe. Tomorrow." Talia's denial is emphatic. Her speculative stare makes me less comfortable. She's all I've got here. She's rescued me once, I'm going to have to trust her.

I feel a yawn coming up and try to make myself comfortable. I shouldn't be sleeping this close to a head injury. What are the symptoms of brain damage? Hallucinations? Seeing people dissolve in front of you?

"Do we sleep here?" Her expression doesn't change at my question. I wonder if the gap or rift between our worlds is still there, if anyone else has discovered or fallen through it. "Okay, I'm sleeping then."

I look around and move to a corner away from her. I'm too tired to stop myself from sleeping, I no longer care about any consequences. I roll over and ignore the stare. A breath and the candle is blown out. A soft rustle of movement and I presume she's settling down somewhere.

It's dark and my ears strain to catch any sound. The image of the man's skull rises and I close my eyes tightly, rubbing my fingers together, remembering the feel of the dust between them. I relive the struggle with the tramp and the fight to get through the grey nothing that brought me here. What had happened to the girl? My thoughts turn darker, what were my parents thinking? Did they think I'd had an early night?

I'll never sleep, it's too cold and my feet are damp. I curl up, preserving my remaining warmth and tuck my hands into my armpits. It's work tomorrow, will they miss me? My eyes become heavy, despite the unforgiving stone floor underneath me. A rock pokes itself into my back and I shift out of its way. I sleep.

Chapter 4

Out of habit she moved quietly, sure footed in the dark. If Daniel had been there, he would have said nothing could be seen. Talia's senses went beyond his, used to the smothering blackness. She scuffed through the streets in her soft shoes, using the air movement as much as her eyes. Lights flickered at each major intersection and she averted her gaze, not wanting to spoil the little night vision she had.

She found her thoughts going back to the nob she'd saved. She'd heard rumours about them but never seen one close up. All the way back she'd been fascinated by what she could see of his clothes not having any holes or tears and his skin clean in a way that suggested a proper wash with servants to draw the water and scrub everything away, not a wipe down with a damp cloth.

Talia shuddered her mind away from the image. She'd been coming back from an unprofitable venture, wary of those out in the mid-point between dank day and the city's self-imposed night curfew and had heard the scuffle. Drawn by the possibilities of looting, she'd intervened at the sound of his voice. She frowned, something about the tone had caught her. Used to reacting on a second's thought, she'd kicked his attacker in the kidneys and tripped him as he'd folded over. One glance at the victim had proven her hunch right, he was worth something.

Her stomach had turned at the familiar face on the floor – Corte – drunk again. He should have known better than to attack a nob or he would have done if he'd been sober. Her leg had twitched to kick him unconscious and stopped at the rolled up eyes. No point in making things worse for him. She'd grabbed the nob's hand and run from the scene before she was recognised.

A lifetime's worth of walking the city led her feet to a building crowded with people. Hovering outside, she scrubbed her eyes and smothered a yawn. She had to stay on her guard, especially here. At the moment, there was no way she could turn up with the nob at the wall and expect a reward for handing him in. He was just useless junk unless she could get to the right person. He'd be taken off her and she'd be given a beating for daring to ask for anything.

She thought about talking to Corte and wondered if she dared after this evening, even if he sobered up and didn't remember anything. This nob had better be worth the lost business, Corte was a useful person to know, he often had the contacts she didn't but his prices were high. She shook her head, she'd have to take the nob with her and somehow she got the feeling he'd not appreciate his worth. The look on his face when she'd handed him the first rat… she had other food but why waste it on him? He must be from high up on the hill to be that naive, maybe the top, and she wondered how he'd got down here. Helpless sod – even the people in this building would have him for breakfast.

Her only option lay in front of her. She shifted uneasily, disliking the truce that held people honest in this area. Dodie didn't tolerate those breaking her peace, it was bad for business. Her lungs gurgled as she took a deep breath and she plunged into the crowd, searching for Dodie.

Noise and light assaulted her senses, attuned to the night outside. Talia flinched as a dog whined, having been kicked and she slid out of the way of its teeth as it snapped. The nob was worth something. Even with another's cut taken out, he would still be worth several months of food and easy living. Talia pushed her way through, caught in the throng. Unable to see over people's shoulders, she was reduced to quartering the room to find the person she wanted.

Finally Dodie loomed in front, a large woman in every respect. She was holding court, a mug of beer in one massive hand as she entertained those seeking her favour. She turned, having caught the flicker of a sycophant's eye. Not much got past her.

"Talia! Darling!" Her voice was as soft as her body appeared, she reached down to pull Talia into a bear hug. As always, despite feeling like a bundle of twigs, Talia was reassured by the presence of the big woman. Dodie had brought her up and introduced her to the underworld. She mock drew her knife and laughed as Dodie snapped out the expected swift hand to block.

"What have you got for me?" Dodie's eyes creased into the folds of her cheeks, almost disappearing into the fat. Talia dug into her pockets and produced a few small trinkets she'd brought. They vanished into the robes Dodie wore. "We don't see you often enough here darling." The endearment concealed a question.

Talia tossed her head in pride. "Got something else. A nob."

"Nobs don't come down here without protection."

"This one did." Talia spat back at the man who'd dared interrupt. "He's a nob all right. Clean as a baby he is... and about as bright." A derisive laugh rose at her crack.

"What do you want?" Talia had Dodie's attention now.

"A name from someone up top. They'll be looking for him, be a reward."

"And my price?" Dodie's voice was a lazy drawl, Talia knew it masked the razor sharp mind underneath. Dodie hadn't risen to the top purely by the weight of her fist.

Talia shrugged and looked at her non-existent fingernails. "Whatja think he's worth?"

Dodie motioned the others away, moving Talia towards a table. She waved a hand and Talia helped herself to a mug and filled it with beer from a pitcher. At a nod, someone passed over a bowl of soup and she was watched as she gulped it down. Despite Dodie preferring to do her business in public, a space surrounded them giving a sense of privacy. The others turned their backs, talking to friends while eyeing the odd couple they made over their shoulders.

"You're too skinny, come and work for me."

Talia shook her head, "I like being independent."

"Stubborn child." Dodie didn't have to pretend a fondness, she loved all her children. Others used street rats like Talia, smaller, weaker and less able to protect themselves. They beat them up, sold them, made them fear the world and made them into bullies and pimps like themselves. Dodie used a different method. She took them in, looked after them and had ended up with an army of youngsters who knew what their life could have been like. Talia had been one of the few to rebel and go her own way. She brought Dodie information when she had it, trinkets when she wanted something, otherwise she attended to her own business. Dodie tolerated her wilfulness as long as she didn't cross her.

Dodie waited until Talia put down the bowl and they argued amicably about the percentage each would get. They agreed Dodie would find a name and let her know in a few days.

"Come and see me soon darling." The words were for everyone to hear. This time the crowd parted for Talia as she moved to the door and she made the most of it, conscious of the protection laid on her.

Outside it was a different matter. She kept the swagger up, past the corner and then slid into the night, aware that others might follow her back to her sleeping place. There was always the risk that someone would find it and use it or find it and wait for her. There'd been that time several years ago when a man had taken a liking to her, not paying attention to her threats. She shuddered, he'd trapped her one evening, caught her when she'd been tired from digging and not checking as she'd wriggled into her hiding place. The warm blood running over her hands, the gasp and shake of a body over her. The first time she'd killed someone. She'd run and curled up in an empty cellar, not caring about the bruises or the dogs sniffing around.

Now she was careful, wide eyes scanning the darkness, head tilted to catch any sound and breathing lightly to prevent her lungs catching at the mess inside. A stumble close by, she froze. A deep cough and the sound of fabric against brick. She stayed still, nostrils flaring and caught the smell of urine. The patter against a wall. A muttered swear word and the man staggered on, nearly brushing against her.

Her feet carried her back to her current hidey hole. She stayed in the entrance, trying to sense if anything had changed. Nothing, no difference in the feeling. She risked her lighter and walked into her territory. All was safe.

Talia glanced down at where the nob was lying. His mouth was open and she briefly considered dropping something into it. He looked young, none of the scruffy half shaven look that most of the boys her age shared. He certainly had the scrubbed look of the few nobs she'd seen behind their armed escorts. His skin was soft, a pinkness on the bridge across his cheeks. She remembered his voice and the pang it had sent through her the first time she'd heard it. It had stopped her replying to his questions while she'd analysed her reactions and then dismissed them as not being important.

Still curious, she leant forwards and abruptly drew back as she felt her lungs curdling for a coughing fit. She moved away and hacked into her elbow, not wanting to wake him. No soft feelings of sympathy for the nob, he was simply better off asleep. Less noise and somehow less pathetic. Only a nob could fall over his own feet and expect to survive down here. She wiped her nose across a sleeve stiff with grime and absently scratched a nail through her hair.

Talia mentally re-arranged her plans for the next few days. She wouldn't be chatting up the traders from across the city as she'd planned, those trinkets she'd found would go to the new cause currently sleeping in the corner. She'd have to find an excuse to get into the inner circle behind the wall. Dodie would give her a contact name, no more. Talia would be expected to find the reason to get to the contact herself, unless she was prepared to pay more. The offer to simply give up the nob and live off Dodie's largesse had been unspoken in Dodie's smile. Talia muttered something at the thought of being dependent and shivered.

She curled up on the pile of rags she slept on, her mind working furiously. She needed a proper bribe. There were still good things to be found in her diggings far in the south of the city. The risks were worth it, few got the items she did – another reason Dodie was prepared to tolerate her.

Her lungs trembled again and she forced the cough down. Someone would pay a lot for him. Talia curled up and blew out the lamp. She stared into the blackness where her prize lay until her eyes closed.

Chapter 5

I wake groaning and every muscle in my body protests against my stretch. It's cold and a thin grey light sifts through the open doorway. My shoulders drop. It's real. I'm not at home in bed with Biggles lying across my feet. I long for my thick winter duvet and the luxury of snuggling for five more minutes. Cautiously I feel the lumps on my head, a dry crusty scab above my eyebrow meets my fingers and the remains of a headache lurk amid the tenderness. I rub the rest of my face, wishing for coffee. What am I going to do? I remember how the grey slid through my fingers until I'd grabbed hold of the girl. I need to find her. I try to recall her face and fail in the memory of sun speckled eyes.

A movement catches my eye and I jump. Talia is sat in the corner, picking her teeth. I suppress the image rising of a baboon from a nature documentary, the unknown ferocity and a native intelligence in both their eyes. I try to tell myself that I know more and fail.

"Morning."

Talia grunts at my forced cheerfulness, wipes her nose across the back of her hand and stands up. "Come on."

"Why?"

"Gotta meet someone."

"Who?" I pluck at my shirt, peeling it away from my armpits where it's spent the night clenched against the cold and heave myself up.

"Someone to get you back to where you should be." I try to hide a flinch as she comes closer. "You don't smell." Her voice is curious.

I sniff and regret it, I can smell plenty and only some of it is myself. Another more urgent feeling intrudes, I need a pee. I scramble up the stairs to follow her outside and move away to give myself privacy. There's no way I'm asking permission. The sound makes me wince, steam rises off the wall and floor from the stream. I try to act unconcerned, inside I feel like Dominic. I turn to find Talia gazing off into the streets, her back to me.

She grunts at me to follow. Talia walks in a purposeful way through the streets, giving wary nods to other people. I'm surprised at the number of people about, still not many considering the size of the buildings lining the streets but it's not quiet on the main thoroughfare either. Somehow I'd expected Talia to dodge and keep to the shadows, instead she's confident, even swaggering a bit. These people look as tough as her. I find myself flinching at the knives worn openly and notice the seamed faces flicking to mine in return, assessing and dismissing.

The mist has dispersed a little in the early morning, a soft glow outlines the buildings. A fine powder falls briefly and stops. I brush it off my jumper and find it's warm, is it ash? I wipe the smears onto my trousers and try not to thinks about the man's skin flaking onto my fingers. I shake myself, it must have been a trick of the light, something to do with concussion. Last night was a bad dream, I'll get home today. I can almost feel Biggles shoving his hard head against me in welcome and his claws scrabbling.

She glances in my direction more than once and then drags me to the side. "What are you doing?" I look blankly at her. "Walk properly nob. You're calling attention to me, making yourself a target. Here." She rummages in the bag slung over her shoulder and a piece of metal is shoved into my hand, narrowly missing cutting me. "You walk like a good time boy, people'll think I've gone soft. Act tough."

Act tough. I've never been good at acting. I clutch the makeshift weapon gingerly, try squaring my shoulders and put my face into an expression of grim determination. A slap stings across my face and I glare at her.

She smirks, "That's better. Now walk."

We keep going and aware of her warning, I try not to rub my face. Something trickles down it and I wonder if it's bleeding, I daren't ask. My mind goes back to home with a pang. My parents would be up by now, I'd have collected the milk from the doorstep and left it in the kitchen. Would they have checked to find out why I hadn't? Lost in my thoughts, I follow at Talia's heels, not paying much attention to the streets around me. I nearly bang into her as I miss her hand wave to stop. Talia mutters something under her breath, I'm sure it's a swear word. There's a group of people in the road ahead and snatches of conversation drift towards us.

"Stay here, and try to look normal." She sighs as I lean against the wall and flinch away at the damp seeping in. I can feel myself flushing, even here I'm not considered normal.

She swaggers towards the group, hand on the knife in the back of her belt. A thin voice greets her casual comment. The group parts and I see a body on the cart of a large woman. Talia peers over the edge, makes a comment and stalks back towards me.

"Come on nob." Is her voice sharper?

"Who was that?"

"No one you'd know." A definite sneer.

"Why do you keep calling me nob?"

"Cos if I chopped you off at the hips, you'd still have a knob for a head." My mouth opens at the unfairness and clicks shut as she turns and walks away, fists tight against her sides. I glare at her back and keep up, reduced to being baggage.

Stinging from this latest comment, I notice the tangled hair and holes in her clothes. I'm stuck following this person, is this the best I can do here? There must be someone in authority who can help. Talia hasn't even told me where she's taking me. Anger begins to burn, first my sister, now Talia. The receptionist and Clive making comments, there'd been others too. Always stumbling, getting things wrong, even the counsellor hadn't understood what I'd wanted to say. They all laughed at me, was I always going to be something for people to sneer at?

I start paying attention to my surroundings, there must be a way out of here, somewhere to get information. Surely someone as grubby and foul mouthed as Talia can't help. I've no sense of direction, was this the way we'd come in the dark last night? Another intersection and a tang of salt in the air hits me. The sea? There are always important buildings next to the sea – customs offices and so on.

Talia is still stalking ahead, muttering to herself. She doesn't think I'm important, she's proven that by her comments. Not so many people in this street, fewer to help her catch me if I run. I slow, eyeballing her skinny figure and make a sharp turn without fully thinking about what I'm doing. The air is still grey in the dawn, further down the street only the outlines of buildings can be seen. This place is dismal even during the day.

I throw down the piece of metal and start running, anger and a wild joy lending me strength. Talia coughs her lungs out like a pensioner on sixty a day, there's no way she can catch me running. I'm fit, I trek up and down the hills daily with Biggles. Dust puffs around my feet as they hit the floor. I feel pride in finally being able to do something she can't. I hear a shriek as Talia realises my escape. I no longer care that she might be able to help me get back home. She denied all knowledge of the rift I came through. Inspiration hits, maybe I can find that girl on my own. She can't blend in here any more than I can.

Something slams into my shoulder. I stumble, putting a hand out to stop myself falling and look behind me in disbelief. Talia stands in the distance weighing another stone. She's thrown half a brick at me. I gape in stupidity then narrow my eyes. There's a limit to her throwing range, I must be close to it. I run again, trying to ignore the pain spreading down my arm. It's harder to run with only one arm working properly. A screech of rage behind me and the other rock clatters close by. She can't possibly throw much further. My lungs are burning, I daren't think how much dust I'm breathing in or the other people I've heard coughing. This sort of stuff can kill you if you breathe in too much.

Another smell of the sea and I turn towards it, working my way downhill all the time. I risk looking behind and see nothing in the narrow alleyways. I must be safe, I've been out of Talia's eyeline for several streets. I slow and start to look around, allowing my breathing to relax. What is this place? Some kind of city, it's enormous. It would have been stupendous if it wasn't a ruin. All the buildings are made of brick, giving it a Victorian steampunk feel. Fancy brickwork shows through the grime. I touch a window ledge, it's covered in the same grey ash I noticed earlier, only here it's inches thick.

It's like some movie set from a dystopian future, a hopeless future waiting for the hero to come barrelling in. I snort to myself – not me. My eyes flick to the windows high up, noticing the broken panes and I wonder what the buildings were used for. I'm not anyone's hero. Talia's proved that. All I can do is run and use computers.

All the films I've seen about rebuilding a future like this. How exactly do they rebuild? These people have nothing, they're living off scraps from the past. I have a horrible thought, is this my world – in the future? I glance around. What had happened to make the city like this? Ruined in places and covered in dust, a war? I go cold, my imagination working overtime – nuclear war? I begin to panic and catch myself covering my mouth and stop. There's nothing I can do. If the city is radioactive, then I am dead. People are surviving here, I can too. Until I find a way home at least.

As I head downhill, the buildings become larger and are in better condition. The rubble is cleared to the sides of the streets to allow for the traffic. Signs of restoration appear, one building is covered in a shaky scaffolding with buckets being hauled up on ropes. Everything is done by hand, men stripped to the waist and sweating in the cool air. The new day begins to show more as I walk. I peer upwards and see smoke billowing out from the chimneys above. Large windows are covered in grime, the same as the rest of the city. Are these factories? I wonder what they could make in such a pre-industrial area.

A plaza opens out in front of me, I can smell the sea but can't see it. A building stretches across the back, blocking the way through, another road crosses from left to right. I freeze as I notice the bodies hanging from gibbets at one end and imagine the baying crowds.

A heavy low thumping fills the square, I swing my head trying to locate the sound and fail. It must be coming from one of the buildings close by. I can feel the rhythmic vibrations running through my feet. I stop in the shadows, trying to work through my options and wonder if Talia is following. I lean against a building to watch and shift away as vibration rumbles through my bruised shoulder.

People walk through the large square, there's little to show if they are male or female. Their clothing is practical and smeared with the dust that covers everything. Grime emphasizes the lines in their faces making everyone look old, including the children. I'd expected them to be bent over and downtrodden. These people give the appearance of workmen doing a job that wasn't to their liking, but had to be done. They walk in small groups, talking quietly. The few children I see stay close to the adults. I wonder if I should ask one of them about contacting the authorities. The bodies swinging in the background trigger a diluted survival instinct, making me aware that this may not be the best option. Maybe Talia had been right.

I twist behind to see if she's caught up and an awareness invades my mind, like a smell of a dream. I turn back to the square, trying to work out what it is. I have a nagging sense of wanting to warn the people in front of me. I can't say what's wrong, just that something is. I shudder and look at the bodies swinging, trying to convince myself that I've been spooked.

The people in the square walk faster, the soft murmur of talk stills. Something is definitely wrong here. Still no sense of panic, simply those in a certain area move, slowly clearing a space in front of one of the alleys. My eyes are drawn to the entrance, a figure stands in the shadows. I can barely see him and yet I know he's there. I squint, and the recognition grows stronger.

It's the grey man, the same figure I'd seen the previous night. I'm sure he's the same man I'd seen by the hedge. The first link I've had with my own world. Maybe he could take me back if I can't find the girl. I feel a sense of distaste, despite my hope that he can help. Why don't I want him to come closer? A lethargy creeps over me, I can see people moving slower, panic starting to show on their faces. Why aren't they moving faster if they're not happy?

The grey man steps out into the square, somehow drawing the shadows with him. A hood over his face obscures his features. The crowd parts further, a ripple in custard. A slow motion movie where the only person moving normally is the grey man. The figure raises a hand, a slow step forwards and he places it on the man's shoulder. A gesture of friendship, a greeting and yet the man staggers and lets out a muted cry.

I see his mouth open and close, the terror on his face visible. The man falls to his knees and topples to hit the floor. In the silence, the sound of his head connecting with the cobblestones makes my stomach lurch. The grey man follows his victim down, kneeling on the ground briefly beside him. I stare, mouth open, this was the man I'd wanted to help me. I remembered Talia's fear the previous night as she'd mentioned the grey man. Frozen in place, I watch as the figure stands, leaving the man on the ground and walks away. The crowd follows his movements, watching him leave and the weight lifts from my limbs.

There's a brief moment where people stare at the body and then they resume their business, walking around him like a pile of rubbish. The square gradually clears. What has happened? Why isn't anyone helping? A determination fills me. I'm not going to be a bystander on this. Only a few people are walking by now and I jump as a loud noise blares. The remaining people hurry away. Some kind of warning? My anxieties about nuclear war are raised again. Where's everyone going?

I'm left in the square with the body. I strain my ears, I hear the clattering and thumping from the buildings close by, nothing else can be heard over the noise, certainly no aeroplanes. What sort of aeroplanes would fly in a world like this? I scan the sky, trying to see through the mist. Nothing. My gaze returns to the body. I've been sweating in the cool air. Out of habit, I pull my jumper off and tuck it under my arm as I walk over. The man is lying huddled on the ground, his face turned away.

"Are you okay?"

I'm back to feeling inadequate. I did a first aid course in university and was profoundly bad at it. I'd passed of course, it's difficult not to. I put my hand on his shoulder, where the grey man had, and feel a thrill run through me. I shudder and wipe my hand off, the dust from his shoulder leaving a smear on my jeans. I take a deep breath and try to roll him over by pulling on his arm. He's lighter than I'd thought he'd be. The arm underneath my hand feels delicate as though made of paper like a wasp's nest.

I trip over backwards as his face finally turns my way. It's desiccated just like the man last night. The skin is stretched over his cheekbones, his mouth wide open, lips peeled back. This man was living a few minutes ago, talking and laughing with his friends. How can he be like this now? This is more like one of those people they find in glaciers. He looks like he's been dead for years. The body rocks and falls backwards as I let go. The weight of the body lands on his neck, twisting it and it tears with a papery sound. Dust sifts out.

My eyes fix in guilty fascination. I can see inside his throat, it's hollow and dry. No living tissue left... the structure of the wind pipe... I find myself scrabbling backwards, trying to gain my feet. I whimper and hear myself start babbling, "I'm sorry, I'm so sorry."

I nearly shriek as a hand clamps over my shoulder. Grey man! My knees turn to jelly and I drop my jumper as it pulls me upright.

"Which do you belong to?" The voice is resigned, the accent is the same as Talia's. I can't reply, my brain is still filled with images of the dead man behind me and the grey figure's strange assault. There's nothing grey about the man standing in front of me. He's my height but stockier. A sleeveless jerkin show arms easily wider than mine – doesn't anyone feel the cold here? I try to turn and point to the man behind and find I can't, his grip's too tight.

He repeats his question and I gape, not understanding. Part of me notices the square filling with people again. They are giving me and the dead man a wide berth. The man holding me sighs and without visible effort, pulls me towards a building. Still in shock, I go without a struggle.

We walk through a small door set into thick double doors and into hell. The noise is incredible in the confined space, the floor is shaking. The building is dimly lit by electric lights, swinging in loops from wires, it's the first proper technology I've seen so far. I can't see the back of the room for the large machinery, tree trunk limbs heaving up and down in a medieval punching and long shadows turning. Violence is in every move. People scurry past as I'm dragged through open mouthed, carrying things and shouting over the noise. Mostly the shouts are to gain attention and then sign language is used to make themselves clear. Smaller figures dart under the machines, I wince as the children slide with inches to spare between the moving parts, one slip and they'll be crushed.

My gaze is drawn to the ceiling and I see material flapping on rollers high up. I trip, and my captor grunts with irritation, lifting me to my feet. I trot up the stairs after him the best I can, his hand still gripping my arm. He briefly knocks at a door and enters. The door slams behind us, shutting out part of the noise. The vibrations shout through my feet.

Dazed from the noise, I see a man behind a scruffy desk, little more than a set of planks nailed together. Different coloured counters are piled on the desk in front of him. He's shifting them around on a piece of paper and calling out numbers.

"Igren. Found him outside. He's not part of a team." My captor interrupts the man with the matter of fact statement, no deference in his voice. I pull my shirt into place and try to look presentable, despite the hand holding my arm.

The man behind the desk looks up in irritation, one finger on a counter to be moved. "Name?"

"Daniel Jones." I feel the urge to explain. "I'm not from round here. There's a dead man outside your..." Words fail me. Factory? Mill? What was the correct word for what was going on downstairs? I hadn't been able to work it out from my brief exposure, I stop at his bored glance.

"You need to prove you're not attached elsewhere, otherwise you will be indentured here. You will find us good masters. You will be fed and watered and have a place to stay so long as you work."

Work? Panic fills me at the thought. I can't work here. It's like the history lessons I'd had at school, people crushed in a moment, injured for life. I had to get home. "Please, you don't understand. I don't belong here, I need to..." How could I explain?

Igren continues as though he'd heard it all before. "We are reasonable people not slavers. You will have a day to tell us who you belong to. A name will suffice." He pauses, waiting.

"I was with Talia, but..." Again, I have no chance.

"Talia?" Igren snaps his fingers and a skinny figure appears from the corner. Ink stains his fingers and the cuffs of his shirt. He asks the man, "Has another clique started? I haven't heard of that one." The new man, some form of scribe I presume, shakes his head.

My heart sinks as I realise Talia must be outside of this system. My voice is a whisper, "She lives on her own." I know no one here. I am no one.

He snorts. "An outsider. Listen boy, unless you can come up with another name within a day then you will be with us. You will get three meals a day. Good meals and a bed. Safety." His voice is cajoling. A man persuading me that working in the hell downstairs is better than being on the streets. I think of the cold dusty city, Talia's thin face as she eats rat and the figure of the grey man and begin to wonder.

Igren nods to my captor. He turns me and drags me back through the din. We walk down stone steps, a damp saltiness making the air heavy and I'm dumped in a cell. He pats me on the shoulder and tells me to think carefully. I stare at the blank wall, hearing the door shut and locked behind me. Vague thoughts flicker without connecting. I'm stuck here, I need to find a way out, someone higher than this Igren or Talia to help me.

Slowly other senses intrude and I pull myself out of my shock. I can smell salt and feel a warmth rising from somewhere, it's strange in the cool air. The wall is solid rock and the thump and grind from the machinery still vibrates, although it is muted here. Everything is damp with a mildewed smell. A small window opens to the outside, no glass in it. The light has a strange quality and I walk over to investigate. My feet splash and I jerk back. It must be a puddle, I can't see much of the floor in this light.

I find a dry way around and look out to see the ocean in front of me. It's nearly level with the window and I realise that on some high tides it must flood my cell. My eyes are dragged out across the horizon. Nothing out there apart from the ubiquitous mist bank and the rise and swell of the waves. I stand on tiptoe and find waves breaking on the rocks in front of the window. Spray dampens my face and my tears slide to join them.

I spend hours huddled up on the steps, the driest place in the cell. The tide recedes, the only way of noting the time. Images of my family, the last happy afternoon I'd spent with Dominic in my shed and uneasy thoughts of Talia run through my mind. When the door thumps open behind me, I jump. The same man puts a bowl down on the step beside me.

"Soup. Eat it while it's hot." He sees me notice the open door and grins. "Forget it boy, just eat."

He folds his arms and leans against the frame. The tattooed vines running down his bare arms twitch with the flexing of his muscles. I'm starving. The last thing I'd eaten had been roast rat, before then? Sunday dinner. How circumstances change, I'd even welcome Sarah coming through that door. I imagine her comments about me being here and wince internally.

"So lad, any names?"

My stomach grumbles and I grab for the bowl. "I'm not from around here. I'm from England. I don't know anyone." I manage to talk around a mouthful. I'm hungry and it tastes wonderful.

He looks amused. "So how did you get here?" At least he seems willing to listen, maybe he can influence this Igren to help me.

I stumble through my explanation, "Look I know it sounds strange but I followed this girl, she went through a rift or portal and I ended up here. I was attacked by this man," I show him the lump on my forehead and he raises an eyebrow. "Talia rescued me and then took me back to her sleeping place. She was taking me somewhere else but I ran." I feel lame, it sounds dreadful. "I want to go home." That sounds worse, now I sound like a child.

He ignores the catch in my voice and asks, "Where is home?"

I put the bowl in my lap, desperately holding onto my hopes, "As I said, England."

"Where is this England?" No recognition, he stumbles over the word and my hopes plummet yet again. Where is England? A simple enough question.

"Where am I now?"

He laughs, "You are in Narith."

"Where's Narith?"

"Narith is here. There is nowhere else." There's a finality to his words.

That does it. No England. No way of getting back home unless I can find the person who brought me here. When my parents discover me gone… what are they going to think? I put the nearly finished bowl of soup on the floor and sink my head into my hands. Will there be an investigation? I nearly sob in frustration. The only thing leading to my disappearance is a pile of grey dust on the footpath outside the orchard. Would they think it was my remains in the dust?

The man gives me a searching look, "Come with me."

He grasps my upper arm and stands me up. We walk up several flights of stairs, the pulsing of the factory working its way through my feet. I'm puffing by the time we reach the top. We stand near the roof of the building, a low wall surrounding the edge. The sea is on one side, the low rise of the city on the other. Both city and ocean stretch as far as I can see into the mist.

"I explored a lot in my youth, then when I came to work for Igren, I travelled for him. There is nothing else boy. There is the city and the sea."

I gaze upwards. Even the day has a grimy feel to it. Smoke from the various factories filter upwards into the mist and the buildings are covered in a black filth. The ocean is grey and blends into the bank of fog on the horizon and I shiver in the wind. The veil parts, a rare occurrence here I guess, and something humps itself into view. A moon – not mine. This is no silvery disc, this is a nauseating blend of oranges and greys. Despite the dirty filter of atmosphere, this moon lurches towards the earth. Valleys and canyons can clearly be seen. It's enormous.

Even though I knew it, a chill runs down my spine at the final proof. This is not my world.

Chapter 6

I watch from my cell window as the water reveals more of the rocky shore, the tides must be huge here. That moon, I shudder. I try twisting the bars at the window and find no movement. I splash back to my step and sit. My warder was good natured in taking me back to my cell, even kindly. He seemed amused at my shock and made me finish the soup to keep my strength up before leaving and locking the door behind him.

What can I do? No one's going to be looking for me in this world. If I'm working here in the mill, then who's going to help me? Those other people were allowed out, would I be allowed to leave if I tell them I'll work for them? My spirits sink – they've locked me up – I don't think they're that stupid. I wrestle my anxiety down. I need to show them I'm trustworthy, that I can do things for them. The higher I can get in this society, the more chance I have of getting out. I rub my face, I need to get back to Talia. She'd had ideas and knew people that might help. Maybe these "nobs" can help me after all.

The day passes, I swing between wild hopes and worrying myself sick. The tide changes and starts the gradual climb back up to my window, the sky darkening. With nothing else to do, my brain twists itself into knots, trying to work out how I got here. I try to remember the girl's face and fail. My home was a world away, the baggy jeans and the fear streaming off her were all I could recall.

Just when I've sunk into yet another hopeless mood, I hear footsteps in the hall. I straighten, telling myself I need to make the best of this and square my shoulders, determined to prove my worth. My warder appears at the door. He's in a cheerful mood, Igren has asked for me. The usual grasp on my arm and we walk up through the factory. It's empty, the vast room is in darkness apart from the oil lamps. Huge shadows wrap themselves over the machinery, a silent picture ready to explode into motion in a moment.

Igren is sitting behind his desk, the pile of counters has been moved to one side. He doesn't waste time. "Any names?"

"No but I can read and write." I figure few can in this world. I see a flicker cross his face and know I'm right. A glee fills me, I can do this.

"Prove it." He snaps his fingers and the skinny ink-stained man scowls and shoves a piece of paper in front of me. He doesn't like having a rival with skills. I try to look casual and panic when I see the marks in front of me. It's not English. They speak the same language, but it's not written down the same.

"I can't read this but I can write… pass me the pen." A nod and a pen is passed. A nib strapped to a thin piece of wood. "Ink?" The scribe narrows his eyes and carefully places a bottle in front of me. I dip the pen and write as smoothly as I can. "This is my name, the date – as far as I know – and my place of birth." It's not come out too badly, despite the ink blobbing.

The scribe picks up the paper and squints. "It's only scribbling. This ain't writing." He looks smug.

"It's in my language." I manage to keep my voice even and he snorts his disgust.

Igren takes the paper from him, turns it several ways. My hopes sink, he can't read. "Looks like it's writing but not ours." He sighs, "If you'd said you were one of Dodie's boys then I might have believed you. You've the right look."

My guard interrupts, "Dodie's dead." Igren blinks and looks up. He shrugs, "I heard she fell over the other day and never got up again. They took her to the kilns yesterday."

"Well, that changes everything." Igren passes the paper back to his scribe and gathers himself, ready to make his judgement.

"I can write other things." I'm desperate, I need to show my worth. "I can add and subtract, do your accounts for you." Inspiration hits. "Just think, if no one else can read your accounts, then it'll be a secret."

Igren looks amused. "I keep my secrets in my head, boy, the best place for them." He nods to my guard. "Get the details sorted and put him to work. Give him the wool bags first with Vihaan, get him used to it." He smiles at me, "I'm not a bad man, if your family finds you then you can tell them that they'll be welcome to join you. Three meals a day and I separate the men and women at night unless they find a man they want to be with. They'll not believe the difference in you in a few weeks."

I'm dragged out in shock. My guard's grip is light as he takes me through the square. I glance at the few people left in the streets. The sun is beginning to set, the shadows darkening.

"They'll be going home shortly. People don't hang around here." His voice is casual.

I can't be forced to work for them, I need to get away. Anywhere is better than this, I might be able to find Talia and apologise to her. I twist and lunge out of his grip. His hand slips and I run, head down, my feet pounding, the blood thumping in my ears. People move out of my way – they're helping – I'm going to get away. I can find a quiet doorway to sleep in tonight, forget the cold. Ideas race through my head, I'm going to do this, I'm going to get away.

Something tangles my feet together and I trip. A laugh from someone close by and I hit the floor hard. I twist to look, my feet have a rope wrapped around them with stones attached, some kind of bola. I try to free myself and a shadow falls over me.

"Don't try that again," he says in a kindly tone. He twists my arms behind my back – there's nothing kindly about the rope he ties around my wrists. His hands are efficient but not rough. "I wondered if you'd run if given the chance. Well, it won't happen again. Up you get." He loosens the bola and peels them off me. He shoves me towards a building, smoke seeping from the windows higher up into the dusk. Inside it's hot, furnaces are burning brightly and the smell of iron pervades everything.

"Evening Darius. I've one for Igren. You got the message?" A grunt and a nod from one of the men. "Need him sorted now. He's a bit frisky on his feet."

Another grunt. My guard shoves me towards a table, face down and leans on my shoulder, wrapping his arm around my neck. I struggle, trying to get air into my lungs. A blast of warmer air runs across my back.

They've ripped my shirt. I can't see, can't breathe. A burning warmth getting closer. I shrink away and begin fighting in earnest. My guard simply leans harder and tightens his grip. The world shrinks down to a small patch of skin on my right shoulder. A scream bursts from me. A searing pain spreads and I faint.

I wake retching. The bruise from Talia's brick is nothing compared to this throbbing open wound. Something cold is slapped on my shoulder and I let out a muffled groan as it seeps into my skin. The pain recedes and I shiver. There's no shirt left on me, they've cut it off my back.

I lie in the same position for what feels like ages, frightened to move in case I pull my injured shoulder. My brain imagines all sorts of injuries, seeping pus and gangrene. My limbs are like putty, they've left me face down. A thin mattress rises around my face and nearly smothers me. I can feel the leather straps attached to the frame underneath. Eventually I manage to turn my head.

Someone's left a lamp in an alcove, just a simple wick in a puddle of oil. I gaze at it. So many things I've taken for granted. Light at the touch of a button, transport, talking to people miles away just by lifting a piece of plastic. I'm back to the stone age, in the ruins of a world that isn't even my own. Tears leak out of my closed eyelids. I've no chance of finding Talia now. Is she even looking for me? Who was it she was taking me to meet? My family are never going to see me again. I'll be crushed in one of those machines or hung in a creaking gibbet.

My self pity session is interrupted by the door banging open. A thread of self preservation kicks in and

I haul myself onto my elbows, wincing at my back pulling. Several more lamps are lit as men come in. They are hard and bearded with grime wiped to the corners of their faces. A few meet my gaze briefly and walk by to their own beds, ignoring me. It's a large room and yet it's filled by them.

One opens the shuttered window, leans out and whistles, another rushes over and they catcall abuse at a person walking in the street outside. Insults are passed between them, casual comments flung across the room. A splattering in the corner and someone yells about not filling the bucket too soon – they're going to have to empty it. The smell pervading the room becomes stronger. Sweat and urine dominate, I try and breathe through my mouth.

I pull myself up carefully to sit on the side of the bed and nearly fall through the gaps in the straps. I'm chained to the bed frame by my ankle, enough length to stand or lie down, no more. Reassured by the lack of interest in me, I twist, trying to see what's been done to my shoulder. It's too far around, I can't see anything.

"Not much on your back is there darling?" I jump and look up. My questioner has a single eyebrow topping off a body that easily weighs twice mine.

"I just wanted to know what they've done." I sound inane and flush.

"Don't worry, it's still nice and smooth." The comment is loaded and I freeze. The eyebrow wiggles at another man, nearly as big.

"What you doing here nob? Been exploring in the wrong places?"

"Get lots of excitement here..."

The comments come thick and fast, they've decided I'm interesting in the same way a small boy would torment a bug. Hard eyes, hard bodies, I feel small and insignificant, my replies are lost in the banter. The man with the eyebrow is the worst, every comment is laden with innuendo. Part of me is saying this man is a sadist, he's enjoying me being terrified. It doesn't make any difference. He's here and I'm penned in for the night with him. I look at the others and they meet my pleading gaze uninterested in my fear.

Eventually one stops the torture by saying, "So, you're the replacement." Not a question. I nod, not quite sure what or who I'm replacing and note the dismissal in his eyes. A clattering bell rings through the corridor and they turn their backs on me to get into their own beds.

"Night night sweet cheeks." A laughing comment in the dark as the lamps are blown out.

I'll never sleep. It's cold and I've got no shirt. My shoulder aches from where Talia threw that rock at me. My other shoulder pulses with every beat of my heart, the painkilling ointment has worn off and the brand is now a mass of hurt. How am I going to explain this to my family? The straw mattress scratches and tears leak out. I'm in a pen with a bunch of human animals. I'm sure I'm going to be raped at some unknown point in the future. I begin to shake, my teeth chattering. Something coarse is flung over me and I jump, a squeal bursting from me.

"Calm it kid. Now shut up and sleep."

The man in the bed next to me has thrown a blanket over me. It smells and is covered in something that's made it stiff. A tiny gift in the stinking night, I whimper and bite my tongue.

My dreams are full of dark streets with unknown danger around every corner. I run, dodging the people with blind eyes and outstretched arms who are trying to catch me – a macabre game of blind man's buff where I am the only one who can see. I have to find a way out, a place of safety... My thoughts dim and focus into a room with a child playing with a toy train on the floor while dust swirls about him. I know that boy and I shout, trying to warn him of an unidentified peril. He plays on, unconcerned. The train loop around, first down one set of tracks, then at a flick of his finger, down another. I watch as the dust gathers behind him, swirling in the unmoving air and looms over his head to block out the light. Dominic flicks a finger to change the points and smiles.

Chapter 7

"Go on, wiggle your arse at him, tell him you're gagging for it. That'll put a stop to him." One of my room mates speaks to me while I'm stood in the breakfast queue waiting to find out what slops I'm going to be fed. I don't have high hopes.

"You mean he won't…?" Desperation fills me, I can't finish off the sentence.

His tone is careless, "Oh he will, but he won't enjoy it as much and he might leave you alone afterwards." I gape, my brain struggling to understand the concept of casual rape.

He pushes at me companionably and grins, "Get your breakfast, you need to keep your strength up."

I'd been bounced out of sleep as a large clanging had echoed through the corridor. Sandy eyed, I was surprised I'd slept. My shoulder was bruised on the one side and I winced as I felt something tear on the other. Everything ached from the rough handling I'd had the day before.

The others were standing, docilely waiting for the door to be unlocked. My tormentor had winked at me and turned his back, I felt lucky to have survived the night unscathed. I no longer smelt the room, the night had inured my nose to the bucket in the corner. I stood by my bed, still chained to it and watched the others waiting.

The men filed out as the door opened and a guard came to prod at my shoulder. He waved impatiently, turned me around and slapped something on the leaking scab.

I asked, "Aren't you going to put something on it? Stop it getting dirty?"

"Air's the best thing for it. You want me peeling the bandage off after it's stuck to you? Keep breaking the scab and it'll get infected. Don't pick at it." He smacked at my wrist as he undid my chain. My protests that I hadn't, went on deaf ears and I was shoved into line with my room mates.

Back in the breakfast queue, the other man chuckles at my reaction to his comments and pushes an empty bowl at me. "Come on Gullible." Smarting, I follow him and have something slopped in. It smells surprisingly good. He laughs again, "Why do you think people come back when they're let out?" He nods at the bowl, "It's a damn sight better than what the freebies get. Now eat, you've a hard day ahead."

I tuck in. A vegetable, maybe seaweed was most of it, with slivers of fish and bread to mop up the juices. Comments are passed around with the jug. I gulp some down, and choke on the sour drink with my first gulp.

"Beer." The Eyebrow leers at me. "It'll put hairs where you need 'em." I feel myself flushing to the rest of the table's laughter.

After breakfast I'm taken through the mill. It's enormous, I hadn't realised how far it stretched past the plaza. The dormitories are on the top floor I'm told, the weaving on the bottom and preparation on the middle. Sheets of material roll high above me, flapping as they dry in the warmer air. A haze of dust hangs and I feel the rumblings of a cough beginning.

The men peel off, used to the routine. I stop, waiting to be told what to do and stare at a vision of Dante's hell, wondering if I can make it to the front door or if there's a back way out. The thumping of large hammers, the rattle of looms and shouts, shriller cries from the women and children. How can this be a life for anyone? I wonder where the wool comes from to make all this material, I've seen nothing but city so far.

Loops of electric lights hang from the ceiling giving a shaky glow, smaller oil lamps throw brighter patches in darker corners. Levers and pistons thrust through the floor, moving smaller cogs to turn different machines. Everything is crude and yet it works – just. I'm fascinated how they've planned all this, all these different machines. I guess they must use the tide for powering both lights and looms, the difference between high and low must be huge. I move closer to an iron bound piston punching to peer down through the hole in the floor, wondering if my guess is right. A crack in the air next to my ear nearly makes me fall into the gap.

"Boy!"

Yet another large man, I'm mesmerised by the whip he's waving. Even the small men, the ones my size, have muscles and an air of competency I lack. He looks me up and down with a disgusted expression. "You're helping Vihaan. Although I'm not sure what help you'll be..." He jerks his head and I slink after.

We walk through the mill to an upstairs room. Square cloth wrapped bundles are being winched through the large double doors in the side of the building. A number of men pull them in and untie them, spilling fleeces out onto the floor. The outer wrappings and ropes are thrown down to shouts below.

"Vihaan." My guide bellows and walks to the next room. I freeze as the Eyebrow appears, several fleece slung over his shoulder like an extra from Jason and the Argonauts.

"This one here's to help you." The foreman disappears and I stand rooted to the spot, alone with my tormentor. He grunts and slings a fleece in my direction. I raise my arms to catch it and am nearly knocked to the ground.

"This way." He swipes another fleece up in one meaty paw and walks through the door to stack it onto a rack. I stagger after him and drop it gratefully. I stare after him as he walks away. He stops and glances back. "This is what you do. Take a fleece from that room, bring it into this one and stack them. Think you can manage?" I nod and he turns away.

The fleeces are heavy and stink of ammonia. My face is frequently buried as I carry or more often drag them to the next room out of the way. Absently I wonder where they are getting the chemicals to clean them from and I jerk my face away as I remember – ammonia comes from urine. My guess is confirmed over the next few nights when I see the unlucky man taking the full pail out.

My arms are shaking by the time I've taken the second load over. The third load is worse, I end up dragging it. The floor is clean here, no dust to contaminate the washed goods. I stop for a rest, my arms and legs trembling, to be yelled at by one of the men hauling the bundles up. Vihaan sets me to undoing the bundles for a bit and then mercilessly hands me another pile when he thinks I've had a long enough break.

Just before the bell goes for lunch, the bales stop coming and the men on the crane lean against the walls to watch us work. The rough conversation is driven by bouts of innuendo aimed in my direction.

Vihaan sees my glances at their comments. "Just tell them where to go and they'll stop – probably." He has half his front teeth missing, making his grin lopsided.

The last fleece is taken by Vihaan and I relax against the open door frame in the hope of a longer break and peer over the edge to see men pulling the carts onto another track and re-fixing ropes. A bell is pulled and the carts begin to rattle away. No engine to be seen, I try to figure it out. The men move out of the way sharply as a loud rumble builds in the direction of the tracks.

Another set of trucks appear and I marvel at the simplicity of the system. A gravity fed railway, laden trucks pulling the empty ones back up the hill. This is how a civilisation claws its way back up, by using simple ideas that work. My own brain begins to work overtime, thinking of all the inventions thought up in my own world before technology took over. Steam engines, harvesters for crops, seed drills...I could help them here. Even if I couldn't remember exactly how to make them, surely someone could take the idea and make it work.

My thoughts are interrupted by Vihaan pushing at me, nearly knocking me out of the open doorway. "Back to work."

My thoughts turn dark. I'm here in the factory, no one wants to know my ideas or even cares that I have them. I grab a fleece and drag it viciously across the floor. At the sound of the double bell Vihaan drops his fleece and grabs mine, leaving me staggering. I join the queue and eat lunch without tasting anything, grateful for the chance to sit and mope.

The afternoon is similar, we drag small cartloads of carded wool to another room on the same floor. No time for a break here. I try and rest for a few minutes and a guard's whip flicks out and touches my back. I dance out of the way to hoots of laughter from the other workers. When Vihaan walks me over to the carding room and gets me to load trolleys for him, I almost forgive him for last night.

By the end of the day I'm walking in a haze of exhaustion. I stand behind Vihaan with my bowl, staring through his solid back. Someone bumps me from behind. I ignore it and it happens again, less gentle this time. At the third bump, I tell the person where to go without looking.

I become aware of the silence as a large hand lands on my head, turning me around. The man it belongs to is the same size as Vihaan, his other finger is raised, ready to poke again. I glare at him from under my eyebrows, totally fed up. I've been dragged into this world without a way back, I've been branded, had bricks thrown at me, been made fun of and worked to exhaustion and now this idiot is taking the piss. I slam my bowl down. The fear and rage comes boiling up and I raise my fists, aware on a level that I look ridiculous. Not caring, I spring forwards and an arm wraps itself around my waist, lifting me to one side.

"Back off fuck wit. He's one of ours."

It's Vihaan. I gape, shocked out of my anger. I swing my head and notice how the workers have crowded around, blocking the fight from view. Of a size, the two circle to the hoots of the others. Two bulls, slow and solid, eyeing each other, each waiting for a gap in the other's defence. They've both got huge work scarred hands and shoulders, anything connecting is going to hurt. The other man's nose is leaning sideways, he's broken it at some point and had it set badly.

I have a sick feeling in my stomach, I didn't mean for this to happen. I'm sure there'll be a punishment for fighting. Will the guards do something to stop this? I look for help and all I can see are the flashes of eyes and teeth, the people watching reduced to a pack of animals, waiting for one to be torn apart.

A few false swings as the tension mounts, I brace myself to run out and get between them. One of my room mates leans a casual arm on my shoulder. My legs buckle under the pain spreading from the brand. He pats my arm roughly and stands me upright again.

A murmur runs through the crowd, Vihaan and the other man nonchalantly turn their backs on each other. By the time the guards appear, I have been integrated back into the queue, away from my tormentor. I stand in line, almost dizzy in relief. No bloodshed, no one injured. The guards stalk down the line, flicking their whips and glaring. The mill workers studiously ignore them, whistling and tapping at their bowls, waiting for food. I try to set my face into innocence, knowing I look guilty.

We sit at our table and Vihaan lands his backside on the bench next to me with a thump. He grins, "You're our bum boy, not theirs" His eyebrow waggles and he knocks me on the shoulder, "Nice try with the pins." He motions with his fists imitating me. I flush, aware my fighting skills are non-existent but return the grin in relief as he picks up his bowl to eat.

Shortly afterwards, we are herded back to our dormitory. I'm exhausted and slump on my bed, fingering the blanket as I wonder if I can fall asleep in front of everyone.

Vihaan minces past, "Fancy anything to keep you warm darling?"

I freeze and then remember his approval of me standing up to the man in the queue. I clench my fists to stop them shaking. "Piss off, I'm tired."

Catcalls from the others inform me that I've impressed them. Vihaan's mouth gapes into a grin and when he takes a breath to reply, a faster man snakes his arm out to catch Vihaan in a neck lock and tells him to behave, they need to sleep.

Shaking the man off, Vihaan chuckles, "There you are darling," and throws me an extra blanket.

I don't know how many days I was there. All thoughts of escape fled from a mind too tired to think by the end of the day. The men teased me good naturedly and I was part of the group as they saw my efforts to keep up. The warmth surprised me, the feeling of acceptance from the uneducated workers. My previous life was another world away. Sheltered and cosseted, the barbed comments that had upset me so much meant nothing. I snapped back replies as fast as they were dished out. The rough ways I lived with no longer bothered me. Animal functions ruled – I ate, slept and defecated alongside them.

I became aware of the talk in the evenings before the lights went out. Grumbles about the work, the factory and the nobs on the hill that kept them down. I ask why they didn't move elsewhere or rebel.

"Look boy, see that?" One of the men drags another's shirt down to show the brand on his shoulder. A brief scuffle between them. "That means we're owned by Igren. Yes, he feeds us but if we run, the first thing that happens is that your shoulder's checked."

"You runs, you gets caught, you gets hung." Another agrees and there are nods from all around.

I venture, "But there's lots of you, not so many guards." The men are kind in their rough way as they explain that I've replaced a hung man. If they all rebel then no one with Igren's brand will be employed. They will starve, simple as that.

That night I sleep very little. This world is so different, there's nothing to stop you getting hurt, nothing to stop any other man from killing you. There's only the fellowship of my dorm mates between me and a harsh death. My bed had been slept in by man who'd lived alongside my workmates, who'd been hung at the gallows and swung in the breeze. I shiver, seeing my own face on the dead man and realise I will never go home.

"Ten day."

The cry of the guard is different to normal. I trot after my room mates, proud that my muscles no longer ache so badly after the long day. The men's normal innuendos are at fever pitch and I find myself in a room with buckets of water, containers of soft soap and crude scissors for clipping beards. I strip and scrub myself with the rest. After washing, water is thrown across the room in high spirits, even the few guards watching join in. I get a face full and throw a bucket load back, laughing at the ribald comments they make about my temper.

My shoulder still hurts if I catch it, but appears to be healing cleanly. I pull my clothes on and wait. I'm given a plain coin, half the size of my palm and a dull silver colour. I flick it over, there's nothing stamped on the other side. I'm dragged along with everyone and men from other dorms join us. There must be about thirty in total when we're let out of the front door.

My questions about where we're going are ignored. The men tramp through the streets and I wonder about escaping. Not many guards, and the streets aren't so well lit here. Maybe I could... I catch the eye of the guard from my first day, he smiles and hefts his crossbow. I quieten my thoughts, I've no second chance of running here.

Any comments quieten as we queue up at a door and I notice some trying to straighten clothes and push back hair. I'm prodded inside by the man behind me and shift to stand next to the wall, it looks like untold luxury after the days in the mill. There are hangings on the wall, polished tables and incense burning. I sink into a chair and watch. The other men are shifting, impatient and yet waiting quietly, there's an expectancy in the air.

A woman appears from behind a curtain. She walks up to a man and kisses him. Murmurs from the other men are muted, respectful. She leads him to a table and they sit. More women appear. Some take their men straight upstairs, others sit and talk or pick up card sets to play games. Not all the women are young, some are older.

The effect on the men I've worked alongside is civilising and then the realisation hits – I'm in a whorehouse. Slowly I rise, wondering if I can slide outside, I don't want to be part of this. I don't care about the crossbows, maybe they'll let me go back. Just as I think I can get to the door, I find a hand on my arm.

"Are you Daniel?" An older woman stands in front of me. I nod, trying to see a way out without dying or worse. "Someone would like to see you upstairs. Have you your token?"

Worse than dying? My mouth dries out and I'm left speechless. Sensing my panic, she tucks her hand underneath my arm and steers me towards the stairs. Starved of female company, any comments made by my dorm mates are mild, their attention is for the women in front of them. I've no chance of running, it would be noticed. I feel the sweat breaking out under my armpits. What is this unknown woman going to expect of me? I can barely talk to the women of my old world. By the time we've reached the top of the stairs I'm nearly rigid with fear.

My escort laughs gently, "Don't worry, there's nothing to be frightened of."

Noises can be heard coming from the other rooms, I'm caught between a desperation that she's a whore and that it's not right and a fascination for what could happen if I let it. I feel sick as we walk, suddenly unsure of what I even want and knowing my own body is betraying me. There is a door at the end of the corridor, she gestures and opens it for me.

I remind myself about the diseases that can be caught and shut my eyes, I can't do this. The decision is agonising. I slide in and take a deep breath to say I don't want to. The door shuts in my face and I turn to face the bed, my heart in my mouth.

Chapter 8

Talia is lying on the bed, picking at her nails with her knife, her dirty shoes on the clean sheets. My mind races to catch up with what my eyes are seeing. Does she work here? Is she a whore too? I look back at the closed door and my muddled thoughts shriek that there's no way I'm touching her.

She smirks and cuts through the fuzz in my head, "You look like a Blubber fish."

"A what?"

"Big mouth." She gapes at me, opening and closing her own.

The familiar irritation pricks at me for the first time in days, "Does she know you're here?" I gesture behind me.

"Course, I asked her to keep an eye out for you." Talia pulls herself up and wipes her nose on her sleeve. "Saw you get caught by Igren's lot, I knew it wouldn't be long until you came here. He's alright is Igren." She catches my look and qualifies, "If you like that sort of thing."

"Why are you here?"

"You ain't from round here. There'll be a reward for you. Igren's one of the good ones but he still can't think past his own nose." She pulls a face and throws something at me. I nearly fumble the catch as my jumper unravels. I pull it on and nearly miss her next question in the luxury of the warmth from a softer land.

"So, you coming?"

"Where?" I start as she opens the shutters and blows the lamp out. "Why'd you do that?"

A sigh in the dark, "You need your night vision nob. Unless you want to stay with Igren. Good food, nice beds. I can get Betha back up here if you want to stay. May as well enjoy what's on offer."

The comments bite. I've spent days taking crap from the men and dealing with it, five minutes with Talia and I'm back to the familiar feeling of not measuring up. "I'm not a nob. Stop calling me that. I'm not as clever as you are here, but just you wait. If you were in my world, the shoe would be on the different foot all right."

"Shoe on a different foot?" There's complete incomprehension in her voice.

I wrestle my frustration down and say, "I'm not stupid. I've taken exams, I've got qualifications, they're just not useful here."

"Egg Sams? I have eggs when I can find the nests." She sounds wistful in the dark and I suppress the urge to groan. Why is talking to Talia always so difficult? She's not stupid, none of the men in the mill were either. It's just a different level of intelligence, they've not had the book learning I've had. Frankly though, I think Talia delights in outsmarting me, she's always pulling the conversation in the opposite direction to the way I expect. Heavy footsteps and laughter come down the corridor and I'm reminded why I don't want to stay.

I fumble my way to the window, feeling for the frame and say, "Just get me out of here."

The climb is frankly terrifying in the dark. There's a slight ledge below the windows for our toes. I lean into the wall and see Talia's outline inching sideways, hooking her hands into gaps left by broken bricks. We sidle past lit windows, hearing the grunts and laughter of my dorm mates with their companions. I barely breathe all the way across to the next building, trying not to think about how vulnerable we are. My arms are shaking by the time Talia grabs my wrist to drag me through a broken window.

Talia can barely see more than I can, and I snatch for her hand as we stumble over blocks and detritus. She pauses at the broken door, peering out to check for the guards and hushes me when I ask if we're safe. My mind is full of crossbows and how easy it is to aim them, remembering how my guard had hefted his with a grin. One figure is in the light at the junction, we wait until he turns to casually wave at his friend. Hearts thumping, we move through the dark shadows in the other direction. Once on the next street and out of sight, we dart into the back alleys.

Talia leads me and this time I trust her – she knows what she's doing. At her insistence, I try not to look at the lights hanging at the intersections. She stops several times to cough, hacking her guts up and spitting. My own lungs ache in sympathy, it's a cough I've heard echoed throughout the factory. I'm blind as she pushes me through a doorway, my shoulder brushes against the door frame. She lights a candle and I shade my eyes, the flame throws wavering shadows onto the wall. Shielding it from the breeze, she motions me down the staircase and I recognise her hiding place.

I sag in relief as she tucks the candle into a cranny, "Can they find us? Will they look for me?"

"Course they'll be looking. You'll have been marked. Here, let's have a look." She spins me around and pulls at the neck of my jumper to look at my back before I can stop her. "Nice." Choking, I wrestle her hands off using several words I wouldn't have dreamt of using a week before.

"Ooh, been mixing with the hard men have we?" I catch a half smile from her in the candlelight and feel oddly pleased. Her expression turns serious. "We've missed the meeting, he won't bother again."

"What meeting?" I can see Talia bite back a remark. "Yeah alright, I'm a nob. But if you don't tell me anything..."

She suddenly grins and her face lights up. She's still not pretty, she's not got enough teeth and is far too skinny, but there's genuine amusement there. "We need to get up behind the wall, to the nob's part and get you back in there."

"I've told you, I'm not from there."

She sniffs, "They'll know what to do with you." I sigh and it turns into a yawn, maybe they will. Someone must know how to get me back home.

We settle down for the night and I find I'm missing the company from the dorm. Despite the warmth of my jumper, the chill still slides its way into my bones. I hunch myself up and slide my hands between my legs, squeezing them to keep the warmth in. More for the sake of talking, I tell Talia in the dark about the men refusing to rebel in fear of the consequences and she agrees to an extent.

"It happened a long time ago when the factories were smaller and there were more owners. It's always been used as a threat to keep the workers in check. A lot of people starved, that's why some of us won't work for them. We don't like being kept in one place with no options." I hear her voice becoming thoughtful in the dark. "Still, that was years ago. The guards only shoot enough to keep the rest behaving, they can't afford to lose them. In theory…" Her voice trails off.

"What?"

"Nothing. Go to sleep." Her voice has become sharp again. I shake my head, it's not my problem, I only need to get home. I don't need the problems of this troubled world as well as my own.

In the morning Talia stuffs a canvas bag into my arms and leads me downhill in a different direction to the brothel and Igren's factory. I've insisted that she takes us to where she found me. I don't care that she's not pleased and thinks I'm interfering with her plans – it's my way home we're looking for.

It's good to be out in the air, stretching my legs instead of the warm noisy factory, even if the air is damp and grey. I stride next to her, shoulders back and nearly whistling my happiness. Talia gives me several sideways glances and I can see her biting her tongue. We stop at an unremarkable intersection and she waves her hand towards the middle.

"S'here." She's not being helpful.

I sigh and ask, "Where was I exactly?"

Talia glowers and points to a window, "There." I move to lean against the wall, trying to remember the exact sequence of events. It's no use, I could have been anywhere in this city. I turn and run my hands over the wall. Nothing.

I speak out loud, thinking it might help us both, "I couldn't grasp the rift until I had my arm around the girl's waist and she pulled me in. It's like a void between our two worlds, a place where we weren't supposed to be. Everything was tight, I couldn't breathe." I paused remembering, "She slid out of my arms before I came through. She was the same size as you." I look over to see Talia stood with her arms wrapped around her waist, hugging herself as though cold.

"Here." I reach out to show her how I'd been pulled through and she twists out of my arms, her face glancing up at mine and for an instant I see the girl from the rift. I stop, stunned by the fear in her face.

"Come on nob. Nothing to be found." The sneer is back in her voice as she walks away and I automatically follow, thinking furiously. That look, now I'm sure that girl was Talia but why wouldn't she take me back? Why is she so adamant that only these nobs can help me? She found me again after I'd been taken by Igren, had she found a higher bidder? I watch her back as she stalks in front. Her clothes are wrong, I'm sure it was blue jeans the girl had been wearing, and baggy over her skinny legs. The hair's wrong too, it's too long. Nobody can grow their hair that quickly. My head aches and I resolve to keep an eye on Talia, wary for any betrayal.

I get left by a wall. I lean, surveying the quiet streets and try to project the same confidence the men at the factory had. Inside I'm a mass of worry as Talia saunters up to a man, not much different to the one who tried to kill me on the first evening. He wraps a boozy arm around her and whispers in her ear. I find myself straining to hear, knowing I've no chance. She coyly slaps him away, a side to her I've not seen before and I realise she's flirting to get information. The man keeps trying to grope her and despite everything, by the time she walks back in my direction, I'm fuming for her.

"What the hell was he doing to you?"

"It's fine, Martie hasn't been able to get it up for years." Her voice is careless. I'm spluttering my indignation, it doesn't matter if he can or not. A horrifying thought occurs – how does she know? My thoughts must be obvious and she laughs at my face.

"What's worse, him having a grope or your bum pals back at Igren's? That bloke who was protecting you, he'd have had you in a second if he'd wanted to. Anyway, I've got a name and a place." She tucks her hand into my elbow to pull me along and I realise I'm embarrassing her in front of her contact.

"Talia?" She grunts in reply, still frowning. "How old are you?"

Her face is a picture as she turns, "Does it matter?"

"Don't you count the years? Every winter or summer or something?"

"Winter?"

"As the seasons change." Her face is still crinkled. "Hot weather, cold weather, more rain, sunshine?"

"It doesn't change. It's always like this."

Fog, mist and a cold dampness that seeps into everything. I feel my spirits sink. "So the whole island's like this?"

She brightens, "Up on the hill it's different. The nobs blocked it off."

"Why?" I haven't had much information about this world, anything might help.

She shrugs, "They keeps the best stuff up there. They have the space to grow green stuff for meat to eat. They give us stuff down here, we give them stuff back."

"What sort of stuff?"

She mimics my face, "What were you making at the factory?"

"You mean the wool comes from up the hill?"

She rolls her eyes at my slowness and saunters in front, making it clear she's bored with the conversation. "Better come with me nob." I sigh at Talia's inability to use my name as she continues, "Can't go up to the hill empty handed, even with you to give back. Gotta find something."

I don't want to go up the hill, I want to go home and I'm still not sure I trust her. What can these nobs do to help? My stomach rumbles, no breakfast was offered this morning, and seeing Talia's thin arms, I didn't like to ask. Visions of cereal, porridge and toast dripping with butter run through my mind as I walk.

I follow her to another part of Narith, more rundown and only the occasional person to be seen in the distance. The quiet intensifies, I find myself breathing lightly, trying to hear through the silence. This city is enormous, the amount of people it must have once held. I try to imagine the streets bustling and jump at the crack of wings from a pigeon-like bird. It even affects Talia, she hunches over and stays to the sides of the streets, not wanting to be seen. She darts into an alleyway, levers a few bricks out of a wall and pulls out a handful of rags. Glancing around, she shoves the bricks back into the hole and walks swiftly out, stuffing the rags into the bag I carry.

Walking up the hill I get more of a sense of the size of the city. The bay is hidden in the mist below and I wonder if it ever lifts. As we climb, the sun shines through stronger until we finally reach an open area before a long building. Talia looks up and counts the blank windows to arrive at a small archway down some steps.

"We're stopping here. Martie says he meets his contact every morning after ten day. We've gotta get in to meet him." She points up at the building in front of us and I realise it's not just a building, it's a wall snaking its way along the contours of the hill. This is where the nobs live. Windows and doors have been filled in, the wall is the height of the buildings down by the docks. I crane my neck and see a figure walking past along the top.

Talia whisks me into the shelter of the archway. There's a wide gap across the top with iron spikes showing in front of the door. We stop underneath them as she bangs on it. I take a step back to get out of the way of the portcullis and she drags me back into line with the peep hole that's just opened. I stand, feeling vulnerable with the weight of the iron balancing above me. A whispered conversation through the peep hole and Talia rummages through the bag I carry to pass something through. The peep hole slams shut and she stares intently at the wood. I shift from foot to foot, waiting and eventually the door opens for us.

I duck through and we enter a small room. A brazier is smoking gently in the corner, coals glowing. Dice and cards are set up for an interrupted game of patience. I feel more like a loose end than ever as Talia is passed something and told directions. Both doors leading to and from this room are heavily barred and an efficient looking crossbow leans next to the man talking.

Talia grabs my hand to walk me into the corridor, her eyes are everywhere and I presume she's storing any information she can to sell. Strings of electric lights show the way through the corridors. It's almost dreamlike in the quiet, there are no windows and the walls, when we pass through doorways, are thick like a fortress. Disorientated, I let Talia lead with the feeling we are walking through the wall, not along it, heading up at every intersection. We get stopped by the few people we meet. Talia shows her token to them, they point out directions and we are left to continue walking.

Finally we come to a winding staircase and Talia glowers at me, "Keep your mouth shut." I sigh as she turns to walk up the stairs, I do little else around her other than follow and be told not to talk.

Another small room, someone is sprawled in front of the fire, his boots on a stool. His hair is greasy, clothes better kept and in brighter colours than Talia's. He's my age, better fed than most I've seen and with a wary intelligence in his eyes. He stares, assessing us as we walk in.

"Where's Martie?" His voice is petulant.

"Not here. You're Bay?"

"I've told Martie to stop giving my name out. Why shouldn't I have you thrown out?"

"I got something for someone. Worth something it is."

Talia stalks around the room, eyeing him as she talks. Half the conversation I don't understand, scraps of comments, rumours. I wonder where this is leading as they spar with words, I can't tell who's winning. Talia has a charm about her when she's talking like this, one that hasn't come out when she's spoken to me. Her hands wave as she talks and her face lights up with a sly appeal.

Bay in turn pretends indifference, his fingers play with a necklace and a shadow shifts under his chair. A large head pokes out and yawns. A dog with the most perfect set of teeth I've seen so far on either man or beast slides out. The boy drops his hand down and pulls the dogs ears gently, smirking at Talia twitching away.

He asks about the factories and I see the flash in Talia's eyes at the sudden curiosity on his face and I realise he's not been down there. She fills him in, including what I've told her about the workers not daring to revolt. Uneasy at the casual betrayal, I shift the weight off my feet and catch Bay's attention.

"What about him, he doesn't look useful."

"Leave him, he's important. He lays out the dead." Bay flinches. I open my mouth to say that actually I only work in the office and shut it again. If these nobs can help then any advantage I can gain for us is good.

I decide to act smart and try to ignore my heart thumping. "I liked your funicular railway." Bay looks blank. "The one that brings the wool down to the mills. It's a good idea to use gravity to pull the carts up after they've been emptied. Wasn't something I was expecting here." I manage to sound condescending.

"Told you he was special." Talia's face is a mirror image of the cat in my shed. Bay is puzzled at the difference between my words and appearance.

I lean against the wall, feigning boredom. "Would be interesting to know how your supply chains work. Obviously you keep your stock behind the wall?" My stomach's churning, I'm dreadful at this sort of thing. Talia's examining her nails, a smirk on her face. Bay tightens his lips, unsure how much I know. I wander over to the fire and leave him to stew. Proper fires are rare from what I've seen and I make the most of it, warming my legs.

Bay narrows his eyes and walks to the shuttered window. "Look," he says and flings it open, making the fire flare.

We're high on the inside of the wall. Well above the mist, the sun shines on paradise. Plateau after plateau of grasslands stepped high up the mountain side. In the distance I see the mountain, cone shaped and smoking gently. My gaze falls to the window sill and the familiar ash covering it.

Small woods are dotted throughout and a lake is close by. I can see the inside curve of the wall, doorways and windows leading out, but very few people using them. The amount of land contained must be enormous. Sheep are scattered across the pastures, nothing larger and I realise I haven't seen any large animals on the other side of the wall either. Any carts here are pulled by hand. Talia is staring, the green is almost hypnotic after the grey of the city.

Bay's come to a decision while we've been gaping. "I'll help you but I'll need something to smooth the way." Talia glances at me once, no doubt weighing me up against the price of another middleman to please. He shuts the window and waves a hand, "You may use my name once more."

Subdued by the riches she's been shown, Talia nods and leads me out. She's silent as we walk. The doorman shows us out with a smirk, the plebs shown their place. At some point I realise we're not going back the way we came.

"Where are we going?"

"Aren't you hungry nob?" I don't need to answer, my stomach grumbles for me. She chuckles. "Need to get some food."

"More rat?" I try not to sound too disgusted, although it hadn't tasted as bad as I'd thought.

"Nah, need other stuff. You eat too much. Here." She goes through the bag and shoves a bundle into my hands. When I look dim, she rolls her eyes and mimes wrapping it around my head and shoulders. "Igren's men'll be looking for you." I cover my head hastily, leaving the ends to dangle over my shoulders like a scarf.

Another square, the fourth edge dropping off into the sea. I peer over and Talia pulls me back sharply. There must be at least a ten foot drop and then rubble below, exposed by the tide. On the other two sides, ruined buildings lead into the water, more gradually appearing as the tide drops still further. The smell is incredible here, salt, seaweed and sewers. At the far end of the square, people are lining up to be served at tables, presenting something. Money? I realise I've nothing to give. I pat my pockets and find the silver coin.

"Is this worth anything?"

Talia snorts in laughter, "Only if you fancy one. Still..." She plucks it from my hand and pretends to flutter her eyelashes at me as I groan. "Don't worry nob," Talia gives me a friendly shove. "I'll get plenty for you."

She sobers abruptly and remains wary the whole time we're in line, tense and constantly looking to see who's around. We reach the front to the queue, Talia hands over a small grey disc, half the size of mine and gets a bag of something. She dumps the bag in my arms and motions me to stay behind her. The bag slops in my arms, it feels like rice and knobbly vegetables.

I shift it into the shoulder bag as Talia stops to talk in a low voice to an old man with a much younger boy leading him. I stand and stare out into the waves. The sun arcs through the mist behind me and they clear momentarily, revealing the city to be a disaster zone under the waterline, ruined buildings are half collapsed shadows as they reach into the distance. The water is oily closer in and reflects the sun, burning my eyes. I squint, a grey smudge on the horizon shows probable land and then the mists roll back in. Talia takes hold of my arm and marches me back in the direction of her home.

"Is it ever clear?" I ask, sparks lighting up my vision. She grunts, still looking for trouble. "What's up?" I try not to look as though I'm looking, knowing I'll fail in her eyes.

"It's dangerous to queue up." We're walking fast. "People want to know about you, where you've been. Where you sleep and if you'll join them." Having met up with Igren, I guess the joining won't be voluntary.

"Those people you were talking to, do you trust them?"

"No. I'd sell them as fast as they'd sell me if I had to."

"Then why..."

"Information. Now walk." We leave the people behind and she begins to relax. We stop so she can check to make sure no one's following.

"What now?" My feet are aching and my stomach is touching my backbone.

She grins and pokes the bag I'm carrying, "Food."

Chapter 9

Talia is a surprisingly competent cook when not forced to roast rat. The bag contains lentils and a few vegetables. The remaining ingredients go into a sealed jar, tucked back into its hidey hole. I wait impatiently for the lentils to cook through.

To pass the time, I say, "I saw the city going underwater."

"Yeah, you used to be able to walk all the way to the mainland once."

"When? How do you know?" The guard hadn't known.

Talia shrugged, not caring, "Someone told me."

"What happened?"

"The waters came up, only the people on the island managed to escape."

"When?" I'm fascinated. I remember reading about the low lying land of the English Channel and the waters flooding the marshes between. I wonder what it must have been like. A huge tsunami wave breaking everything in its way or just the waters rising relentlessly with the people fleeing in front? I shudder, die fast or die slow.

She shrugs again, "Dunno, it happened a long time ago. Nobody believes me." Disgust fills her voice, it's the end of the conversation as far as she's concerned.

A mug is produced and dipped into the thin soup. I see her wavering and motion for her to take her share first, despite my own hunger. She doesn't hesitate, barely waiting for it to cool. She slurps at the dregs and fills it again for me. I find myself gulping it down in a similar way and she laughs. It steams and fills my belly. We share the rest of the pot and she swills the cup out, tucking it upside down into a corner to drain.

She stands and stretches, "Come on."

"Where are we going?"

"Diggin'."

We walk for what feels like miles. With Biggles on a lead and breakfast inside, I'd happily walk for hours. The soup has filled me but also sloshes alarmingly in my stomach. I glance around, the scenery hasn't improved, just become more ruined. More sky shows through empty windows, rubble across the streets. A huge viaduct marches across the skyline, one of the few structures I've seen in good repair.

"What does that do?"

"Carries water." Her replies have been short all the time we've been walking, she doesn't want to talk. I'm also uneasy, too aware of eyes watching from the doorways or is it my imagination? A gleam of teeth and a shadow moves. Talia stoops, grabs for a stone and throws it. A yelp and a dog skitters away. She grunts her satisfaction. My wariness increases. When was my last tetanus jab? I try to remember the symptoms and I step more carefully, keeping an eye on my footing.

This part of Narith is stepped into the hill, a series of house sized buildings half buried in a land slip rather than the factories I'd seen so far. We pick our way between the houses, the streets must be buried metres deep. So many of them are falling to pieces. The tsunami, a huge moon and the smoking cone in the distance across the plateau lands – was this earthquake territory as well?

There's nobody around, I've not seen anyone for ages, this part is deserted. Talia stops and glances about, she doesn't appear to be taking any chances. She catches my hand and drags me to a window. I'm larger than her and have to squeeze through. She tests each step she takes down a half rotted staircase. At one point we climb, sliding our feet into holes in the walls. Talia guides my feet, I can barely see now. We move down with every step and I become conscious of the weight of the earth above me.

The staircase comes to an end and she pulls at me, to go through the bag I carry, not bothering to ask. A candle is lit, illuminating the room we stand in. Earth and rock, the walls are thick with decay. Plaster is coming off the walls in lumps, and large cracks showing through the brickwork. Another gap in the floor to the side of us, the wooden steps long gone.

"This lot's been cleared out years ago." She catches my look, "We're going further in. The rest were too chicken. There's good findings down here."

Too chicken, I gulp. I can see the earth tumbled around one end of the room, the black space of the empty stairwell close by. Water drips, it's quiet here or would that be quieter? Outside in the street had been quiet enough. Little to be heard of the factories working to supply the nobs on the hill and only the occasional wisp of smoke betraying a fire.

"What sort of findings?"

"Stuff." She moves towards the stairwell, the candle wavering. Our shadows are huge, supplemented by the stains into grotesque figures. She carefully drips wax onto the oddly shaped plate she'd taken from the bag. I realise its purpose when she clenches it between her teeth, the candle pointing away from her face. Talia clambers down like a monkey. Given the choice between staying on my own in the dark and going further into danger, I follow.

The climb isn't as bad as it looks. The earth slide has come into the stairwell and we shift around larger rocks. Talia stops in an opening and takes the plate out of her mouth. "Stop here."

She breathes heavily and places the candle on the floor, readying herself for a coughing fit. We're in the room below. The earth has broken through in one corner, swallowing it slowly, inch by inch.

Talia wipes her mouth and picks up the candle. "This way." She leads me through a rectangle of blackness. It's a warren down here, a whole buried city.

To hide my nerves, I start talking quietly about the subject that's been bugging me since I got here. "What do you know about the grey men?" She glowers at me and I'm not sure if it's me speaking or the subject.

"They been leaving dead bodies all over the city for years." The whites of her eyes show in the candlelight. Her voice is tight. I don't blame her for not wanting to talk about them, I've only seen them a few times and the results scared me.

"One got to a man before I was taken to Igren's factory. Everyone ignored him, what happened to him?"

"Don't you know?"

"Why should I?"

She stops to consider me. "They look like you." I think back to both the grey figures I'd seen, I couldn't remember much, only a dizziness that pulled. Their faces had been mostly hidden by the hood, I'd no idea if they looked like me or not. Talia's face is a pale circle in the dimness, the soft candlelight kind to the harsh lines and dirt on her face. We have a moment when we're not fighting, she's as curious as I am. Then she snorts and breaks the moment, jerking her head. "This way."

Another stairwell, this one tighter. One breath from Mother Earth and we'll both be taken into her cold embrace.

"Here." Even Talia's voice is quieter, the usual edge gone. She wriggles around a corner and I see the signs of digging. She grabs for the bag again, pulling out a trowel. She moves the earth aside with short sharp sweeps, shifting larger rocks with a practised hand. Without being asked, I hold the candle up to help and she nods her approval.

Something catches her eye. A careful flick uncovers a tiny figure, no larger than her hand. It's corroded and green with age. Talia picks the soil out from around it and curls her fingers to pick it up. She motions at me to open my bag and places it inside, with more care than I've seen her use yet.

"Is it good?"

She shrugs, "Maybe. I'll clean it off and see."

She scrapes the removed earth into a spoil heap behind her, moving forwards slowly. A patter of soil and another gleam is revealed. This time it's long and thin. Talia's trowel traces the outline. It's bigger, something intricate. I find myself pointing out the specks in the dimness. We're both absorbed in the discovery. It's big, small cogs and wheels can clearly be seen. It's some kind of machine. I can see the gleam in Talia's eyes, she wants this. I share her feeling I also want to take this home and wash it, I point out parts she wouldn't have noticed as she scrapes away. It's so complex, my fingers are itching to mend it and make it work. Several figures are on top and traces of paint still show in the candlelight.

Talia leans back to shake her hair out of her face and points to the overhang above. "Need to clear this."

She slices decisively and I jump at the groan as the earth shifts, the terror of being buried alive rising to squeeze my throat. Talia's eyes and trowel are everywhere, catching planes of earth to let it patter harmlessly onto the floor. A muffled sound and the pile in front moves, a trickle of water pools from the base and finds its way past my feet. The machine is covered, I'm sure it's twisted beyond repair.

I'm sweating. "It's gone, can't we leave?"

Talia shakes her head, "That stuff's worth something."

She jumps back as the soil heaves and rushes towards us. Totally unnerved, my voice breaks as I squeal. The earth stops by my ankles.

I say with as much authority as I can, "Talia. I'm leaving."

"Fine. Leave."

She takes the candle from me, goes back to the pile where the machine is hidden and starts scraping. I'm left in the dark of the doorway, staring at the dark earth in the candlelight. Talia's having to dig one handed.

I don't want to stay. The black stairwell looms in my mind, how can I climb back up knowing she's down here? I imagine trying to bargain with Bay without Talia when I don't even know what to ask for. I thrust my hand in the bag I carry, a few smooth cylinders meet my fingers as well as the figure she'd found earlier. She has the lighter in her pocket. I have nothing without her. I grit my teeth and edge closer to help, trying to keep an eye on the pile in the dim light. Sweat soaks me in the cool air, I want to be out of here as fast as possible. We work swiftly and lever the contraption out in one piece. It's caked in mud and there are several small stones wedged between the rods and cogs. Talia is chortling to herself.

"Right. Can we leave now?"

She nods and cradles her prize. I have a sense of pressure, of something waiting to change and I don't want to be here when it does. We reach the first stairwell. I stare upwards, how the hell are we going to get that thing up there? My nostrils flare and I begin to shake, I want to get out of here, a primitive fear of being trapped is starting to rise. I steady my breathing, panicking isn't going to help.

Talia appears unaffected and refuses to be beaten by something so mundane. She rummages through the bag and takes out various long scraps of fabric and ties it to my back. It's awkward but I can climb with it on. She takes the plate in her teeth and points out the handholds to me.

A groaning crash from next door. Talia jumps for the first handhold and scampers up. I'm a second behind as the earth pours in from the room we've just left, a bubbling river, an animal intent on smothering us. Something gives on the other side of the stairwell and I'm following Talia up with the earth boiling at my feet, cursing the machine strapped to my back, the slight weight now dragging me down. The earth attached to it calling to the earth rising beneath. I'm alone in this hell, searching for the circle of light above, one wrong move and I'll drop into the pit below. I scrabble for the handholds, finding them by more luck than design. The feeble light disappears and I feel a scream rising at the smothering darkness.

The edge of the stairwell, I heave myself over into the circle of light and nearly freeze at the world shaking around us. I can't hear anything. Talia mouths something, grabs my arm and pulls me sideways. Adrenaline spurs me on, helping me to dodge obstacles and balance across broken beams. For once my feet are as nimble as Talia's and my determination rises, we will defeat this beast and come out alive. Talia's hindered by trying to shield the candle as we run a different way through the buried rooms. The hill is grumbling all around us.

She stops, another landslide is in front, the patter of soil saying it's new. A last crash from behind and everything is quiet. All I can hear is the blood pounding in my ears and my panting. Talia begins to cough. I close my eyes, my knees weak. Safe, for the moment.

My feeling of safety doesn't last long. The earth has come through the rooms behind us as well as in front. We have two candles apart from the one that's lit. Talia paces, her face is grim, mud streaked across her forehead. The land slip's a major one. Everything groans, threatening to move further if we try to dig across the top. A room and a half is all we have between us and a chilly death. Water trickles down, adding to the worry. If there's a stream coming through, then everything is going to move again. The fact that it's cold and we have no food are now minor worries – we are unlikely to die from either hyperthermia or starvation.

I state the obvious. "Unless you have any ideas, we've no way out."

Talia's eyes flash in the candlelight, she starts to speak and then stops herself. Something about the way she looks at me, it's almost as if she's biting something back. The fear in her eyes, I think back to the intersection where I tried to take hold of her waist and the way she'd looked up at me then. The two memories slot together in the same way my arm had fitted around her waist. Was Talia somehow that girl who brought me through?

"Talia." She snarls wordlessly as she paces between the two rooms like a caged animal. I take a deep breath, "Talia. Can you open a rift…?"

"Shut up!"

The scream is deadened by the weight of the earth around us. There's something in the force of her denial, she's completely on the defensive. This isn't the Talia who told Bay rumours and half truths to get what she wanted or the one who flirted with drunken Martie, she's shaking. Her fists tighten and for a minute I think she's going to charge me. I raise my hands but refuse to step back.

"You know something." Her eyes are wide, showing the whites. I'm right, I must be. She's scared. Tough, if there's a way out of here, then I'm going to take it. This place is scaring me too. "Talia."

"You don't understand. I can't do it." She sinks onto the floor, just outside the circle of light. My hope builds, she's lying badly now, I must be onto something.

I feel like a shit bullying a skinny girl, maybe a few years younger than me.

"I saw you."

"No." She's shaking her head, twisting her fingers. "No. I'm a good girl. I got told not to and I haven't." When I crouch down next to her, she clutches at my shoulder and peers into my face. "I can't. He'll find me."

"Who?" She goes silent. "Talia. We've got to get out of here, we'll die otherwise. I'll protect you." How the hell I'm going to do that, I don't know. I can't even protect myself in this world. She curls into a ball, sobbing. The water begins to trickle faster, a pool forming by the wall.

This is bad. Something's scared Talia badly enough to make her cry. I guess not much does that, however I'm also not keen on staying here, is the wall behind us beginning to bulge? I can't tell in the candlelight. I light another and the circle grows. Talia's hunched on the floor, her face pressed into her knees, a bundle of rags and bones. I wrap an arm around her and pull her close.

"Talia. We aren't going to get out of here without you doing what you've been told not to do." I wince as I try to follow my own sentence. That wall's definitely bulging. I rub her arm briskly. "Just the once, okay? Maybe whoever it is you're scared of won't notice."

She raises her head and looks into my eyes. I try to look reassuring. "Come on," I say. I can feel her shaking. There's a damp stain under my backside, the water's coming in faster. I help her uncurl and stand up. She sniffs and wipes her eyes.

"I shouldn't be doing this. I got told not to."

"Who said so?" I keep my eyes on her to try to give her the confidence I don't feel. I imagine the pressure of the earth behind the wall, waiting for something to give.

"Mamin, before she disappeared."

"Try. I told you, I saw you doing this. Take me home Talia."

Talia closes her eyes, sweat beading her forehead, her hands up in front of her. She concentrates, feeling for something. Her eyes pop open, tears streaking her cheeks, "Can't." She's got a childlike desperation in her eyes, she wants me to believe she can't do this. She's got nothing left inside to hide behind.

I stand behind her and put my hands on her shoulder and for once she doesn't shake me off. "Come on. I saw you do it." I coax her, "Hold your hands up again, I know you can do this."

She shakes her head, "I don't know where to go. It's not safe." Her shoulders are slumped, hair hanging over her face.

"My world's safe. I saw you outside our orchard, don't you remember?" I see her face twist and remember she doesn't know what an orchard is. "Okay, I'll describe the woods on the hill where I live then. They're like the trees we saw out of Bay's window, only there are a lot more of them. I walk there every morning with Biggles my dog."

I rub her shoulders gently as I talk about the tall straight trunks, the brown leaves between the paths and the fresh air when walking before breakfast. The views from between the leaves out over the valley and the roads in the distance. How Biggles loves to race ahead and look back at me, his tongue hanging out in a smile.

I tell her that I'm worried that my parents have missed me and my voice catches. A longing sweeps over me, I want to go home.

Talia raises her arms decisively, her face is set, mouth pulled down. Her fingers run over the air and suddenly catch, a grey line appearing. The air in my lungs stops, she can do this. She's breathing harder now, pulling at it. I stand behind her, watching for the eye wrenching light. She grunts with the effort and a decided split shows in the air. The ground underneath us starts to rumble, the air pressure changing as a smell of soggy earth rises. I move to help and my hand passes through the split, unable to touch it.

"Get your leg into it and pull. I can't help yet."

She groans and twists her body into the gap. It shifts reluctantly with a familiar wet sucking sound echoed by the soil starting to move behind. A loud crack, the bricks in front of us begin to shift. In a panic, I grab for Talia's waist and let her pull us through.

Chapter 10

Once inside the split, I find I can grasp it. That same feeling of being somewhere I shouldn't, of the rift trying to reject me back into a space that doesn't exist anymore. I think of the earth collapsing into the rooms behind us and shudder or try to. I hold onto Talia with one arm and push futilely into the rubber with the other. She seems to turn, a blind mole seeking its way through vibration. The muscles in her waist are tight with determination and unlike me, she moves, wriggling and shoving in one direction. All of a sudden the resistance is gone and we're no longer swimming against the current, rather we are being spat out in a more convenient direction. The same stomach turning feeling as the rift peels apart and we push through to fall into a heap.

I gasp in the familiar smell of beech woods. Last year's leaves rustle underneath me, crisp and dry. I look up to see the familiar green and blue lace of my own world and close my eyes in relief. Tears leak out and for once I'm not ashamed, Talia has got me home.

A muffled noise makes me turn, Talia is sobbing quietly into her arms. I try to move and against all logic, find a large amount of mud has come through with me. Shuddering, I kick my way free of it and remember the contraption still strapped to my back. I can't undo the knots, I'll need a knife to get through them. I crouch close to her and she looks up, smearing the tears away with a muddy hand.

"You did it. You got me back." I can't keep my excitement out of my voice.

Talia refuses my hand and stands up, looking around with one shoulder higher than the other. "Never been here in my life."

I roll my eyes and get my bearings. We're a little higher than the usual path I take, it's about half an hour's swift stride downhill. It's early morning by the look of the sun, with that tingle to the air saying late spring is turning into early summer.

"Come on." I hitch the mess of mud and metal higher and turn to walk down. Talia is still staring, her mouth a thin line. I stop and say, "This is my world, I know what I'm doing here."

"This looks like that place where the nobs live. Like Bay showed us."

I try for a reassuring smile. "We never did get to see your nobs."

"They're not my nobs." A snarl.

I sigh and go back to her, "Tell me about them while we walk. There's nothing to fear here, no need to hide." Her eyes are big and I look down at us, coated in mud and grime. Nothing to fear. Most normal people would avoid us and then call the police. Especially Mrs Pickles, she got the Neighbourhood Watch going and knows everything that happens. My heart sinks as I remember that we will have to sneak past her front window.

Talia walks close to me as we head downhill – not quite on my heels – she leaves a purposeful gap as though proving she doesn't need to be this close. She doesn't quite pull it off, flinching at every sound. I'm basking in the clean air. No factories, no mist, only the smell of leaves and farming.

"The nobs live on the hill." Her voice cuts through my thoughts. "They live behind that wall made from broken down houses. They trade with us." She spits on the ground, leaving a grey mark oozing on the brown leaves. "They have everything they want."

"If they have to trade then surely they don't have everything."

She snorts her disgust at my reasoning. "They have the best land behind the wall. I talk to Martie. He's one of their contacts, looks after them and gets them what they want. It's warm up there on top. They have animals, grow lots of food and make the lamps for the streets. We only have the fish and the mills."

"You have tidal power." She looks confused. "You know, the water wheels that power the electric lights and they need the factories to produce goods. You should be on even footings with them, why aren't you?"

"The mill owners are in with them, they stop people from rebelling."

"You mean they keep them indentured – keep them tied to the factories?"

She grunts, "People are afraid."

Having heard the men talking in the evenings I agree and wonder how long it can go on before it all collapses. Yet Talia wasn't completely innocent in this, she'd been happy enough to sell on information to a nob's nark when it suited her. I shrug, not my world, no longer my problem.

We reach the edge of the woods. The lane begins and Mrs Pickles' house appears, sitting in its perfect cottage garden. Following my example, Talia ducks almost to her hands and knees and scuttles under the eyeline of the hedge. I hope Mrs Pickles isn't in her garden, if she sees me and Talia then it'll be all around the village. I fumble for an inane story about being knocked over by Biggles to explain the mess I'm in and hope it won't be needed – nothing can explain Talia's state.

Her curtains are shut. I breathe a sigh of relief and drag Talia away. The pile of ash is still spread across the footpath and we both give it a wide berth. I shove Talia over the fence and hear Biggles galumphing up the path.

I bang into her as she backs into the fence and all grace gone, fall flat on my face. Biggles takes the opportunity to jump all over me, panting and licking while starting the few deep woofs that will morph into a full on howl that there's a stranger in our midst. I grab his head and put it into my shoulder, turning it into a play fight. His strong spaniel body wriggles, pushing at me. I wince at his claws, I need to get them cut. I try and smile at Talia through the tears of his head hitting my chin.

"Good boy Biggles. This is Talia." I snatch at her shrinking hand and give it to Biggles. He decides she must be a friend and makes a leap in her direction. "Down boy." I grab his collar to stop him jumping all over her. "It's okay, it's just Biggles, he won't hurt you." She shrinks away, holding her knife. "He's friendly. I know this place, remember? Put it away."

I haul on his collar and pull him towards the shed. In the distance, the house is in darkness and the curtains aren't open yet. I wonder what time it is, Mum's normally an early riser. I wonder how Biggles got out, I normally keep him in with me. Saying that, I'd not shut him in the night I'd left. I start to panic about how long I'd gone and if my parents have called the police to report me missing.

I nod Talia in and firmly shove Biggles out. He stays by the door with a mournful expression and I wince at the familiar smell of cat. I look around, catch sight of the open window and hope it's a residual smell, then notice Talia's expression. She's looking around the shed in wonder.

"Sorry, it still smells of cat."

"It doesn't smell at all." She sniffs and I remember the stink of the world we've just left. She's grimy, her clothes are stiff with dirt. I can't leave her like this, she's going to need a shower and clean clothes. "Are you rich?" I shake my head, start to explain that I can't afford my own place and stop when she says, "Only rich people can afford to live like this." Her eyes are big, taking in my bed with the thick winter duvet and pillows. Even to me they have the look of luxury after the last week or so.

I find my scissors and cut the contraption off me and rummage through my drawers, pulling out clothes for myself and find a few items that might suit Talia.

"What's this?" A spitting hiss answers her question. Talia's hand shoots out and she seizes the cat by the scruff of its neck, dragging it out to hold it dangling. The cat, sensing it's in the presence of sterner stuff than myself, hangs limply and utters a pathetic pip.

"Good eating on a cat." She turns it around speculatively. I struggle to stop myself grinning and open the window wider. It's not had the chance to do anything nasty. I take it from her and dump it on the grass. It glowers at Biggles and stalks away, mortally insulted.

I pick at my jumper, the mud from the landslip hasn't done it any favours. "I'm going to have a shower, stay here."

The shower is a recent addition to the shed, an absolute godsend in these circumstances. Dad and I'd considered a toilet but had decided it was too much work, hence Dominic's need to go outside. How long ago was that? I need to find out and feel the knot of worry tighten, my parents must be beside themselves.

I look in the bathroom mirror. My face is filthy and I feel years older than when I'd last looked at myself. I also need a shave. Carefully I peel my jumper off to look at my shoulder and wince. The brand is a mass of scab, the edges scarlet. No sign of infection, I prod at it gently. It's not large, but there for the rest of my life. A lump rises, I'd never been one for tattoos and now I was marked.

I strip and let the water run over me. Absolute luxury. I bask in the steam and scrub the days from Narith away. The bottom of the shower turns grey and something about the grey stain disturbs me. I quickly swill it down the plughole.

Talia's standing in the same spot when I come back. She looks out of place, almost a cartoon character in my normality. Is this how I looked to her in her world? I show her the bathroom and start the shower. She looks dubious but I convince her when I show her the old clothes I've found in my drawers. She touches them gently and glowers.

"Don't come near me in here or I'll cut your balls off." I feel those parts of me shrivelling to the point where she'd never find them. I leave her and the bathroom door slams shut, barely missing me.

I wait, looking at the normality I've not had for – how long? A week? Longer? I see the shed through Talia's eyes. Clean, warm and safe. My whole world is safe, no one would kill or hurt me to survive. Food was a surety every day. The office where they could only cut me down verbally. I could feel myself swelling with confidence, compared to the people I'd met in Talia's world, they were nothing.

The door bangs open, interrupting my thoughts. Talia with her hair hanging over her eyes, stalks in. Her mood is vibrating through the room, I can tell she's daring me to laugh at her new clothes.

"We'll have to do something about your hair, here." I hand her a hair brush and she looks at it in the same way as I look at the cat's leavings. "Here," I repeat and take it from her, tentatively stroking the ends. Her hair is a matted mess. The temptation is just to drag it through. I reach for scissors to cut through the larger knots and she has her knife up before I can cut. I smack her hand away firmly and continue, refusing to respond. She's shifting constantly, I end up cutting off a lot more, trying to keep the mop as even as possible. I turn her around to look at the front and bite back a swearword. Without realising, I've chosen the same clothes worn by the girl I followed through the rift.

She scowls, "What?" She's been in a foul mood since we've arrived.

"I've seen you before." Talia sneers. I look down and realise the only difference is that her clothes are cleaner at the moment. "I saw you, with your hair like this, dressed like this the first time I followed you through."

Her face, pale from living under grime, is full of the angles of starvation, I notice the lines around her mouth and between her eyebrows. She's not so much younger than me, she's just small. My clothes look fashionably baggy, making her into a tiny truculent rapper star. How can this happen? Those clothes have been in my drawer all this time and her hair's never been that short. Biggles gives a joyful bark outside and I hear Mum call. I freeze, unsure what to do. Talia's eyes narrow and she draws her knife. Mum calls again.

"Stay here."

Outside, I want to fling my arms around Mum, pick her up and spin her around simply for us both being here and yet I don't. Something's wrong, she's not bothered by my having been away. An oddness prevents me from asking and I find myself standing with my arms crossed, trying to look casual. A comfortable conversation happens, nothing to say that I've been missing. I desperately want to find out what's happened and yet find myself in a conversation about normality – she wants my washing and can't understand why I won't let her get it.

I manage to put her off for the moment, mentioning the cat being in there makes her smile. There's no way she can come into the shed, goodness knows what she'd make of Talia being here. As I turn to go back to the shed, I casually ask the date. She sighs and smiles, it's Monday the second. The day after I left. To my relief Mum goes back inside the house, not noticing my shock.

I'm left reeling, at least a weeks' worth of working and skulking in Talia's world has taken barely any time here. What is this, some kind of magic or has Talia brought me back in time as well as space? The thought of Talia brings me back to my current problem – what am I going to do with her? She's got no passport, no identification. People will ask questions. Hell, Mum will be asking questions if she sees her and Mum will come looking for washing when I've gone to work. I glance at my watch, seven thirty. I have to go to work. Despite everything I've been through I quail inside. I hate it, the petty conversation, the smirks. I far prefer the cool quiet of the morgue – no one answers back there.

Back in the shed, Talia's behind the door, hiding from view. This world isn't right for her either, she's too wild. I need to hide her, at least for today until I've had a chance to think. I talk while I make up a bag of food.

"Right. I'll need to hide you somewhere." Inspiration hits. "There's a cave system in the quarry on the hill. You should be fine there. Just try to look normal if anyone walks by." I look pointedly at her knife. "We don't carry those around here. You'll have to leave it." Her reaction is typical, ignoring my open hand, she stuffs it back in her belt. I decide I'm not going to push my luck. "Just keep it hidden, okay?"

I take a jumper out of a chest of drawers and give it to her, it's not going to rain today. "We'll take Biggles for a walk and I'll show you. I'll come and pick you up tonight."

"What you doing?"

I grin and give her the satisfying answer of "Stuff." She shuts her mouth and pulls the jumper on back to front.

We sneak out, the best anyone can sneak with a brown spaniel bouncing around them. Mrs Pickles is in her garden and I manage a weak grin and a wave. She comes bustling over to speak to us, in pretence of being neighbourly. I can barely get a word in edgeways. She keeps glancing at Talia and I wince internally at Talia's expression – it wears the same bemused horror I felt when given the rats to carry. Eventually Mrs Pickles works her way around to asking Talia where she comes from. I start to splutter my way through an explanation and am cut off by Talia.

"Oh, just passing through. Come on Daniel." Her voice is casual, making it clear she doesn't want to be here.

Mrs Pickles looks at me and humphs, "Well, it's nice to see you with a young lady for once." Her tone makes it clear she doesn't regard Talia as a young lady for a minute. I groan internally and allow Biggles to pull me away, knowing that Talia's presence will be reported throughout the village.

The day passes in a blur of worry about Talia and her being found. They're short of hands down in the morgue again, for some reason they can't get people to stay. Clive's been making jokes to the receptionist about everyone downstairs being strange. He's right, but they're strange in a way I can understand. I offer to help out during a break and Mr Davies appears pleased. He talks pompously about undertaking being a good career as we walk downstairs.

I take a split second to decide, "Actually, I'd be really interested."

He looks surprised and mutters something about me having to take a pay cut and start at the bottom. A reckless feeling fills me and I find I don't care about the money. I have a place to sleep and food to eat. I can wait and anything is better than office politics.

One of the other undertakers notices my hands while I'm rolling up my sleeves and says they look competent. I glance down at my hands under the water as I wash them. They aren't the great square spades Vihaan had, they're slender with long fingers and yet with the nicks and scratches from the mill, they have an air of being able to do things. Competent was a word I'd never have given myself. I feel a pride build inside and notice the pointed glances at Clive walking past and shrug with a smile. Clive with his comments couldn't touch me this morning, he's got nothing on Talia or the men at the factory.

Following instructions, I find the work soothing and start thinking through my problems. Talia can't stay in this world, she's going to have to go back. Then I realise that I don't want her to go back into danger. I'd worry about her going back, she's got nothing. Those grey men as well, what if she got caught?

"Sometimes it can take courage to step sideways into a world you don't know." I gape at the remark echoing my thoughts and then realise my boss is talking about me moving into the morgue.

I drive home in a thoughtful mood, stopping to buy a pizza. Layer out of the dead. I like the idea of becoming that person, thinking about the look of respect in Talia's eyes.

Talia. What am I going to do? I wave a hand at Mum, showing her the pizza box and leave it in the shed to dash up the hill, ignoring Biggles' imploring look. I'm panting by the time I get to the quarry. No one there and I shout Talia's name, no answer. Maybe she'd been spooked by a walker. Maybe she'd gone back to her own world without me. A sense of loss fills me, odd and spiky as she was, I still need to know that she's safe.

I make a loop, passing the place where we'd come through the rift. The pile of mud seems larger than I remember. I slow as I come closer, it's definitely larger and greyer. It looks dustier, less of a pile of mud, more of a pile of clothes. I give myself a shake – it's just mud – nothing to worry about. Something runs through me as I stare and my sweat chills in the breeze. The creases and lines in the mud twitch, becoming an arm. A foot stretches out, rustling the leaves. My breath catches. A grey man, in my world.

I'm rooted to the spot as the mud re-arranges itself before my eyes, the body bending at impossible angles, sucking itself higher. A fall of mud from the shoulder solidifies to form another arm. A burst from the chest rising up to form a head, the face hooded and deep in shadow. The same recognition fills me, I should know this person.

Terror stops my feet from working. I stand there, all plans wiped clean from my head, seeing in my mind's eye the man in the square and the sound of his head hitting the floor. The figure in front of me is eerily quiet, only the rustle of leaves under his feet where the weight changes as he forms. I watch in fascination at the mud curving to form the stitching around the elbows. Such detail. The mouth is all I can see under the hood.

It looks young with no lines and it's partly open as though concentrating. Mine echoes it. The same lethargy fills me as it had with the first grey man, weighing down my arms and legs. No choice about running, I would stay and see what he wanted. A calm fills me as I contemplate my destiny. An arm begins to stretch in my direction. The image of the desiccated corpse from the square rises in my mind and I brace myself, unable to think of any alternative.

Something hits me. Grabs my arm and shoves me into a stumbling run down the hill. I slide, still in a daze. Someone pants in my ear as they drag me through the bushes, heedless of the thin saplings whipping into our faces. I fall flat on my face, forgetting to break my fall and look up at Talia. She's pulling at me, tugging on my arm. I stagger to my feet and clumsily try to remember how to put one foot in front of the other.

I swing to look back and see him striding downhill. Nothing seems to bother him, he walks down the slope as though it were flat clear ground. The brambles slide through the mud of his body. My mouth opens as I clearly see one go through him and out the other side. I meet his eyeless gaze and he pins me into one place for a split second. Then I hear Talia, a thin frightened keen coming from her. She's swearing at me, at herself, tugging on my arm and dragging me onwards.

I let her lead me, conscious of the presence behind. Something is sucking the fight out of me, I shouldn't be this tired. Talia's breath is coming shorter. She's going to start coughing shortly, she can't keep going like this. I can't keep going either. I trip again, this time in one of the many small streams that come down the hill after the rains. Talia begins to cough, a deep hacking sound. She lets go, unable to hold her ribs and keep me moving.

I drag myself out of the wet and begin to crawl. I can't get to my feet. I'm going to die like that man in the square. Talia is bent double, unable to do more than cough. This fit's bad, the lack of air drives her double.

The grey man arrives at the same steady walk. I lay on the leaves and gaze at it. I can do no more. I wonder if it will carry on walking once it has killed us. Talia has fallen to her knees, her face puce. It's only paces away now. It raises its hand and takes another step towards us.

Chapter 11

A deep gasp beside me. Talia has finally drawn a breath, the coughs dying into a spasm. Her lungs heave with the effort of bringing oxygen back into her body. She stares, exhausted. Neither of us can do anything, we are both going to die.

For a split second the figure seems uncertain. A grey foot is raised and plunges into the stream, less than six inches deep. I watch the water run up the leg, it loosens the mud, cracks widen and collapse. The figure falls, splashing across the stream, landing inches away from my leg. The mouth opens and drowns as the water enters it. I twitch away and find the strength flooding into my limbs as the rest of the body is sucked back into the wet. It takes moments and then nothing left but a thin grey stain spreading downstream.

Birdsong comes into my ears, a light breeze ruffles my hair and leaves scrunch beneath my body. I gape at the shafts of sunlight, becoming conscious of the sweat drying and a thin pain across my forehead. I touch it and my fingers come away red. A branch must have caught me and I'd not noticed.

"They can't touch water." I jump, surprised out of my musings and lean back onto my elbows to look at Talia. She's recovered from her fit and has a satisfied look on her face.

"Doesn't it know not to go near?" I can't give it a sex now, it feels inanimate to me.

"Don't seem to. Best thing to do if they're following you. Deep puddle'll do it. Running water's best. One step and poof!" Her arms spread wide, demonstrating the disintegration.

"How did it get here?" She shrugs. "Did it follow us? There was that pile of mud on the path when I first saw you. It's still there, will the same thing happen with that?"

Talia looks puzzled, "It looked the right sort of stuff but it wasn't the same."

"How can you tell?"

Another shrug, "Just can. They sometimes do that, fall into a heap and then when you walk past..." She waves her hands to show something growing. "Didn't know you had them here."

"We don't." We didn't, at least not before I'd met Talia. Nothing normal about mud or dust animating and walking around killing people. I shiver and despite the shock, my stomach grumbles. The practicalities of life insert themselves. "Let's go back, I've got some food to introduce you too." I grin, "and it's better than rat." She restricts herself to a snort and follows.

We arrive back at the shed to find Mum's left a note pinned to my pizza box. They've gone out for the evening and I breathe a sigh of relief at not having to hide Talia from them.

The pizza goes down very fast. Talia, licking her fingers, insists on wanting to clean the contraption she'd found. I pull it out from its hiding place and take it down to the bottom of the orchard to put the hose on it. Gradually gears begin to show through the slow trickle of water, a clockwork mechanism appears and two figures on a pierced base. The handle is missing so I get my screwdrivers out and fiddle with it. Talia hovers, showing anxiety over her baby. Biggles is told to sit and wriggles ever closer until told to move back. I notice he shuffles over to Talia in the hope of a fuss and she ends up unconsciously burying her fingers into his fur until he falls over in ecstasy.

I grease some parts, clean off others, moving them gently to clear the rust. I reach underneath, showing her how the rods move the dancers. She sits and watches, for once her eyes unguarded. I find a piece of wood, drill some holes and attach it. Holding the base down, I encourage her to turn the handle and the figures dance stiffly.

"I could get some enamel paint and make them look pretty if you like." I can see Talia struggling. She doesn't want to let me do any more. She wants to keep her prize for herself. Having seen her world I can understand.

"I need it for Bay." She doesn't. She wants it for herself, a small piece of prettiness in a world of grey mist.

"No you don't. We don't need to go there again. You've brought me home." I wait and watch her screwing herself into a knot. "I need to paint it. This part here and here are rusting, they won't last long otherwise." I touch where the rods are holding the dancers. "I'll put it in the shed where it'll be safe for the moment." She nods and stands, putting her hands behind her back. I pretend not to notice the tears filling her eyes.

"All right nob." The insult isn't quite in her usual tone. I smile, take the dancers and tuck them inside the shed.

I come back with my own twisting stomach. The presence of the grey man in my world has firmed my decision, I can't leave Talia to go back on her own.

I stop in front of her and say, "We need to go back and find the source of these grey men."

Such simple words. My heart's sinking already, I've only seen part of the city. That guard, he'd travelled around the island and told me there was nothing else. I'd seen the plateau lands and the wall surrounding them but I want Talia to be safe. We have to find out where the grey men are coming from, especially if they're coming into my world.

"Why?" Seeing my confusion, Talia asks, "Why do you want to leave here?" A skinny arm is waved. "You have everything." I see my world again through her eyes. Clean and safe, with lots of food and no need to run and hide. The privilege of being brought up here means I can see its problems but to her, it's paradise.

I feel awkward, "We're friends, aren't we?" Her mouth hangs open, the concept hasn't occurred to her. I try to make her laugh, "Isn't there a fish that does that?" I open and shut my mouth imitating her.

She clicks hers shut. "Nob."

I snigger and throw a stick at her. Biggles launches himself at it and we end up in a three way romp that the spaniel wins easily. He runs off to gnaw at his prize. I lie panting in the grass and become serious, "I am going back with you, you know that, don't you?" She looks down at the grass and lets her hair cover her face as she nods.

I go back to the shed and stuff a rucksack full of anything we might need. A warm hoodie and food that will keep for several days. I've not been able to sort out time off work for the next day, it's too short notice. I'll just have to hope Talia would be able to bring me back in time. I snort at the thought. I have a time travelling friend, of course I'll be back by tomorrow. I just need to worry about the enemy dehydrating me, nothing much. I pick up my rucksack and we both take a deep breath to battle our way through the rift.

The familiar lurch and we are back in the city, fighting the nausea. I'm more wary this time, I've brought the thumb stick I use for walking in the winter mud. Talia nods her approval at the competent way I swing the shoulder high staff while walking.

The contrast to my world this time couldn't be greater and I'm more alert, expecting trouble. Grey walls show in the lamps at the intersections, scattered rubble to trip the unwary, and the streets are deserted in the night. Talia snuggles into her borrowed jumper and walks off with the expectation of me following. I shrug my hoodie on, pulling the neck up to keep the chill out and hurry to keep up.

Back in her cellar, I tell Talia about my day while she checks out her hidey hole, stalking around, picking at items and sniffing at them. I'm enthusiastic about my decision to become an undertaker. By the look on her face I can tell she's still not sure of the term and I try to qualify it with the comment she'd made, "You know, a layer out of the dead."

She flinches and says quietly, "Those grey men. We call them the dead, that's what I thought you meant."

My mouth opens and shuts with nothing coming out. She'd thought I could do something about one of her world's nightmares and I'm nothing but an office worker. My heart sinks, "I'm sorry."

Her mouth pulls up into a bitter line, "Doesn't matter, we'll find them." We spend the rest of the evening barely speaking until she curls up into a corner to sleep and I lay staring into the dark, worrying.

We start searching the city the next morning in a despondent mood. It's a hopeless task, neither of us know what to look for. We decide to start searching close by and we quarter the district over several days. Talia uses her contacts, asking questions and we look at piles of dust and mud and poke rubble heaps. Word on the grapevine comes floating back reluctantly, there is little to be heard. Talia is visibly twitchy as the deadline for meeting Bay passes.

I begin see the city as a catastrophe waiting to happen. Everyone relies on the shaky network of factories, fish farms and the energy from the tidal waterwheels. The largess from the nobs in power on the hill is resented. Mutterings of rebellion are constant in the messages Talia gets back. New bodies are left hanging in the gibbets, evidence of the small scale riots testing the boundaries.

Nothing is wasted here. Those richer will pay for goods or services, the poorer work in the factories for food and somewhere to sleep. No sick days, no way out – you work or you die. Talia is good at scavenging for buried treasure from years past, the only reason why she's not working at the factories like the others. I ask what her parents had done for a living and stop at her scowl. Other people are in cliques outside the factories, staying together for survival and trustworthy companionship.

The constant mist, the dust and the cold shortens lives. Faces are hard and I hear Talia's cough echoed in other people. The sea, to my surprise, is warm and full of fish. When the tide goes out, the stubs of buildings are revealed, the basis for the fish traps in the bay. There are very few boats to be seen, those I see are guarded well.

We sit and watch, perched on the edge of the square, feet dangling towards the water and chew on the stale biscuits Talia has traded for. My food is being eked out. I've let Talia save it for other times and ignore my stomach grumbling. I can go back to my soft world, a few days hunger won't hurt me.

Shouts of "Shark!" come from the figures wading in the water. The seaweed is harvested from pontoons further out, they also help with cover for the fish. Yet more factories manufacture the fish and seaweed into food to eat. The smell of rotting fish and sewers rise and I no longer notice. My clothes are a mess again.

Narith rises behind us, up into the mist hiding the plateau. Above us like an unseen omen of doom floats the nightmare moon. Smoke adds to my despondent mood. There is a precarious order here which will be extinguished by a final flare of rebellion. I can only hope we find the source of the grey men before it happens.

Chapter 12

Talia took a deep breath and concentrated, feeling for the part of her that knew what to do. She raised her hands and parted them. The seam appeared, a grey line in the air. She turned to Daniel, checking that he was still asleep in the corner. Her eyes wide, she forced herself to keep her breathing steady, it wouldn't do to let him wake and see this. She had to do this for herself, had to know if she could do this on her own.

The lack of progress was frustrating. She was too used to making her own way in life, leaving the things that didn't matter for day to day survival. Daniel had changed that the day he'd offered her his help. She couldn't let him be better than her.

She let go and the line stayed, wavering in the candlelight. Talia placed her fingers within and tugged, pushing her way inside. It was harder this time without the urgency of fighting to survive. She wriggled and cursed in her head. Spots appeared in her vision with the lack of air. She struggled, desperate to get through and she felt the void give way as she blacked out.

Talia woke to the sunlight beating across her face. Leaves crackled underneath her, dry and crinkling with age. She was in a dip, trees high above, a breeze rustling through. Everything was green and blue above and brown below. No dust. She ran her fingers through the leaves and dropped them, watching as they fell.

She was struck again with the cleanliness. No smoke or dust. Daniel's world. It felt safe here, despite its strangeness. Shaking off an unaccustomed guilt at leaving Daniel sleeping in her own world, she got up to walk down the hill. She wasn't far from the track from Daniel's house and on impulse she set off down it.

Flashes of light caught Talia's eye and she watched with her mouth open at the sight of things hurtling along a thin grey ribbon a long way away. The thin trail of sound made a shiver go through her. She rubbed her eyes, unused to looking into the distance.

Ducking under the hedge to avoid the old lady's house, she walked along the track. She could see the trees, the or-chard he'd called it, over the hedge. She tried the strange words in her mouth as she walked. Despite being helpless and soft, Daniel knew things. He had an air about him – when he wasn't tripping over his own feet.

She reached the gap in the hedge and peered through to meet the gaze of a small boy. He stood, hands clasped and watched her with a serious face. Small and clean, he regarded her with an air of having known her for years. Talia backed away, frantically trying to figure out how he could be both asleep in her own world and also stood in front of her. The only solution she could think of was that she'd somehow gone back in time to his world. Daniel was a child, too young to protect himself. A moan escaped her and he cocked his head, turning slightly to look over his shoulder.

Another sound caught her ear, not quite a sound, a feeling of ripping. A grey man was coming, she'd brought it to where Daniel was unable to defend himself. Despair hit Talia and unthinkingly, she called his name, knowing he couldn't reply from her world. She had to keep it away from him, she could feel it pushing through from where she'd entered. Sobbing, she ran towards it.

Talia reached the path with her lungs gasping from the uphill run to find it pouring into the clean world like the contents from a sewer after heavy rain. It forced its way through and built itself higher, the dust running upwards and sticking. Boots and legs, she recognised them now, they were Daniel's. The belt, the odd jumper – hoodie he'd called it and a blanket covering his shoulders making the cloak.

It was immobile for a moment. She swung her head wildly in panic, no streams could be seen here, no water. Terror squeezed her throat shut at what she had to do. She had to stay between it and Daniel, he was a tiny serious boy. Tears made her vision blur and she wiped them away with a jerk. She'd never felt protective about another person before. There had been other children at Dodie's but she'd always ignored them. Daniel was different, he was clumsy, awkward and yet he knew things she didn't. She'd scorned him to begin with, now she had to protect him.

Time had run out. The body jerked and the hole snapped shut with a wet sound. The lethargy hit and Talia stumbled while trying to look back at the same time. Her only option was to run downhill until she found another path. She didn't have the energy to run up, away from Daniel. She skittered downwards on all fours until she could lever herself back onto her feet, breath coming in short gasps, panic wiping her mind. She'd never been this close to a grey man without water before, she'd always run hard and fast at the first sight.

Talia didn't know where to go, panic made her mind go blank in a way it hadn't before. All thought of Daniel fled her mind, she had to keep it away from herself. The ground levelled into a dip, the difference making her legs give way. She spotted another track down below and scrambled to her feet. The grey man strode on behind, steady and unforgiving. It never sped up or slowed down, simply turned to face the direction she was running in.

The track led uphill towards the grey man or down. Talia choose down, hoping to find a stream or a pond. Her lungs ached for air, the years of muck stopping her from breathing deeply. The path was full of dips, hidden by the leaves and her legs jarred every time she hit one. She stopped to spit onto the floor, wheezing and looked over her shoulder. She'd lost it behind the twists of the path and the large prickly bushes. She closed her eyes for a brief second, she needed to think, where would water be? She'd have to keep heading downhill and hope to find something large enough to drown it in.

A sixth sense made her turn to look at the bush behind her. Something grey was pushing through, less than three feet away. The shock made her gurgle and she choked. The grey man wasn't following her along the path, it was hunting her in a straight line. Coughing the saliva from her windpipe, she turned to run, stumbling as she tried to look at the same time. The grey man re-formed itself as it walked through the bushes, the cracks smoothing over and disappearing as she watched.

Talia ran, the track blurring in her eyes and her feet hit black stone – the lane – she'd gone the wrong way. She was leading it towards Daniel. Tears squeezed out and blurred her vision further. She called out, trying to warn him and choked on her own voice, despairing at the feeble thready sound. She tripped again, skinning her knees and she fell into a ditch beside the path. The green plants covering it weren't as soft as they looked. The leaves stung her as she fell down the short bank squealing.

A splash, the plant stems broke and she was lying in water. The shadow of the grey man was above her, the figure bending to reach out. A moment was all Talia needed, she scooped up the green stinking liquid she sat in and threw it. A splatter made a hole deep in the body, others followed it. Talia ignored the burning of the nettles and threw water as fast as she could. Craters formed as each droplet hit. No emotion showed around the mouth, no sound came as it retreated. Dribbles ran, pulling details out of place and the man took a step away. Talia redoubled her efforts, tears running and blurring her vision. A pause and it disintegrated; a pile of mud left on the black stone.

Talia panted, her lungs heaving and shaking from the adrenaline rush. She could hear voices in the place where Daniel lived, she had to hide somewhere. A moment's thought brought the quarry to mind, she'd be safe there. She pulled herself out, shaking her hands and scraping the worst of the green slime from her hair. She remembered the shower Daniel had made her have with clean water and soft fabric to dry herself on. She gave the soggy pile of mud a wide circle and crept up the path, remembering this time to sneak under the hedge at the old woman's house. The quarry was dry and warm in the sunshine and Talia allowed herself to fall asleep.

She woke with a jerk from a dream. A hazy recollection of sitting on a woman's knee chanting a counting song, touching fingers in time and laughing. Tears filled her eyes, she hadn't been able to see the woman's face – had it been her mother? Dodie filled most of her memories, a larger than life personality, with a meaty fist clouting you around the ear if you didn't behave. The comfort of someone being on your side in the dangerous streets. The other woman had been tiny like herself. Talia strained her memory to see her face and saw nothing.

A brief flash of anger filled her, Daniel had no right to have her feeling like this, no right to ask about her parents. Those that were too soft didn't survive in her world. The dead place inside worked, nothing got in the way of it. She firmed her lips, he was weak, a whimpering thing that wouldn't last five minutes under pressure. She reminded herself of his face at the dead rat, the way he'd shrunk back when she'd thrust it into his face to carry.

Talia decided to walk back to see if the pile of mud was still there, she intended to throw more water over it, just to make sure. She'd dried out while sleeping in the sun, bits fell from her hair and she brushed them off with care. She touched the clothes gently, they were warm and well made, nothing like she could afford in her own world. Talia gazed at the sunset for a moment and shook herself. She needed to move, it would be dark soon and she'd be dead if she didn't toughen up again. Staring at the thin silvery disc coming over the horizon, she snorted her disgust, even this world's moon was pathetic.

She found her way back down to the track, past the place where the grey man had found her and Daniel the first time and dissolved in the streamlet. She cursed at not finding the same stream when the second grey man had come through and frowned when she found no traces of mud from the first grey man. She bent to check, the grey mud would be obvious in the brown here. Had she come the wrong way? She walked a little further and came to the lane. Nobody in the garden and she checked the pile of mud – it was lifeless. Talia walked on further to where the track opened out into a wider lane. A strange smell lingered, something about it touched a part deep inside and she found a terror rising that was nothing to do with the grey men.

Talia turned before she could whimper aloud and had another shock when a tall figure sprawled his way over the fence. He was brushing himself off, looking down the lane away from her. She stood half dreaming until the figure turned and Talia had trouble stopping herself from screaming. This wasn't right, she'd seen him as a young boy only several hours ago. The irrational thought flashed through her mind – how did he have this magic to change his age? He was also asleep in her cellar, her mind twisted into knots trying to work it out.

Forgetting her earlier resolution to be tough, the strange feeling about the lane and coming face to face with Daniel, completely un-nerved Talia. She had to get away, and she couldn't do that in front of him. She ran for the safety of the woods. She ran, knowing that Daniel would chase her. Awkwardly, as he was in the middle of the path, she pushed past him and despite her determination her eyes flicked up and caught his.

A familiar protest caught her heart as she plunged on. Everything clicked in her mind like the figures dancing on the contraption she'd found. It had happened last time, it would happen again. Large animals loomed over a fence and she flinched away from them. The sound of feet pounding behind her and a swift glance showed that he was closer than she thought. Too tired, a corner in the lane – maybe she could get around it and open a rift before he got to her. She raised her arms frantically, tugging the air open and pulled, unable to turn to look over her shoulder again as she caught herself in the rift. Her foot lashed out as she struggled and she felt it hit something yielding. Maybe this time she could get through…

An arm around her waist made her gasp, forcing the breath from her in the nothingness. She wriggled and the fingers tightened and then slid away. Talia fought to get the easiest way through, thinking about how she'd found him being attacked by Corte. She stumbled out onto the street and into a man's arms. He bellowed in surprise – Corte!

She groaned, she had to get out of here. Daniel would come through in a minute and she would see herself if she stayed. Memories flickered of that night and the person she had been. Vicious in terror, she gave two fast punches to Corte's stomach while gasping in the night air and she opened the void again, heading back to the time she'd come from.

Talia staggered in exhaustion and hoped nothing would follow. The fear of Him sending a grey man to follow her twice in an evening might be too much. She didn't know who "He" was, only that she shouldn't have gone through the rift and that "He" could follow. The memories crowded behind the shut door in her mind, shouting for attention in a language she couldn't understand. Damn Daniel for clearing the dead place away, it had kept her away from that door, stopped her from thinking about it.

She leant against the wall in the cellar and stuffed her sleeve into her mouth to try and stop the coughing fit she could feel coming. She could barely keep her eyes open and yet she needed to stay awake, to check for pursuit. A bucket sat close by the door and another at the other end of the room, the water covered in a thin layer of dust. Not for drinking, no one would drink that muck. It was enough to disable a grey man, to give time to run.

The break opened close to the wall and she staggered to her feet, grasping for a bucket. It hit the grey man as it came through, rendering it into a pile of mud. So close to her sleeping place, she'd have to move. The dirty water spread over the floor and pooled into the corner. Daniel was still asleep in his corner with no idea of what she'd done. Talia sank to her knees, knuckles stuck hard into her mouth, hoping he wouldn't see the pile. She'd led him here. She was responsible.

Chapter 13

Another day, another fruitless search. We're in an area Talia doesn't know so well and nobody likes talking about the grey men to strangers. Talia is having to do a lot of persuading to get any information. Rumours are starting to spread about us and people drift away the minute we're spotted. It's not good. Talia mentioned something about a "Dodie" being dead and that her clique's broken up. It's almost as though it's a personal insult that she can no longer use them as a source of information.

We walk slowly back, tired from more than just the day's walking. I mentally run through the last few days. Yesterday was wet, a damp drizzle that Talia refused to do much in. She pointed out, quite fairly, that the grey men won't be moving in the rain so there's no point in getting wetter than we have to. She also insisted on moving to a different cellar and her only explanation was a muttered comment about being found if we stayed. We got soaked walking there and I'd wished for my waterproofs. A miserable day was spent huddled close to the brazier. There's something the matter with Talia, she's been out somewhere during the night, her clothes are a mess. I ask her once and get snapped at, almost like she did at the beginning.

We've decided the source must be fairly close by to her old hidey hole, we've heard less and less about them the further we move away or maybe it's just people don't want to talk to Talia. I've sketched out a charcoal map on the new cellar wall, detailing the streets and the parts we've checked, making notes of what we've heard. It's a huge task, so many of the buildings are ruined, some streets are a mass of rubble and others aren't places to walk down for different reasons.

I rub my eyes, feeling the tiredness slow my pace. I wish we could take a break, go back to my shed in the warm and immediately feel guilty. Talia can't take me back without a grey man following us through. I mutter a phrase I learnt from my dorm mates and tell myself to deal with the discomfort. Talia stops in front of me and I nearly bump into her, absorbed in my thoughts. My swearing increases as I see at the dread in her face. Bleary, I turn with her and see a figure rising from the rubbish right behind us. One arm is outstretched in our direction, the face covered by a deep hood.

My thoughts go from zero to sixty in less than a second, there's no space to move, no time to run. It's within touching distance already. My knees are buckling. It's one thing to be searching for something like this and another to actually find it.

I begin babbling, trying to engage it in conversation. "Who are you? Speak to me. Who do you work for? Why…?" No response, the figure is eerily silent. It's mouth open in concentration and it moves like an automation, no human grace or skill in its movements. Terror overwhelms me, it's too close. I hear Talia whimper behind and don't think any less of her for it.

I swing my staff in panic. There's not enough space to swing properly but anything to keep it away from me. A hand lashes out and the staff is caught in a vice-like grip. I can't break away, the lethargy is making my knees weak, driving me towards the floor. Talia grabs for my other arm, trying to pull me up. I stare into the depths of the hood and I'm caught in the eyeless gaze of death. The polished wood under my fingers turns rough, cracking as the moisture flees. It snaps like a twig under the pressure and I'm left holding the broken end. A blindly swinging hand connects and grasps it again.

My mind's screaming that I must get free, that I mustn't touch it. Talia is dragging clumsily at my other arm, shouting something I can't hear through the roaring of panic. I cling to the staff, I can't unpeel my fingers. I'm being brought closer, the other hand is reaching out for me. Instinctively I fling up my hand to block it with the vague thought of holding it back. In my mind's eye, all I can see the previous victims, how they staggered. I'm going to die.

My fingers clutch at nothing, they go right through the sleeve and dust sifts through my fingers, streaming downwards. The hand drops into debris and the mouth gapes under the hood. It stretches, and turns back over itself into a yawning hole as the arm dissolves onto the floor. The head rolls back and the spine arches. No sound comes from it, simply a whisper of disintegration. The powdery dust trickles over my arm, it's warm with a disgustingly intimate heat. I stand and watch, stupid in shock.

A jolt of something runs through me and I fall heavily, the remains of my staff clanging onto the floor. Talia's arm is still around my waist and she drops with me. The body collapses into a pile at my feet, the clothes falling into the same mess of grey dust. No skeleton, nothing inside to make it walk. The dust stirs lightly in the breeze and I hold my breath as though it might infect me with the same disease.

I pull myself up onto my backside and stare at Talia, my brain unable to process what has happened. There are smears of dust on my fingers, I brush them off – unclean.

Talia's face is awe-struck. "Layer out of the dead."

"I didn't do anything." Abruptly an energy sparks through me again, making my stomach roil. I lurch to my feet as it races through every muscle in my body. It's dirty. A loathing for it fills me and darkness shadows my vision. Filled with the absurd feeling of wanting to get away from my own body, I turn and run hard. Not looking where I'm going, I slam up against a brick wall and without warning, a brief glimpse of something deep in a cellar stains my mind. It's black in there but I can feel the presence of something centuries old and its hunger for power. Talia scrambles up and follows me, her eyes wide.

I don't want it near me, I want to go home and hide under my duvet, shut myself away from it and yet it's in my own mind. I'm cursing myself for being a coward but it scares me to the point where I feel like a three year old lost in a crowd. I'm snivelling and I can't tell Talia why. Two sides of me in conflict, one wanting to run away hard and the other says – well what did you expect? Gradually it comes to a close.

"It's over there." I point in the direction of the wall, I swipe the tears off my face, feeling the sting of grazes. "Underground somewhere."

Talia looks, only seeing the wall and points at the building. "You mean in here?"

I shake my head, impatiently, "No, further away. I can't tell precisely, we'll have to keep looking."

"You could always do that again if we can't find it. They can't hurt you." Her voice is hesitant.

"No!" I shout the denial. I can't do that again. I feel unclean in a way that's nothing to do with the dirt I wear from living here. This is more than skin deep, it makes me want to rage and hurt. Talia backs away, her hand on her knife.

She's never been this wary of me, I've always been the useless one. I take a deep breath, try to smile and fail. "We need to deal with this tonight." My smile twists, "Otherwise I'm going to be too scared." She nods at my honesty and comes to slide a hand into mine.

I no longer care about the coming night or my tiredness. I have an urgency driving me. I close my eyes and try to feel the direction it came from, then open them and start to walk. Talia walks beside me, quiet and uncomplaining.

The wall looms above us. I'm lost, the sense of direction I had has gone. The mist is luminescent from the nightmare moon riding above. I shiver and pull up my hood to hide in the depths.

"I'm cold." I sound like a child and for once Talia doesn't make a biting comment. I realise she's shrunk into herself. All this time she's been frightened of these dusty men and I've vanquished one with a touch. Me. The person who can barely put one foot in front of the other without falling over. I remember my thoughts the day I ran away from her about the city needing a hero. Maybe I am a hero.

I shake my head. Too often heroes die horribly. I don't want to be a hero, I'll settle for a quiet life. A pang of homesickness rises, despite knowing I can go back at any point doesn't stop me wanting a normality where nobody's out to kill me. Even living here is violent. I look at Talia, small and tough, her knife or tongue ever ready to lash out. I can't compete.

Talia sniffs. The smell here is awful but then it is in many places. She waves a hand, keeping me at a distance and trots further down the alley. I follow more slowly, wishing for my staff. She stops at yet another dark doorway, half blocked by rubble and points down with a querying tilt of her head. I shrug, I can't tell anymore, all I know is that I don't want to go down a black hole in the dark. Anything could be down there. I know I'm being a coward. It's easy to decide you're going to save the world, less so to actually do it when it means risking your own skin. I feel the familiar tiredness hit the back of my knees and screw a tiny amount of courage up to nod.

"It's in there." My voice is shaking.

Talia's eyes are huge as they meet mine. Taking a deep breath, she finds her lantern with a stub of candle in and lights it. Holding it up, the light fills the sockets of her eyes with darkness. Her mouth is firm.

"I'll go first."

She starts to refuse until I point out that I can deal with the grey men, ignoring the gibbering inside me shrieking that I don't want to. I want to be at home in my shed, with Biggles' head on my knee. I feel more than hear a hissing, like a sand timer in reverse. Something is building itself down there. I scramble down into the black hole, the light behind me throwing my shadow into the room.

A grey lump lies close to the door. We both jump, ready to run and realise it's a dead body, mostly desiccated. It holds the remains of an axe, the metal pitted with rust. I need a weapon, something in my hand to reassure me that I'm not helpless. I take the axe and heft it, recognising the rough feel of parched wood.

Dust is kicked up by our feet. I hold my breath, not wanting to cough and I try not to think about the terror building up. I have to do this, I have to act. If I don't then I'm going to run away and never come back again. The lantern throws a shaky light onto the walls, not helped by Talia climbing over the rubble.

The cellar is wide, blank windows suggest it was once at street level. There are openings in the walls to other rooms, piles of bricks across the floor and the ever present dust. A sound escapes me, a whimper. I bite my lip, thinking of the scorn Talia would pour if she heard it. No other noise apart from Talia's harsh breathing and the sense of something building. No life here, not even the rustle of a rat.

The dread fills me as I begin to walk towards a doorway. My feet are being pulled in that direction. I know what is there and I fear it. Talia has hold of my elbow. Her fingers are tight and her skinny body resting against mine. The whites of her eyes catch the candlelight. The fatigue is growing, I drag my leaden feet, scuffing through rubble. My knuckles are locked around the axe as we move through the doorway and into the next room.

A man is standing in the lamplight. He is my height, slim and grey like the dust on the floor. He is nothing special, certainly not the horror I'd expected lurking in this cellar. His head is covered by a cloth hood, a cloak is over his shoulders and his hands are spread apart. He is the image of the grey men we have seen. My eyes are drawn to the dust growing from the floor, it glows from within and I watch, fascinated. The body grows and sways and the man sways in time, the hands shaking.

"Daniel..." Her grip tightens.

"Not now." Twisting away from Talia's hand, I lurch towards the figure and its toy in a stumbling run, no longer thinking about being a hero, just knowing I have to stop the building of this new facsimile.

My hand touches the dust man, it holds for a moment and collapses. The same spark flashes hunger between the two of us. The hunger is an ancient evil, tarnished with contempt and underneath lies a very human terror. The man cries out in pain and raises his hand to grasp me. The voice is eerily familiar, a rustling croak from dust in his throat. He moves fast and grabs my wrist. Talia screams from behind me. I stand, frozen to the floor. The grey from his hand shifts and begins to stain my own skin, spreading up my arm. I can feel something writhing, squirming up against my flesh. I try to pull free but his hand is a vice, gripping mine.

Terror fills me and I feel his own terror infecting both of us, I want to hold my head at the pain of both our terrors merging. That tendril between us creates a connection and something squeezes down it. It's over in an instant and yet I feel it's every move, a lump of something pushing its way in. It wraps a hard rind around itself, protecting itself deep inside me. A sudden drag at my arm as though he is trying to pull away and yet he's not moved. I feel the ripping sound of a rift opening and his grip loosens.

"Daniel, don't let him get away!" Talia's voice comes from a distance. I twist to grab his sleeve, I can't let him escape. The stretch increases, shaking me and making my teeth rattle. Our combined terror, the disgust of this creature holding me, the thing worming inside. This creature can't be allowed to get away. I want to end it, I have to stop it. My voice cracks as I scream a challenge to the fear I feel and hammer the axe down over the hood. The tearing flesh and bone that shouldn't be that fragile. The spark of a life blowing out and the rise of sanity – what have I done?

The face turns and catches the feeble candlelight as the man slowly collapses at my feet. A disintegration of body parts, desiccating into dust like the men he had created. I stand, swaying and I choke as my brain processes what I'd seen. Blackness threatens at the image of the hood falling down from the man's head, and my own scared face looking back at me.

Chapter 14

I have killed a man. I drop to my knees, trying not to vomit. My hands are deep in the dust from his body and I jerk them into my chest. The wildly inappropriate phrase comes to me… ashes to ashes... and my lips peel back in a grimace as I gag through the bile.

It doesn't matter that he was the enemy. Doesn't matter that he sent men to desiccate innocent people. I killed him, I put an axe through his skull. The expected jar through my arm that didn't happen, the way the corroded metal had sliced through his skull and the sudden disintegration… He had my face. Why? What perverse soul could take on the face of their attacker? A line of spit drools from my lips and lands in the heap.

A shadow falls over me and I flinch to find Talia crouching in front. The lantern in her hand shows the light is a little dimmer than it had been and yet I find it difficult to look at it. Every muscle shows she wants to throw herself at me, fighting her own natural reticence. She's terrified and I hold my arms out to bundle her up with a desperate need to comfort both of us.

Talia shifts closer and hesitates, "What's that?" I look at the grey stain coating my fingers. I rub at it with my other hand and it spreads, not coming off. It itches slightly and I feel my breath coming faster. She moves back, pointing down. "Look."

The dust is on the move. How can it be moving? The enemy is dead, he's not controlling it anymore. My eyes are drawn to the movement on the floor, becoming lost in it, my panic sucked into the soothing motion. Eddies and currents swirl in a parched ocean of grey. The wet dimple from my spittle is a whirlpool, the dust coiling around it.

I follow the dust's movement to my walking boots and am jolted out of my fugue. They are covered already, particles are creeping over the rim of the leather onto my socks. I rub at the dull sheen covering the brown leather, it doesn't come off.

Panicking, Talia finds her water bottle and empties the contents over my hand and shoes. On the floor, the wet holds the dust, swirling around the droplets. On my hand and shoes, it's stained into my skin. I scrub my hands under the film of water, nothing changes. The dust has sunk under my skin and under the leather. I stare in sick fascination, seeing the whorls of my fingerprints and the hairs on my arms outlined in grey.

Talia scrambles away, dropping the lantern, her eyes wide. The candle gutters and nearly goes out, sending the shadows swinging wildly.

I struggle to my feet and reach out, "Don't leave me here!" My voice cracks. She stops in the doorway with the lantern between us.

We watch, as a grain at a time, the dust rises to cover me. I can't stop it. The prickly itch runs up over my skin, between my clothes and inside every crevice, absorbing the sweat running down me. I slap my clothes in an effort to stop the progress. Puffs of dust rise and are drawn back into the gravity of my body. I try to take a step and discover my feet are tied to the floor. I can stand but not move. I can't walk. I'm rooted there, next to the heap which shifts itself towards me. I try to stick my knuckles in my mouth to stop the whimpers and snatch my hands away at the grey stains.

As the tide reaches my neck, I squeeze my eyes shut at the thought of them being invaded and hold my breath. The tickle of dust enters my nostrils and I sneeze, frantically pawing at my nose. I feel myself swaying from the lack of air. The second I open my mouth, it's like a hand holds it open and the dust sweeps in to coat and dry me out. My tears as the dust climbs over my face are absorbed. In despair I open my eyes, staring at the candle, seeing spots develop in my vision and watch the cellar descend into a haze.

Like a light switching off, I know when the dust stops moving. I feel tired and hungry, the adrenalin of the hunt and fight drained. I try to smile at Talia who is watching warily from the doorway. "It's stopped. I'm okay Talia."

She's not convinced. I don't blame her, I don't dare mention the lump inside me. It's hard and thuds a split second later than the beat of my heart, putting me off balance.

"You look like one of those grey men. I tried to tell you earlier." Her face turns thoughtful, "Apart from the cloak that is."

I twist to look at myself. Hood over my face, thick boots, I am the image of the creature in the cellar. He'd had my face, I wrestle the panic down. I pull my hood down sharply in a small victory of difference. "We'll find a way of sorting this. I'm fine. Honest."

"I'm going to another hole I've got." She looks meaningfully at me, "Not one you know about."

"Don't leave me." The words burst out. I need her, the feeling rises from within, she's someone I depend on.

"You're him. I can't trust you."

"Talia!" Desperation makes my voice crack.

Her face softens, "I'll be back tomorrow. I need to sleep." She puts the lantern on the floor and slips out and I'm left alone with the guttering candle.

I begin to shriek at her to come back and stop. I know there are people who take advantage of those less able out there, people who would knife me without a thought. I decide to curl up in a corner and find I can't move my feet off the floor. A part of them has to be in contact with it at all times – I'm chained by the dust. A fear rises, I don't want to go outside now. I can't defend myself, I can't run. I slide myself over to the wall, one painful movement at a time and curl up, grateful for the presence of something solid behind me.

I fall asleep and dream of my shed in the orchard. The wind in the leaves, the filtered sunlight and the scent of decaying apples. A deathly silence, with no Biggles running to greet me. I push open the shed door and find Dominic sitting in the cellar room, playing with his train set. He's frowning and holds a piece of track up to me as I enter. I fall to my knees in the dust and take the piece to place it in the last gap and complete the circle. A dread creeps over me as a movement catches my eye, the dust on the floor is swirling. My eyes are dragged into the darkness behind where something is rising. I try to warn him. I can't move! Dominic is oblivious, watching his train going round in circles. I struggle to get a noise past the blockage in my throat and see his hand move to change the points and at the same time the figure steps forwards.

I wake with my face pressed into a pile of rubble, still shaking. The candle's gone out. I've fallen over in my sleep, I begin to lever myself up and nearly fall over as my arms give way. Dominic, my family. I may never see them again. I squeeze my eyes shut, trying to stop the tears falling and find I can't cry. My tear ducts are blocked. The inhumanity of this is the last straw, I curl up with my mouth open and croak with helplessness.

Gasping the dry sobs out, I open my eyes again. A grey haze is in front of my eyes, I can see the edges of the room clearly, despite there being no light. My stomach rumbles and without thinking I concentrate, a new need filling me. My hands begin to warm. I pull them apart, my fingers trembling, my nails start to ache. The strain builds through my arms, making me clench my teeth to stop them shaking.

The dust builds in front of me, shifting into a pile. The panic rises as I watch, feeling ill as the dust solidifies. Feet, legs, the movement of individual grains like a stop motion camera film, shifting ever higher. The waist, the ribbing of the hoody. The arms falling down in a waterfall, the rumpled sleeves becoming visible. No cloak bursts from the shoulders as the head grows this time and the hood is down, exposing my face. A facsimile of myself. My mouth is open as though concentrating, I look young. The grey man that had been stalking the city all this time and this time I am the one who has made it. A word develops from behind my teeth, I clench them, not wanting to say it, fighting the need. It wriggles, sliding out, tickling my tongue. "Go."

I collapse into a pile, all my strength gone. The grey man bows his head and walks away, feet making no noise against the spotless floor.

I can feel it walking through the night. Everything avoids it. Flashes of sight come to me, buildings, the occasional frightened face. It's walking with a purpose, it knows where it's going without me guiding it. I shiver, the last building I recognised, it's on the way to Igren's factory. At least the men will be safe indoors. I think through the list of the men I know there. I'd hate anyone to be hurt, even the Eyebrow.

I try to relax, I've never seen a grey man force their way into a building. They've always seemed to take the closest victim outside. My heart stops at the sight of a line of men walking back to the factory. It must be the ten day trip to the brothel. The figures grow larger, I want to shriek at them, warn them. Why can't they see the danger? They are getting nervous and looking around, maybe they will notice. Forgetting the lethargy the grey men generate, I will them to react, to run. I've never seen a grey man run. My stomach clenches at the slowing line of men, they must run.

Vihaan is on the end, alert in a relaxed way, he's laughing and joking with the other men. I recognise the way he's gesturing as an innuendo directed at the person next to him. There's a pause and he fills my vision. Is there are flash of recognition in his eyes? I see a hand rise to place itself on his shoulder and his face twists in pain. I try to shut my eyes, but can't stop seeing what happens. His mouth is open and his eyes are wide. His face shrivels, becoming parchment. The silent inner shriek of death. The hand drops and he falls out of my sight. I sit upright, staring into nothing as the grey man turns to walk back the way it came.

The view is stronger as though the grey man has more energy, sucked from its victim. Mentally I shake myself, energy taken from Vihaan, a man I knew for a week and who in his own crude way, looked after me. My facsimile walks swiftly now, I can feel it coming back. My body wants what it holds. The anticipation builds, I lick my dry lips, feeling sick. This craving fills me more than the upset over killing a man. I find myself raising my arms eagerly as the grey man returns. He reaches out and touches my palms. A jolt of energy and he dissolves back into the dust on the floor.

I lay back on my pile of rubble. Disgust wars with terror, competing with the complete satiation and the warmth filling my body. My mind is racing, I killed another man. I no longer care about the rough teasing and the first night spent in terror of his advances. Nobody should die like that. Did I mean to send it towards him? Was there something inside of me that actually wanted to make him suffer? I gag, trying to throw up the contents of my stomach and fail. I stare at my hands, try to scrub the stain away and fail again.

The warmth coils down into the centre of me and the lump shifts, sending out a tendril. A thin line of hatred. As I watch, it grows, puts out roots and anchors itself. A thin wail bursts out, the only release I am now allowed. There's a kernel growing inside of me. A small knot that shouldn't be there. It's not me. It's feeding off the life of the dead man and rooting itself in the dark earth of my soul. It gathers its control over my body, flexing muscles without my permission and exploring me. Alone in the cellar, in the dark, I watch it grow and whimper.

Chapter 15

"Where's it gone?"

The grey filter of light coming through from the other room hasn't changed, although Talia has said it's afternoon. I've tried not to complain about her not coming back sooner, at least she's come back.

Talia walks around me, close to the wall with a bucket in her hand. Water slops over the edges and I notice her knuckles, white on the rim as she puts it down. Another has been placed near the entrance. I flinch, a darker haze rises from the buckets. I know it's only water and yet it raises a terror inside.

"It came back. I killed someone."

I'd told her I'd made a grey man and that I was somehow responsible for all those deaths before. I was almost crying again. The fits of rage and fear had exhausted themselves through the long night and I'd spent the morning waiting in a fudge of tiredness. The thought of sleeping and what I might do in my half drowsy gave me the shivers, so I stayed awake, swaying slightly until I'd heard Talia's light step outside.

She sits on the pile of rubble opposite, far enough away to run if necessary and puts her sharp chin into the palm of her hand. Studying me, she asks, "Can't you control them? Stop doing it now you know how?"

"I don't know. I caught myself doing it before I'd realised it was happening."

"So maybe you could stop."

Hope rears its head and plummets again as I felt something shift inside my chest. The thing inside had quietened down after its exploration. I daren't tell Talia about it, I don't want her to leave and I can tell she doesn't want to stay.

"Maybe," I mutter.

She huffs and begins taking items out of her bag. Food and her little brazier. "You need to eat."

I watch as she cuts the vegetables, wiping her nose on the back of her hand, skinny legs akimbo in her baggy jeans. There is something else about her, something I need. The ghost of a whisper runs through my mind. I concentrate on the cooking and remind myself that I'd not eaten since the day before. Nothing comes from my stomach. I remember the feeling of Vihaan's life force shooting through me and felt it lurch. I want more.

Before I can stop myself, I say, "I'm not hungry."

Talia turns to give me another long look, "You prefer sucking the souls from people then?"

That was nasty and far too close to the truth. I find myself snarling back, "Tastes better than your cooking."

"Fine."

She flings the pot in my direction, water, carrots and lentils go everywhere. I cry out as my arms go up to shield myself from the wet. Water all around this fucking place – the thought isn't my own. The pot hitting me is the final straw, I bury my face in my arms and dryly sob as the water is absorbed. I raise my face as Talia moves to touch me and stops at my hand rising to block her.

"Stay away." I feel terribly alone.

She sighs and picks up the pot, rifling through her bag to find more food. "I'll do some more. I need to eat, even if you don't." She doesn't pick up the vegetables off the floor. It's not like Talia to waste anything edible, I think of the grey man rising from the dust and agree.

Talia hunches over the lit stove and watches the contents bubble. I stare at the shadows dancing on the wall and find myself desperate to see blue skies and green trees. This cellar is depressing, more so with the grey haze covering everything. Can I control the grey men? Despair hits, how can I survive without them? The smell of the food is making me feel ill and I daren't tell Talia. The steam coils towards me. Unconsciously I shuffle back, the sole of one foot in contact with the floor at all points.

"Can't you sit properly?" The question catches me out and Talia repeats herself.

"I can only take one foot off the floor at a time."

Her eyes narrow, "Makes you slower." I don't like the satisfied tone she comments in, as though she's pleased she's found another weakness. The anger flashes through me and I bite back a snarl.

When I'm able to control myself, I ask, "What are we going to do?"

Talia's shoulders sag as she pulls her sleeve down around her hand to hold the small cup of soup. "Dunno." She brightens, "Maybe I could talk to Bay. They might know something up at the wall. The nobs know all sorts of things."

Memories of men with pickaxes surge into my mind. The pain of the bright lights they carry and the rush of energy both boiling towards me and dissipating in different directions. The prison holding me contracting into a feeble fleshy shell.

"No. Please don't tell." I gasp the words out in the terror of being found in this state and with no way to protect myself. The grey men could only do so much. The last thought trails away and I open my eyes to see Talia's regard.

"Hmm." I don't feel reassured. She finishes her soup, shakes the cup out and yawns.

"Is it that late?"

"No. I was busy last night. Food don't grow on trees you know."

I open my mouth to say fruit does and shut it again. Arguing isn't going to help. I'm tired too. I shuffle into a more comfortable position. "Aren't you worried about being in the same room as me?"

Talia settles herself down next to the wall. "I've got my buckets." She curls into a ball and stops the conversation.

I'm left with my own thoughts. I want to go home, why did I come here to be the hero? Talia's streetwise enough to deal with anything. Without me, she wouldn't be in this position and I'd be back in my shed. I slide back into my fugue, staring at the walls and at some point fall into sleep and dream of a past not my own.

The cold of the obsidian throne flows through me, tremors shaking my hunched body. A pile of gold and rods of rare metals sit in front of me and I raise a hand. Other, colder hands reach out of the ground to pull a man downwards, the others remain kneeling as he's dragged halfway into the stone floor. My voice is reasonable as I point out that gold and riches were not what I'd asked for. The man's whimpers grow softer, unable to take a breath, the stone cutting in every time his ribs contract.

One distracts me, tells me that I've misunderstood and freezes as another hand reaches for his ankle. He's a brave man, he stands there and tells me that this is not simply decoration that they've brought, it is parts of a machine to help free me. I lean forwards, snarling at the pain keeping me immobile, snarling at the knowledge I now have of their duplicity. Nothing shows but sincerity in his eyes. A final sigh from the floor beside him and he continues to hold my gaze without flinching. I am desperate, my twisted body needs a cure, I can kill anyone, I can do anything but heal myself.

They build the cage around me, explaining with lies to show how it will heal me, to enable me to get off this mountain peninsula. The curse that holds me, that gives me this power is held within this shattered body. I will rise like a star at dawn to come down on the people of the mainland, my stomach warms at the thought and a stone hand comes out of the wall to grasp the arm of a man working next to me. He shakes as I explain in detail what will happen to him if he is lying.

Both in the dream and in real life, my feet cannot resist the call of stone. I cannot move, the limits placed on me, bound as I am to this throne. My authority lies in my stone men travelling the trackways and appearing out of nowhere. They are my loyal lieutenants, unstoppable by any blade or distance hold a continent to ransom, nowhere is safe from them.

The cage is finished, I ask questions in excitement, fingers crawling across the shifting carvings on the arms of my throne as I brush them. One of the men is sweating. They answer the best they can. I will feel heat, a light and then I will be free. I am a fool. They trap me with my own weakness.

The light comes, the heat and then the cage fuses, the men holding onto the rods, sinking into ash, their bones incandescent. I scream as the power streams out of me to encase me in a ball of light. I clench my fists, waiting to rise into the dawn and the mountain shakes above me, the vents blowing steam into the air. The ground sinks, the mountain falls and buries me in my cage.

I half wake to stare into the dark room, raging at the fate that has left me broken in mind and body. My abilities are stolen further, centuries later by the men with lights and pickaxes and are now so shrunken that I can only pull dust not stone into my own shape. My fingers press against the unyielding ground and I curse, longing for the madness of my black throne. I cannot even open the trackways, weak as I am now, I can only send a single minion through an opening made by the thieves and then it clangs shut in my face. This half clinging to life revolts me, one day I will be free, one day they will pay. I sink back into dreams of gilded cages and thwarted power.

The need pulls at me before I wake. My hands part, I need food. It strengthens and my eyes open to see dust sliding across the floor, the ripples fascinating me in my drowsy state. The dust begins to pull itself up and my fascination turns to horror. Talia is sleeping across the room, my gaze swings to her. Even without a decent light I can see she's been crying. Shame fills me, I didn't hear a sound.

The dust climbs higher. How do I turn this off? A struggle within my mind, trying to find the switch. My limbs aren't my own, I can't stop this. What's left of my mind is screaming at Talia to get out, to run. The facsimile grows in the gloom of the cellar, lit by the fish oil lamp that I barely notice, consumed by the desire flooding through me.

A pressure builds inside my mind. Alien thoughts sweep through – she has what I need. I can see a golden light in the gloom, it sparkles around her. The cracked, crusty skin of an ancient oily want fills me. That golden nectar she holds, it's rightfully mine. A part of the energy that was mine, that was used for years to imprison me now lies next to the wall, encased in a meat skin. My lips draw back in anticipation.

I scream inwardly at myself – I'm Daniel! This isn't me! All those grey men I'd seen when around her, they weren't coming for me. I'd never been in any danger from them. They'd wanted Talia. The grey man turns as the dust climbs, seeking her. I can't hold it back, I've no control, a passenger in my own body. Slack hands burst from the sleeves and clench into fists.

"Talia." I force her name out. Her eyes open immediately to dart around the room and meet mine. Her foot lashes out as she scrambles up and kicks the bucket out of reach. My heart wars with terror and exultation as it tilts and half falls over, staining the floor.

"I need you." The words are dragged from me. An all consuming desire rises at the life in her. The light she holds, I want to smother it, feed on it. I haven't seen one like her in years. So few of the thieves are left, what is left in the larger population is now weak, unable to do more than sustain me for long. I remember with satisfaction the feast I'd had years ago, of another woman and the power coursing through me as she died, a brief gleam of what I once had. My mouth opens in hunger at the memory and I bat away the feeble horror of my host. I begin to drag myself across the floor, the dust swirling around me.

I twist inside, fighting a losing battle as I raise my arms to command my doppelgänger. Talia backs away, despair in her face. She's in the wrong place for the doorway, she'd got too cocky with her buckets. Guilt hits me as I realise I also didn't warn her. This being inside of me has been sneaky and wormed its way around to block her off, it's made me do things without being aware of them.

I can feel myself being assessed and the contempt generated by my weakness. My body isn't strong enough, I'm dismissed as a means of locomotion. So much energy expended simply to exist, no way of moving, chained to this room. The thoughts crawl through my mind, grey fingers prodding every sensitive space.

Talia trips over backwards, scrambling away from the door. The grey man steps forwards, swipes at her and misses. I can no longer move, drained and held into place. Everything is quiet apart from Talia's ragged breathing and the scuffle of her hands and feet. The grey man is expressionless, a monster attempting to touch and suck the life out of its victim.

I begin to hope against all reason as my facsimile fails to grab Talia. It's clumsy, and I can feel how the being is enraged at the stuttering control it has. Thoughts flick through my mind that aren't mine. I want to be sick at the stain running through them. I catch a glimpse of a smooth stone figure from times past, recalling the expressionless assassin and how it would move instinctively to catch its victim and quail. Rage flows through me at being forced to be this helpless. I should be able to catch this insignificant person easily. I snarl, forced to wait for my minion to bring her to me. How dare she cause this trouble, many greater than her had once sat at my feet vying for the honour of giving themselves to me.

Talia's moved behind me. I'm held and I can't turn to see her, I can only hear the shuffle of her feet. I imagine her twisting out of the way, shifting constantly until I hear her breath catch. A muffled cough and my heart sinks. I've heard that cough too many times, the precursor to a major coughing fit. She moves to the other side of me and I can see her chest heaving with the effort of containing the cough, her movements jerky, her face reddening. She bends over in her fit and the part of me that isn't me laughs in exaltation.

Her fingers close around the rim of the other bucket and flings it, her throat closing as she chokes. Her aim is bad, it hits the side of the grey man, only half going over it. For a moment it stands, no emotion on its face and then it sags like a sand castle in the tide, slopping and dissolving. Talia sinks to her knees coughing and the backlash of energy hits me.

I scream in pain as it courses through my body, igniting every nerve end. The fury of the being inside me thwarted. No, it's no longer something inside me, it is me. It uses the moment of shock to delve deep inside, merging itself, taking advantage of every point in my memory where I've been put down and laughed at. I can feel the rage growing, the hatred, I will make them pay.

My sister, Clive, the receptionist. Talia. The darkness deepens around the edges of my eyes and I feel the thrill of finally throwing off the chains of convention.

"Run." The tiny remaining sane part of me forces the word out and the last thing I see is the flash of Talia's eyes as she obeys.

Chapter 16

Talia turned to run, Daniel was no longer her friend, he was something hunting her. She ran in a panic, scraping herself against a wall, the rough surface taking chunks out of her arm and stumbled over the rubble pushed to the sides of the streets, unaware of anyone she passed. No one could help her, she had no one to turn to. Who could kill her friend? Her vision blurred, the friend that wasn't her friend anymore.

Talia ran to get space between her and the thing was stalking her. Her lungs burned and she wheezed with the effort of breathing past the obstructions. Finally, chest heaving, she had to stop. She collapsed against a wall, no longer caring about the clothes she'd been so proud of. It was all her fault. She bit down hard on her hand, the pain cutting through her desperation. If she hadn't gone through the rift then Daniel wouldn't have followed her. He was going to die. Tears streamed down her face as she raged, she couldn't help him and it was all her fault. Daniel was dead – she corrected herself – Daniel was alive and trying to kill her.

A whisper of dread and she turned to see the unhurried stride of the figure turning the corner down the end of the street. Something more than the tiredness of bad lungs and running dragged at her limbs. The panic to find safety called and she summoned the void without thinking. Snot ran from her nose and crying, she scrabbled at the air, finding the break and not caring where she might end up. Talia sobbed aloud, knowing every second brought it closer. She had to find safety, somewhere close by where she could find the time to think and defeat it. She needed water.

She could feel her need pulling and within the void she turned, knowing without knowing which way she needed to go. Safety was close by. The void spat her out and Talia stumbled into beech woods. She bent over, coughing hard and it threatened to finish off her brain through lack of oxygen. Her stomach rebelled, adding to the splatter on the ground. A stream of gunk ran out her mouth, spotted with blood.

Snivelling she stood, wiping her mouth and rubbing her eyes against her sleeve and she stared around. Birds sang and she caught the flicker of wings as one launched itself upwards. Talia turned to follow its flight and gazed at the wide lake behind her – the safety she'd been looking for.

She stumbled forwards and felt the break loosen as something came through. The body poured onto the ground. Thigh deep in the lake she stood and watched with dead eyes as her friend built himself up in front of her. His mouth was slightly open as though concentrating, the hood in folds around his neck in his pathetic defiance of what had happened to him. The dirt that had been clinging to his shoe mirrored in dust. She sank to her knees, the water rising to her waist, passive in the knowledge she was safe for the moment. One step forward and her nightmare dissolved.

Talia waded back to the shore to allow the sun to dry her clothes. A tear trickled down her face, she swiped it away, not wanting the weakness. Her legs betrayed her by giving way and she fell into the ground.

Why had she let him come back? She didn't care about anyone else, no one else mattered. She ran through the list of contacts she had, the only other person she'd cared about had been Dodie and she'd pulled away from her in the last few years. Daniel's casual question about her parents hurt, she couldn't remember them. Dodie had filled her life and she was dead. Daniel was dead as well.

The pressure built inside her head, Daniel was dead. Her ribs heaved and she sucked in air to scream into last year's leaves. Talia scrunched them into brown dust in her fists, beating the ground with tears streaming down her face and fell into another coughing fit. She buried her head into the leaves, staring. Brown dust, not grey, still giving life unlike the death the other dust from her world gave. She cried herself out as she hadn't in years.

As the tears slowly gave way, she tried to remember past the blankness in her mind. Nothing, the past was a locked door, nothing leaked out. Limbs shaking from the unaccustomed emotion, she began to pull herself together and looked round. This was Daniel's world she stood in. The trees standing straight and tall, the leaves shivering in the breeze. She rolled over to lay on her back and gazed up at the blue sky between the green leaves. Her mind span in circles, trying to work out how the grey men could have had Daniel's face before he'd even come to her world, and how she could save him. The sighing of wind through the branches soothed her, speaking of a time before the isolation of cold streets and grey cities. Exhaustion claimed her and she fell asleep.

Talia woke with a jump. The shadows had lengthened and she stretched stiffly. The sun highlighted a thin path through the trees. Almost drunk with having slept deeply, she decided to follow it. Relaxed in the knowledge that nothing could hurt her here – Daniel had told her so – she hummed as she walked, a thin thread of a melody. The fragile peace held as she scuffed her way up the narrow track. It led to a lookout point, the view widening. The trees were cut off below. She hurried to see why and stopped dead in her tracks. The mist lay in a thick blanket below the trees, the outlines of the wall could be seen and the tops of buildings further down.

Dread washed through her, this wasn't Daniel's world. She was inside the wall, in the nobs place. She had to get out of here before anyone saw her. She didn't fit in, anyone would see that in an instant. She hesitated, unsure if she would draw another grey man if she opened a rift again so soon.

She was even more in shock when a voice said close by, "This is my favourite place to watch the sun go down." She spun around to see an older man, dressed in blue behind her. She twitched away as he smiled easily and came to stand close by. "My apologies, I disturbed you." He waved a hand at the view, "Do you like it?"

Talia nodded, mind calculating rapidly as she assessed him. A silver chain hung from his neck, several rings on his fingers. Obviously a nob, and a wealthy one too. She had to play along, distract him and then get away before he called a guard. She'd be lucky if she got away with a beating. On a bad day, bodies were hung from the top of the wall.

"You can see the other shores from here on a clear day. I like to come here and think of the past, when the waters weren't as high."

"You remember it?" Talia forgot her wariness.

He laughed, "Not even I'm that old. It was hundreds of years ago."

"Mamin said..." She stopped, she'd had too much teasing about it.

"Said what?" He waited expectantly, reminding her of Daniel, interested in things everyone else wasn't.

"Mamin said she was told about someone walking across to the mainland."

He chuckled, "It must have been a very low tide, and he still would have had to swim the last part. It's deep in places."

"She told me there were bridges and roads." Talia's eyes misted over, so few memories. Those she had, she guarded jealously.

"And now nature is reclaiming the city. Water, trees and ash." His eyes surveyed the landscape. "Where did you pop up from young lady? I would say that you're from down below." His question and tone were friendly, Talia still tensed. He laughed lightly, "Don't tell me you snuck inside." A smile quirked the side of his mouth, "It happens. Are you hungry?"

Emotions warred within her. He might be able to help Daniel, he obviously knew things. Past experience told her that he also might be trying to trap her, she hesitated further.

He chuckled, a warm sound, matching the surroundings. "My name is Kenderick. Stay by all means if you like, otherwise you can follow and eat with me and my family. Please be aware that the guards sweep the area close to dusk. You'll want to be away by that point."

The tip about the guards lowered her defences, "Do you know things?" She blurted it out, unsure how to start.

"What do you need to know?" She eyed him, desperate for help. He had an open stance, she couldn't sense any threat coming from him. His hands looked capable but he didn't have any weapons that she could see. He cocked his head and said companionably, "Come and talk. Let's see if I can help." He walked away without looking to see if she followed.

Talia hesitated once more and followed him down the hill. Steep steps cut into the hillside brought them down quickly to where the wall was close by, a sweep biting a chunk into the greenery. It was lower on this side, only a storey high and built into the hillside. The windows were glazed – no threat of them being broken from this side – and there was the same smear of ash over them, unseen in the woods. Doors showed at regular intervals, all shut. Kenderick headed for one slightly off the trail.

The door opened into a large workshop, the windows showed the view towards the hills and an inner door pulled close. Kenderick pulled a string and the lights came on. She jumped, these weren't the pale feeble lights of the city, these blazed, chasing away the shadows. He watched with an amused look on his face as Talia swung her head around, assessing the area before she walked in.

"Please excuse the chaos in here. This is my workshop, I seldom allow anyone to tidy."

Talia caught the reference to servants and shivered. Her sharp eyes peered everywhere, catching sights she recognised from her digging. It reminded her of Daniel's rooms, full of interest, the familiarity reassured her.

"I've seen those before." She pointed at a couple of mechanisms on a workbench, the tools surrounding them and a book open in front. A pen and inkwell were tucked in the mess.

Kenderick came to stand next to her, "They come from the city, people bring them to me. I take them apart and work out how they move."

"And write it down?" Talia's finger hovered over the book, not quite daring to touch the creamy pages.

"You have quick eyes young lady. Look." He picked up the closest mechanism and turned the handle. Rods moved and pulled. Talia was pleased, it wasn't as good as the one she'd found. A pang caught her at how Daniel had helped mend it. His voice interrupted her thoughts. "I believe we have a lot to learn from the ancients who built this city. Where did you see these?"

"I dug one out… once." Despite her pride, self-preservation caught Talia before she talked about Daniel repairing it.

"You dig? Splendid, would you find things like this for me? I will pay well." His eagerness was infectious and Talia found herself nodding. He rubbed his hands, "Now, I'm sure we've got something for dinner. You said you were hungry?"

The inside door banged open and a boy came in with a large dog. Talia dropped her eyes and shifted slightly out of his line of sight.

"Bay, how many times have I told you to knock?"

The boy looked sulky. "Dinner's waiting Father."

"We have a guest. Please be nice to her." Kenderick waved his hand, "This is Bay, my son." Talia's mind raced, making connections. She realised that Kenderick hadn't asked her name but Bay might know if he'd bothered to ask the doorman the other day. She'd not lied about her name in case Marty had asked. Her shoulders tensed, it wasn't good now she thought about it. Kenderick hadn't asked because she didn't matter to him, if you didn't matter then you were dead. She tensed, she had to get out of here.

Bay glowered out of habit and then stared. Talia's hopes plummeted as he said, "You're Talia, I asked about you at the small west door. You came to see me the other day with that boy, he wasn't from round here."

Kenderick's voice was mild, "Which boy? You didn't mention this Bay."

Bay flinched. "I was going to tell you. She had this boy she thought was one of us. Never seen him before."

"He could have been someone's son you hadn't met. You should have told me. It could have been useful."

A whine entered Bay's voice, "She was going to come back. She offered to get me something good for you." He twisted, "She said the boy was a layer out of the dead."

Kenderick stilled and asked sharply, "Who was this boy, Talia?"

Talia tensed further, she didn't like the way this was going. She'd wanted to ask about the grey men without mentioning Daniel. He was helpless and still her friend, despite wanting to kill her. She slid her hand towards her knife. The door to the outside was only a few steps away. Maybe she could get out and run. Talia allowed her voice to become sullen, refused to glance at them in an attempt to look surly. "Just a stranger I met. He told me he was a nob, wanted to get back in here."

"Interesting, but I don't think I believe you." In mid-sentence Kenderick shoved Talia backwards. The edge of the table caught her ribcage, making her gasp and drop her knife. Taking advantage, he leaned further, digging it in and grabbed her hands. She swore as tools pinched and slid underneath her back.

"Now, that's not nice young lady." He kicked her knife away, and leant over to rummage through the mess on the bench behind. Talia struggled and felt her ribs creak at his weight holding her down. A manacle clicked around her wrist. "I knew these would come in useful again. Bay, bring that mutt of yours here."

Kenderick pulled her up by her wrist and she kicked out at him. He was faster than he looked, a long arm flicked out to give her a smack around the head that made her stumble. "Less of the swearing please."

He dragged her over to a ring on the floor, ignoring the table corner banging into her hip. Her head ringing, Talia launched herself, attempting to distract him before he could chain her up. Kenderick picked her up, easily avoiding her clawing fingers and wrapped his arm around her. The lock clicked shut through the ring and chain. Bay had been the struggle watching through angry eyes, he took hold of his dog's ruff and dragged it forwards. It whined and snapped at Kenderick who flicked out a length of chain, smacking it on the nose. As it cringed away, Kenderick looped the other end of the chain around its neck.

"That's better. You won't be going anywhere until we've had a chance to talk. Bay, you had better eat your dinner in here. Wouldn't want Fangs to get upset and attack our guest." Kenderick reached out to ruffle the dog's ears and it cowered. Talia felt the same way. His voice and stance hadn't changed, it still held the same calmness that had tricked her into trusting him earlier.

Kenderick left and Bay followed, smirking. Talia shifted and the dog growled, evidently thinking she was the person responsible for it being chained up. Remembering Daniels' dog, she tried talking to it and shrank back when it refused to believe her false friendliness. She didn't blame it, she eyed her knife left casually on the floor in the corner and decided she'd happily slit its throat given a chance.

Bay swaggered in with a plate and the dog settled into a position of guarding her while keeping an eye on the food. Bay's eating seemed to go on for ages, she suspected he was enjoying himself tormenting her. Talia's stomach grumbled as the dog snapped up the various titbits thrown to it.

"You and my dog. You've both got the same expression. Do you want some too?" Bay waved a piece of meat at her. Drool pooled at the dog's feet. Talia shook her head. No way would she take anything from him, unless…

She tried smiling and knelt, holding her chained hand out to him. "Help me."

Bay shook his head. "Father would kill me." His voice was matter of fact. "I'm only tolerated. He killed my two older brothers when they got in his way." He dunked the meat he'd been waving into his mouth.

"What if I helped you kill him?"

His mouth paused in its chewing as he considered her offer. "He's too fast."

The dog growled as she waved her hand, "There are three of us." She narrowed her eyes, "Allies?"

Bay's mouth resumed its chewing, "Maybe." The sound of a door slamming in the next room made them both jump.

Kenderick strode in with a book in his hand. "Marvellous how a good meal can restore your mood." He pulled out a nearby chair and began to flick through his book, ignoring the fact that Talia hadn't eaten. "I do a lot of reading. The ancients were very fond of writing information down. I have scribes who hunt down old books. Tell me, how did you get in?"

The question caught her out. She stammered and recovered, "Same way I got in the first time." Talia nodded at Bay who was still stuffing his meal, "Through a door." She shivered at the bland look Kenderick gave her. This man was danger on a whole new level.

"I saw how you defeated that grey man, not many know to take cover in water. Yes, I happened to be passing when you came out of those bushes. Who was that boy Bay spoke about?"

"I told you, I thought he was a nob. I was after a reward for bringing him back, then he disappeared on me. Bastard." She muttered the last word, hoping it would sound plausible.

"Hmm." The gentle sound gave nothing away and yet Talia was aware of Bay's wide eyed look. "What do you know about the grey men?"

"Nothing." She stared at the floor. "Found out about the water by accident, one walked into a puddle in front of me." This at least was the truth.

Kenderick crossed an ankle over his knee and placed a finger on the creamy page. "Let me tell you some history you may not be aware of." Talia prepared herself to be bored and mentally sat up when he began.

"The grey men are an ancient scourge of this city. However, we had a long period of time when they weren't so common. There was the occasional sighting, never any cause for alarm. I did a lot of research when they started to be seen on a regular basis about twelve or thirteen years ago, trying to find out why."

Kenderick settled himself for a long talk, confident of his captive audience. "I found out that many centuries ago, miners disturbed something. A being so evil it was enclosed in a forcefield generated by its own magnetism. The forcefield exploded when the miners triggered it and many died. Those further away survived and discovered they had a wonderful new talent."

He paused and stared down at her, "A way of travelling through space. Of course it came at a price. They were hunted down by the being through their own trackways, by the grey men it made. My theory is that it wanted something they had. Those that could, fled and the ancients made this city an island to trap it here. Many skills were lost and since that point we have been declining, scrabbling for survival." His fists clenched.

"Why didn't they all travel off the island if they had such a talent?" Talia was fascinated, despite herself.

Kenderick recovered and smiled, "I'm sure some did. However, the miners were part of the underclass at that time and loath to leave families and familiar surroundings as all such people are. Such a waste..." Talia bristled at his casual disparagement. He ignored her glare, "They also discovered in time that the trait was passed on to their children. Why are the grey men active once more?" The question came unexpectedly.

"I don't know." The answer was shocked out of her. He stood, placed the book carefully on a table and walked towards her. Talia shuffled back, ignoring the dog's rumble. She twisted away, at the end of the chain and he caught her arm.

"You spoke of your mother being able to walk to the mainland. That was hundreds of years ago. It could never have been done at any other point." Talia shook her head violently. He couldn't have seen her come through, he'd have said otherwise. He wanted to know if she could do it. The frantic thoughts raced through her head as she felt her arm twisted. She swore and kicked out.

He avoided the flailing kick easily and twisted further. "Your mother, did she bring you through? From the past?" He gripped Talia by the throat, pulling her onto her toes. Talia shook her head again, she could remember nothing. Pain lanced through her neck from his fingers, he was cutting off her air supply. Weak as a kitten she pushed frantically.

"You may as well tell me." The calm voice came from far away as lights started to flash in front of her eyes and the squeezing tightened. She was just going to pass out when she was dropped on the floor. She lay there, fighting her own clogged lungs to draw breath and barely heard the servant call again from the other room.

Kenderick nudged her ribs hard with a boot. "Think about talking. I will be back shortly." He strode out of the room, leaving Talia gasping in a pile on the floor.

Chapter 17

Talia rubbed her throat – this was just like that man who'd followed her back to her cellar – she'd knife him too, given the chance. She tried to convince herself she could but the noise of her chains shaking gave her away, she was nothing but a bug to Kenderick, something to be studied, used and then squashed. Bay had forgotten his half eaten meal and was staring at her, mouth open.

She forced the tremor out of her voice and said, "So, you just going to watch him kill me?"

The whine was back, "I can't stop him. He'll kill me instead."

Coward. The contempt rose, helping to clear her mind. "I'll tell him you knew my friend as well, tell him you knew all about him." Bay flinched and Talia started plotting. That book had information in it, maybe it could tell her how to defeat the dust holding Daniel. She took a risk, hoping he wouldn't tell his father, "My friend, he's more important than you think. He can beat your father if I can contact him. That's what he does for his friends. He gathers the dust and makes them into men." Inspiration hit, "He's the Lord of Dust."

"That's not what father said."

"That's because your father doesn't know everything."

"Why isn't he helping you now?"

Talia smirked inwardly, she'd got him. "'Cause he needs to know where we are, and for that I need to be free. It's simple." Bay's mouth worked as he thought. She held her shackled wrist out and he slowly reached for the key on the table. "Come on, you want to be free of him too," she coaxed.

She sat up as he undid the lock on the floor. Talia left the chain snaking towards the loop, hoping it would still pass a cursory inspection. They heard the noise of Kenderick's boots crossing the wooden floor in the next room.

"Now undo your dog," she hissed, pointing at the chain attaching her to the dog. Bay, looking frightened, shook his head and flung the key back on the table. The dog shifted at Bay's movement and the chain moved with it. It hadn't realised yet that it was only the chain connecting them together, not the ring on the floor. She swore under her breath, he was an idiot, but at least she could move. The dog showed its teeth and growled gently, daring her to try. Ideas raced through her head, no time to grab her knife, it was still in the corner, she was going to have to use what she had. She had to get free of the dog, which meant she couldn't leave Bay or it would attack her. Talia avoided its eyes and crouched, feeling for the break. She'd only have one chance at this. She took a deep breath and tensed her muscles, ready as the door opened.

Bay cast one look at the door and panicked, shouting, "Father!"

Kenderick saw the free loop of chain and reacted swiftly, diving towards her. Twisting, she ripped open the rift with her free hand and Kenderick paused for a split second, shock making his chin drop. The dog shrank away from the man and Talia scooped it up in both arms and dragged it through with her. The practice she'd had in recent days held. She could feel the holes made in earlier times, where they went and how far. She didn't want any of them. She tucked her limbs into the breach and twisted sideways. Kenderick's roar was distorted by distance.

Talia came out behind Kenderick and heaved the dog at him. Scared and disorientated, the dog attacked, drawing blood. A large fist connected into its ribs and it squealed, cringing away. Another blow caught Talia and she was thrown across the room to land, half dazed against the workbench. Her arm was nearly dislocated from the weight of the dog, lucky for her it was also trying to get as far away from Kenderick as she was. Bay was curled up in the corner, arms protecting his face, shaking. She pulled herself up, a chance, that's all she needed, she had to distract him.

Talia reached behind her and threw the first thing her fingers found. Tools, the book, anything. Scooping items up, she flung them, not caring if they hit her target. She backed away, a pace at a time, she daren't look at the table she was pulling items off, she could only hope there were enough in reach. Kenderick batted them away, shielding his face. The room had felt so large when she'd first come in, so full of tools, now it didn't feel large enough. She saw the thin line of the break begin to re-open. To hide the flicker of her eyes and the gasp from Bay, she redoubled her efforts. The contraption took two hands to throw and Kenderick roared with rage. The body slowly built behind them – too slowly – she had to keep him distracted. The dog pulled at her wrist, the chain biting as it tried to get away and she whimpered at the pain in her shoulder.

She moved further back and came to a standstill at the end of the chain. Talia swore, the dog had retreated under the table, she had no way of getting it out without being caught. She reached back and her fingers found nothing, a brief glance was all she could risk. She'd thrown everything on the table. Kenderick's eyes lit up and he lurched towards her, hand outstretched. Talia dropped to the ground and his fingers brushed her shirt. She felt the lethargy hit as the grey man began to move and Kenderick finally realised something was happening behind him. He turned and the grey man reached out a hand to place it on his shoulder. Kenderick fell to his knees next to her, staring up at her friend standing above him. His mouth gaped and stretched, his skin became drawn and tightened against his skull. Talia stared, she'd never been this close to a grey man's victim.

Too close, she shuddered herself back into moving. Talia dragged the dog out from underneath the table, her hand twisted in the dog's thick ruff. Too cowed to snap, it slunk, tail between its legs. She grabbed Bay's arm and shook him. Bay stared, eyes wide as he watched his father succumb and she pulled them both towards the door.

"Come on."

The key was in the lock, she twisted it out and looked back. Daniel's face was impassive as he absorbed Kenderick's life. The lethargy lifted the further away she got. She pulled Bay out of the room, him scrambling on hands and knees while he stared backwards at his father's slow disintegration. Talia threw her weight against the door and got the hanging chain caught. She pulled it out, slammed it shut and locked it.

Outside, the birds sang and trees rustled. Talia's sweat dried in the breeze and she shivered, thinking of the nightmare trapped in the building next to them. Bay sat against the wall panting, his fingers in his dog's ruff.

"That was a grey man. How did you do that? Can you summon them?" His eyes were wide.

Talia sank into the grass close by, her mind still racing, she mustn't let him get the better of her. She allowed herself to smirk and ignored the question. "We need to get away. I don't know if they can open doors. Are any doors open in the other room?"

Bay shrugged, "Could have been. Father doesn't let his servants disturb him during the evenings unless it's important, but I'm sure someone will come in at some point."

Talia rubbed her face and the chains clinked. She waved her wrist at him. "Can you get this off?"

Bay shook his head. "The key's in the workshop. How did you do that? How did you make the grey man come?"

"I told you, my friend helps me."

Bay flinched, "You won't let him come after me. I did get you free – here." He looped the chain from his dog's head and bobbed his head, backing away again. Power filled Talia, she'd not had anyone afraid of her before. She chinked the chain, running it through her fingers. This was how the cliques formed, people being afraid of you, thinking you could do things for them, protect them.

Bay's words intruded, "We could overthrow the system now Father's dead. He was important. So many people depended on him despite the fact they hated him for keeping them guessing what he would do next. You said people down there wanted to rebel. There aren't many of us left up here, I know the sorts of things that could help. Your friend could help us. No one could stop us." Wrapped up in his own power fantasy, Bay gazed unseeing at the hillside.

Her friend. It jolted her back to reality. Daniel was the Lord of Dust, ashes filled her mouth. She had to help him, she couldn't leave him like he was. Somehow she kept her own voice light, "Nah, sounds like hard work. You have a go."

"Really?" Bay hesitated, "You could always join me later, I wouldn't stop you."

As if he could, Talia barely stopped herself from snorting. "I prefer doing my own thing, but we might join you later." The promise of "we" was enough. Bay nodded awkwardly and ran off, the dog following close behind.

Despair filled her after Bay had left. Lord of Dust. He wasn't her friend, he was searching for her and would kill her if he found her. Now the adrenaline had stopped pumping she shivered. She wanted her friend back desperately. She'd not had much in the way of friends before. Most people she knew were acquaintances, she only used them for information. Dodie she'd liked and respected, but she'd never allowed anyone to become this close to her. Daniel had managed somehow. Soft and pathetic he'd wormed his way in.

A need filled her for the Daniel she'd known. She wanted to be in his world, not this dangerous imitation. A man's call from further down and she remembered Kenderick's warning about guards patrolling at dusk – she had to get away. She let her need dictate and pulled open the break in the hope that Daniel wouldn't be able to summon another grey man this quickly. The track to Daniel's world was there, well trodden and inviting. Her need pulled in a different direction, she wanted her friend in his own world, someone to help her.

This time was harder, forcing her way along a line that the void didn't want her to take. She could feel the other line. It was almost a road, well lit, welcoming, a safety at the end. There was nothing for her in that direction. The tenuous call beckoned and her lungs compressed with the effort of keeping her alive in a place that didn't want her. Eyes bulging, she found the way through from sheer bloody-mindedness.

She fell into the leaves, flopping over to stare at the deep green tinged with gold, laced in front of the blue sky. The air was warm and dry. Daniel's world, clean and bright. She let herself unfocus and drifted mentally, not caring if the grey man found her. Her Daniel was no more.

A bark roused her. Still used to the danger of dogs in her own world, Talia checked for her knife and groaned when she remembered it was in the corner of Kenderick's workshop. No branches within reach to climb and this area was open, she crouched lower trying to make herself less obvious.

A solid dog appeared out of a dip, a leg to each corner of its body. Bouncing on all fours as if on springs, a smile on its face, tongue hanging out. Everything smiled in this world, she felt the tears tug.

"Talia?"

As though in a dream, Talia raised her head. He stood at the top of the dip, behind the dog and walked cautiously towards her. He was wearing different clothes, stupid in shock she couldn't think of anything else. She screwed up her face, trying to think. Her Daniel was back there, trying to kill her. This couldn't be Daniel in front of her. Her brain refused to think. She'd never been at a loss for words like this before, she'd always known what to do.

He was looking at her oddly, "Talia? What's the problem? Why are you here? I've not seen you for months." He looked around sharply, "Do we need to worry about the..."

"You're dead." The words came in a whisper but they still cut off his sentence. His mouth hung open.

A ripping sound and they both turned to see the slender line appeared in the air behind them, Biggles came bounding up with a stick. Daniel swore and attached him to a long rope. "Come on, there's a stream this way." His voice was firm. Talia stared, this wasn't right. Daniel had never been like this, this determination had never been a part of him.

Daniel snapped his fingers and Biggles sat by his side, head up, waiting for his next command. He held his hand out and Talia took it, feeling light headed. A shallow stream puddled into a wide pool, they crossed over and waited. The grey man appeared. Daniel swore again at his own face in clear view. They shifted back, Daniel keeping his hand on Biggles' neck. He whined, creeping close. No slowing of its stride, it plunged itself into wet death and within seconds, all that was left was the grey spreading downstream.

Daniel's voice shook, "That's not something I want to get used to." Talia perched on a stone, wrapping her arms around herself. He came and sat next to her, letting Biggles off his lead. "Talk to me. Tell me about it."

She went through the events leading up to him becoming the Dust Lord in a quiet voice. This Daniel listened, staring out across the treetops on the hill beneath them. Everything poured out, leaving her flat and empty. When she'd finished, she sat, drained, listening to the wind in the leaves.

"We need to go back."

"No!" She wasn't going back, she couldn't take him into danger, she couldn't risk losing him twice.

"Talia, Listen to me. I can remember parts of what's happened. It happened months ago here. That's why I was surprised to see you, I thought we'd sorted it all."

She sniffed, wiping her nose across the back of her hand. "What happened?"

Daniel hesitated, "There's a haze over my memory but I do think we need to go back. I was found six months ago in our orchard, lying in the grass. I've never been able to work out why or why I hadn't seen you again. Apparently I'd been missing for several days. Biggles found me." He silked his fingers through the spaniel's ears. "I was in hospital for ages while they tried to find out what had happened." He grinned, "They were really upset about the marks on my back." He pulled up his shirt, "Look, the brand's healed."

Talia stared at the neat brand, final proof that she'd done something strange in her travelling. "But how can you be here and there at the same time?

"I don't know. I do have some memories but not nice ones." Daniel shuddered.

"Does that mean I saved you?" Talia leant forwards intently.

He waved his arms in frustration and disturbed Biggles, "I don't know. I know it didn't want me. It took someone over at the first opportunity. It was desperate, it knew it didn't have long to live. It was nothing more than hate and a wanting to live and destroy. I wasn't strong enough to stop it, but I was strong enough to hide. To let it think it had control." He shuddered and his eyes glazed over. "I need to stop it, I have to. I was hoping you'd come back. The things it… the things I let it do..." His face brightened. "I'm sure I remember seeing you when you came through, you were a child. You were being given to a large woman."

Talia's mouth hung open. Come through where? She strained her mind backwards and could only remember the sound of her mother's voice, the sea and collecting seaweed in buckets. Then there'd been Dodie and the grey walls of the city. Nothing in between.

Daniel was still thinking out loud, "We need to find out how to stop it."

"We can't. Kenderick said that it would be after me. It..." She paused, "You want something I've got."

"It's not me."

Talia jumped at the snap and peered at him. His face was set, his jaw tight. Talia dropped her eyes to the leaves. "Sorry," she muttered.

Daniel took a deep breath and carried on his thoughts, "From what Kenderick said, it became active after a long period of dormancy. I wonder if he's right, I wonder if it's something to do with me seeing your mother coming through." Biggles came wuffling up through the leaves and flopped heavily on his lap. He wriggled ecstatically as Daniel absently rubbed his tummy. "There was a woman, she must have been your mother, don't you remember?"

"I can't remember. All I can remember is her telling me not to jump." Her head hurt and she turned away, desperate not to show her eyes filling up. Why couldn't she remember? What was wrong with her?

"How did you know what she meant?" He pressed her gently. "I can remember seeing you being held by a man, then it goes fuzzy, like a dream. I've got a glimpse of your mother's face, nobody else's. Do you know where she is?"

Talia felt the tears gather and it came out as a wail, "I don't know, I don't know. She left me. I don't know why." She felt herself curling into a ball of shame and an arm came around her. Daniel pulled her into his arms.

"You found me again. You can find her." Talia sobbed in his arms, the hurt of years soaking into his shirt.

"How? I can't even remember what she looks like."

"How did you find me when you thought I was dead?"

Talia sniffed, wiping her streaming nose across her arm. "I reached for you, for the person you should have been."

"Then you do the same for your mother. Feel for her."

"I can't."

"You did, Talia do you remember telling me you couldn't jump to begin with? You didn't just take me back, you also took me back in time, my parents hadn't missed me at all. You got us out of that hole, you can get us out of this one." He gave her an extra squeeze and pulled her to her feet.

Talia looked around, "Now?"

"Let me get Biggles back first. I don't want him wandering off. Want to come down with me and I'll sort those chains out?"

She nodded, not wanting to leave him. Biggles grabbed his stick and Daniel amused them both by throwing it as they walked. To her surprise, she had it dropped at her feet. Biggles sat waiting with an adoring expression on his face. She bent to pick it up and jumped back as he licked her face. Daniel laughed. She stared, she wasn't used to him being this confident. He'd changed, he wasn't the weakling she'd known before.

He waved down at the small cottage at the start of the path and peered over the hedge to see if anyone was in the garden. "Mrs Pickles saw us and thought it was your fault I was in the state I was."

Talia bit her lip, it was her fault he'd followed in the first place. They snuck behind the hedge and into the orchard, Daniel grabbed a bag and filled it with food.

"Know what you're like." he said when he caught her looking. Biggles was shut in, bribed to keep quiet with a treat and Talia marvelled again at a world so rich that it could afford to have special treats for dogs. Daniel examined her wrist and went to find some tools.

They walked down to the end of the orchard, out of sight of the house. "This shouldn't be difficult, it looks like it's been cast." At her look, he qualified, "It'll have a lot of impurities in it." The manacle shattered with a few blows. She rubbed her wrist as he scooped up the chain to hide it.

"Right." Daniel put his hands on her shoulders and Talia forced herself not to think of his grey reflection doing the same. "Think of your mother coming through to your time. What do you remember about her, tell me."

"I remember..." She closed her eyes. "I remember her holding me in the dark, being told not to jump, that it was dangerous…" She turned herself around so she was facing away from him, feeling the comfort of his warm hands. "She was frightened." A wondering caught her, she'd never realised what the edge had been in her mother's voice. She took a deep breath and allowed herself to sort through her memories, casting her mind past the red and black of her closed eyelids. A trace of a whisper beckoned and she raised her hands.

Chapter 18

They stumbled through the opening, it was a shock to be back in the ash covered streets after the warm colourful autumn. Daniel was disappointed, this looked exactly the same as the Narith he'd jumped into last time. Everything was still grey and black, the mists coiling through the night and the sudden pattering of disintegration in the distance that always made you jump.

"Where are we?"

"Wait," Talia began to cough and Daniel held her upright. She wheezed, "That's Cobalt Street up there."

"So, have we gone back in time to when your mother arrived? I can't tell, it all looks the same to me."

"That place," she pointed to their right at an imposing building. "A couple of years ago a rival clique tried to start, Dodie made an example of them. She had the whole thing burnt down around their ears." She shrugged at Daniel's look. "They were dealing in children, Dodie objected to it."

Daniel rubbed his face and tried not to think of Dodie's straightforward approach to something she didn't like. So they had come back in time after all, he'd expected differences he could see. "In theory, your mother should be here." He looked around, seeing nothing in the gloom, then rummaged in his bag and clicked something on. A beam of light flashed across the alleyway. "Should have thought of bringing a torch sooner." He gave a grin, ghoulish in the light.

"This isn't far from Dodie's." Talia looked thoughtful.

"So where's your mother?"

A scuffle in the darkness, Daniel flicked the beam of light into an adjoining alley and a slender shadow moved. He grabbed Talia's wrist, pulling her forwards. A flicker in the light of the torch, he swore and ducked at the brick flying through the air.

He waved his hand sending the light wavering, "It's okay! We don't mean any harm." A stream of swear words answered him. "Look, I'll stop here. I've not got a weapon, I just want to help. What's your name?"

Silence. Daniel had left the beam to one side to stop it blinding the woman against the wall. It rested on a small bundle of rags. To his horror it became a child in the light, the dirty hair turning translucent. A small blonde girl, not much more than a bag of bones hunched in the corner.

Why wasn't she moving? "What's wrong with her," he whispered.

"None of your business." The woman was all aggression, a knife out ready.

"Please," he stammered. Talia – the other one – had frozen, with her wrist limp in his hand. He pulled himself together, "Look, we can help you. We know about the grey men."

The woman's head jerked up and stared at him. She was dark haired, with Talia's thin face and light build. The same darting feral intelligence in her eyes – like Talia she was a survivor. "Why?"

"We need the knowledge you have."

"Fuck off, I'm not dealing with the likes of you no more." The answer came back as quick as a slap.

Daniel moved forwards and the woman stooped to pick up another brick with her free hand. "Please, we're not your enemy..." Desperation filled him, how could they talk if she wouldn't trust them?

They all felt the rift begin to open. The only one that didn't react was the child. She stared into space, huddled against the wall. Daniel was sure something wasn't right, she should be more alert than this.

Talia's mother turned slowly, dread in her face. Daniel waited for the figure to come pouring through like sand and started when he saw long fingers pulling the edges of the rift apart. The rift was a black jagged split in the light of the torch beam. A foot appeared, thin and angular, the toes spread wide. Was this the original being? Had it followed Talia's mother through the trackway?

Talia's mother shook herself and scooped up her daughter. She backed towards them, keeping the emerging figure in view. "You wanted to help, then help." The child was silent in her arms, a bundle of nothing.

The grey man had nearly squeezed out of the rift. Rags covered it, hiding its body. It moved differently to the others, not a slow automation, this had a grace more like a predator.

"I can stop it." Terror screamed through at the thought of touching this thing. Daniel felt the familiar lethargy overtaking him. He took a step forwards and raised his hands.

"No!" Talia knocked his arm down. "It's not you, look!" She swung his arm with the torch over the creature's face and he saw bulging eyes and a domed skull. Its foot hit the floor and he watched, fascinated as it crumbled slightly, bits flaking off.

The seam snapped shut. The creature stumbled and a tremor ran over its skin. It turned towards them, its blind eyes searching. This grey man was different, more skeletal, its hands curving into claws, rags hanging and obscuring the rest of its figure. Daniel wasn't sure what was worse, the flashes of detail in the light of the torch or the knowledge it was there in the dark. Talia's mother stared at Daniel and then at the monster as it began to walk deliberately toward them, flakes of dust dropping off with each step.

Daniel was frozen to the spot. The lethargy felt worse this time, tears rose in his eyes – he didn't remember this. Frantically he ran through his memories and failed to get through the mist. He was sure they were supposed to do something. He could only remember a small figure in the gloom, not this nightmare in front of them.

He felt a hand close around his elbow and Talia began to pull him backwards, babbling under her breath that they had to move. He wasn't sure who she was talking to, her or himself. His mouth opened and he staggered as the child was shoved into his arms. His arms closed instinctively around her, cradling the light weight as he would Dominic. He dropped his chin onto her head and smelt the sea. He was so tired, why didn't he give up? Let the grey man have him, that was obvious what was supposed to happen. Why else would it have his face in the future?

One slow step at a time, Talia dragged him and the child backwards. He could hear her whimpering, the slow shuffle of their steps. A shadow flitted in the torchlight and Daniel remembered the last member of their party.

"Run." He forced his head up and saw Talia's mother, face snarling as she stumbled towards the figure, her knife raised as she gasped, "Take her and run."

"No..." The word was torn from him. This was the woman they were supposed to save. She could have told them the information they needed to know. No time to get her to trust them. She couldn't do anything to hurt this monster. Surely she'd know that.

The grey figure appeared to hesitate and then casually raised its hand to grab her wrist. The torchlight showed grim flashes of the scene, jerking at each of the steps Talia forced him to take backwards. He watched the silent flickering film as the woman gasped and sank to her knees. He expected her skin to desiccate. Instead, the grey man's own skin moved, flooding over hers. A muffled gasp came from her and she dropped the knife. Every detail of her clothing and features became outlined in the dust. The grey man shrank, pouring itself onto her.

She arched her back and opened her mouth to silently scream and emitted a golden light that didn't reflect on the alley walls. Cracks appeared in the grey to shine a pale gold in the darkness. Talia had stopped moving backwards, he could feel her resting against his shoulder, muffled sobs coming through. He closed his eyes briefly and held the child tight.

Through a misty gaze he watched as the small grey figure collect itself, stand upright and move towards the closed rift. It paused, raised its head as though sniffing and then turned to stride the other way. No random shuffle, a purposeful stride from the slender figure of what had been Talia's mother.

Talia cried into his shoulder in a way he'd never seen her do before. He shifted the silent child into one arm and held her in the other. Both Talia. Daniel stared down at them in shock. This wasn't going how it was supposed to happen. He felt his brain go into meltdown.

"I remember you being given to a large woman. What happened? I can't remember." He frantically ran through his memories of a different past, one where they'd won – they must have. Why would he have been back in his world if they hadn't won? Why couldn't he remember properly?

He turned to look at Talia, mind grasping at straws. She'd brought him here for a reason. She was going to sacrifice him to the Dust Lord, to get her Daniel back but he was her Daniel. His mouth began to move, eyes wide. His voice cracked, "Please..." He gathered himself, she was the one who'd just seen her mother die. He closed his eyes and forced the words out, voice shaking, "You need to take me to the Dust Lord. I need to replace the Daniel you know."

Talia turned to look up at him and slapped his face, hard. "Don't be fucking stupid." she hissed, the tear stains running down her cheeks. "I need you."

The night was eerily quiet in the face of her admission. He gaped stupidly and collected himself as she took his elbow. After a few steps, she stopped. "I don't know where to go. This isn't my city."

The sky was beginning to lighten in the pre-dawn. Talia shivered and leant against him. Daniel wriggled down until he could sit on a pile of fallen bricks and held his free arm out. She hesitated and curled up against him. The child remained a bundle of rags. He shifted her into a more comfortable position. He wondered what it would be like to wander his own world, twelve years before his present time, seeing familiar places and people that weren't the ones he knew.

"Are you okay?"

"I'm fine," she snapped.

Daniel shrugged it away, he wasn't going to argue with her at the moment. She was far from fine. Come to that, he wasn't fine either. The misty parts in his memory were worrying him. He'd assumed they'd been from defeating the Dust Lord in some kind of way, a sort of fairy tale he hadn't been allowed to remember. He had to sort things out in his head. "Was that him? Was that the thing Kenderick was talking about?"

"Dunno. Certainly wasn't one of the grey men that we had. Those actually looked like you."

"You said Kenderick had books on this. Did you manage to read anything useful?"

"How should I know what's in them?" Talia sounded grumpy.

Daniel realised she probably couldn't read. He rubbed his face, "We need to get back into his rooms so I can look. Maybe there will be more information. Can you get us back there?"

Talia shook his arm off and stood. "Probably. I'd rather go in through a proper door than jump and have another grey man wandering around. We need to leave quickly though, before it can raise another of those things." Talia raised her hands to get ready and paused, tilting her head, "I can feel another track." At Daniel's look she said, "It's not mine. It goes back a long way. I can't see the end of it." She trailed off, awed.

A shiver ran through the child and Daniel looked down at her, "We need to do something with you first."

He laughed ruefully, "I mean with her... You know what I mean. We can't just take her with us. It's dangerous."

She thought for a moment, "We gotta get her to Dodie."

"Why Dodie?"

"She brought me up. She's the only mother I remember." Her tone was vicious in grief. She grabbed his elbow and marched them both down the alleyway. Daniel cradled the child as they walked. She was so light in his arms, maybe it was shock keeping her quiet. She didn't snuggle, just lay passively accepting his embrace, like a small animal not wanting to call attention to itself.

A building loomed in front, one of the few he'd seen with lights showing. They'd seen no one on their way, the lamps had been lit at every intersection. In fact there'd been more of them, one of the few changes he'd been able to notice. Several men loitered round the doorway, bursts of laughter coming from them every so often. Daniel guessed they were to keep undesirables away.

"Wait here." Talia darted away to speak to them before he could say that he'd go with her. The door was held open by a man and she disappeared. Daniel leant against the wall, watching the darker figures with narrowed eyes, wondering if he was succeeding in looking dangerous. Was this the right thing to do? Wouldn't it be better to bring this child into the future? She didn't feel much larger than Dominic. His protective instincts began to stir as the door slammed open again and Talia was followed out by a large woman. A flickering shadow caught his eye at the intersection, a figure watching them under the lamps. He couldn't quite make it out. He stared at it and stopped as the woman with Talia walked up to him.

"You." A finger pointed in his direction. "This is the last time I do anything for you." Daniel's mouth fell open, he'd never met this person before. The child was plucked out of his unresisting arms. "I'll take her. No promises though."

The woman turned, robes swirling. The child, resting her head on Dodie's shoulder, opened her eyes for the first time. She met his gaze and he shivered, they were blank.

"Come on." Talia began tugging at his shoulder, "We need to leave."

"Why?" He resisted, torn between wanting to help his friend as a child and the person stood in front of him.

"She said something," Talia hissed. "It was subtle, but I recognised the signal from when I grew up with her. I've seen it happen before. Come on, do you have to be a nob about this?" The old insult jolted and he followed her gaze, the men loitering around the door had doubled. Daniel backed away, trying for a nonchalant walk and stumbled over his own feet.

"Why? I thought you said she'd help?"

"Yeah, but we're an attachment to the child and she doesn't like her children having any other attachments." Talia walked faster.

Hair rose on the back of Daniel's neck, "What are they going to do?"

Talia muttered something rude under her breath, "Somehow I don't think you'll like it." A catcall came from behind and a metallic sound that made Daniel's blood run cold.

"They've got knives? They're going to kill us?"

She nodded, "They'll have worse than knives. At the moment they're playing a game. Let them think we're playing by the same rules. Once we're behind the corner, run. They'll try to cut us off in the next street. We'll go down the alley instead."

"Can we get out that way?"

"No." Talia's face had a grim smile, "But I can get us away."

Chapter 19

A smell of smoke greeted them as they walked out of the mouth of the alley, mixed in with the usual dead smell of the old city. Shouting could be heard in the distance. Daniel looked around, still expecting to see the men waiting for them after so many years.

"Are you sure Dodie will take care of her?" He'd had to ask the question before they'd jumped. The memory of those eyes, he hoped never to see the same look in Dominic's.

"More than most would. I'm here aren't I?" The answer had been grunted while Talia gripped the sides of the rift. "Ready?"

They stumbled over the pile of rubble that started at their feet as they'd come through – the wall at the end of the alley had fallen in the years between the jumps. A couple of shadows flitted over them and Daniel barely stopped himself from the indignity of squealing at the bats. It had been a close thing, a slender bolt humming past the entrance to the alleyway as they'd scuttled in. The men had laughed at the thought of them being trapped with no way out. Daniel wondered if they'd waited outside long before investigating.

"Let's move away from here." Daniel didn't want to know if a new grey man was going to come through and didn't want to deal with it. Talia slipped her hand into his as they hurried. "What the hell is going on?"

More people ran past, an anticipation fizzling through the air. "It should be curfew at this time of night. This shouldn't be happening." Talia frowned. "Let's find out." They followed the figures running down the hill towards the sea front. "Down by the mills." Talia was all ears, trying to listen to the snatches of conversation, "Some sort of gathering."

"A riot?"

"Look!" Talia pointed to the gaping hole of the cargo doors where several bodies swung. Daniel stared and gagged at the blackened faces in the flickering light of the torches. "It's Igren, they've actually rebelled. Idiots." An admiring horror was in her voice. Daniel recognised the guard from his first day in this world, the vines twisting down his arms no longer moving. A chill went down his spine, they'd stepped back into anarchy. A ragged cheer went up as someone bent to pick a cobble and sent a corpse spinning with a well aimed throw.

The crowd swirled around them, pushing them on. "The square..." The mutter was passed on, a macabre game of Chinese whispers, the content changing every second. The nobs had cut off the supplies... they were going to be starved out... the mill owners had tried to keep people working... There'd been a riot down at one mill... the owners cut down... It had spread... people had had enough of being kept down... They'd blocked off the railway... were going in... They had a nob on their side... he was going to help...

Talia pulled at Daniel's shoulder, "This is serious, we need to get out." Daniel nodded and they tried to push through and failed. Too many people were moving in the same direction, any other way was impossible.

The electric lights were no longer working, the night was lit by torches. Why was it that a crowd looked more like a mob by torchlight Daniel wondered. Was it the way the light flickered over the faces? The shadows hiding the eyes except for the flash of whites? He could feel the suppressed violence ready to leap from one figure to another, waiting for a spark of ignition.

The square was already packed. Someone had started a bonfire at one end and a silhouette was on a box in front shouting, "I can tell you where to fight. You can smash the walls, smash any who oppose us. Paradise is within your reach. Sunlight, green grass, a place to raise your children. No one can stop you. No one can force you to work for a pittance in the mills, split up your families on a whim. Every man and woman for themselves..."

"Kill the bastards!" Several shouts of agreement as the figure paced on the makeshift stage.

The firelight caught the speaker's face and Talia said, "It's Bay."

Bay had discovered his father's gift for words. A scrawny young man with angry eyes, he charmed the mill workers, egging them on. Daniel shuddered, even the women were hard and muscled from their work. Tools were being passed from hand to hand amongst the crowd. No weapons but items people were used to handling, tools that could be vicious in the right hands.

Daniel looked at Talia, "What's he doing? This mob'll tear everything apart."

"That's the idea." An older woman had overheard them, "They stopped paying us, so we stopped the mills and turned the lights off. Now we'll turn them nobs off too." She slapped a pair of carding combs together, the long spikes reflecting red in the firelight. She turned to scream her agreement into the crowd.

He lowered his voice and bent closer to Talia's ear so no one could overhear, "He's gone bonkers. From what you said it's all farming up on the plateau. This lot've no idea of how to live up there without help. They're going to need the people they're planning on killing."

A roar and Bay was picked up to be carried through the crowd. He waved his blessing as he passed people, reaching down to touch hands, calling out encouragements. Daniel's height allowed him to see various mobs peeling off into the streets, following Bay's instructions to start distractions by storming the wall in different places.

"You know him. Let's get to the front, maybe we can stop this." Talia snorted at Daniel's idea, but tried to wriggle through. The crowd pushed forwards, people shoving from the back as others gathered to leave. A scrum of people with sharp objects flashing in the available gaps, no way were they going anywhere. The thrill of fear ran down Daniel's spine – mob rules. Anyone could get torn apart and no one would lift a finger to help. The crowd's noise became louder and he peered over the heads and shoulders, Bay was coming their way. He bellowed, waving at Bay and gave up, it was impossible to catch his attention, everyone was shouting his name.

"Hang on." Daniel motioned to Talia, shifting her around to pull her onto his shoulders. Her place was immediately taken and he swayed with the extra weight as someone shoved into him. Talia waved, higher than the rest and caught Bay's eye.

"Whatcha doing Bay?"

"We're bringing down the system." Bay's eyes were drunk with power. He clambered down from his willing carriers and came closer, "It's chaos up there with Father dead. That grey man you brought in, it's going through everything." People pressed close, anxious to hear his words.

Daniel went cold. How many people could it take? What would happen by Bay letting this crowd in as well? They had to stop it but Daniel knew that the threat of the grey man alone wouldn't stop them. "Look, capture the people. Don't kill them." His voice sounded a thin streak of reason in the noise of violence planned. "You need them."

Someone snorted and Daniel rounded on him, any fear forgotten. "You. Do you know how to farm? Look after animals and stop them getting ill? Do you know about any diseases they catch? What about crops? You need those people up there. Yes, storm the wall, stop the inequality, but don't kill the people. Otherwise you're killing yourselves in the long term." The muttering increased, they were working themselves up to overthrow authority. Daniel knew they didn't want to hear.

Bay frowned and his face lit up, "I've just realised, this is your friend isn't it?" Talia nodded warily. He leaned forwards and flinched away as Daniel glared back at him. He grinned and flung his arms into the air, a mad glint in his eye, "The Lord of Dust is on our side!"

The circle around them widened and whispers started. Daniel hunched his shoulders with Talia still on them. She shifted and he allowed her to slide down.

Some of these people would have lost friends and family to the grey men.

She twisted to hear as Daniel said quietly, "This was going to happen with or without Bay. The system's cracking up. He's just a convenient figurehead, they'll get rid of him when they don't need him." Bay wasn't one of the mill workers, he'd not worked next to them, they wouldn't trust him.

She nodded, "Seen it before, when a local clique broke up. It wasn't pretty."

Daniel gave it one last try, "You're getting your own back by breaking everything Bay? How many people are going to get hurt?"

"Does it matter? We'll do things our own way, when we've cleared the old lot out." The comments came from one of the muscular men around them and the hair on Daniel's neck stood up with the blatant acknowledgement that Bay wouldn't be needed. He watched as Bay turned to laugh and agree with the man, not realising what Daniel had.

Daniel muttered, "Let's get out of here." They began to move sideways, hoping not to attract any more attention.

"Where are you going? You're going to help us!" Bay's voice cut through the talk.

Talia grinned hopelessly, "We need to prepare. To get the help you need."

"You're sneaking away." He addressed the crowd, "Make sure they come with us." Several people came closer hefting weapons. Bay raised his voice again, "The nobs in the walls haven't the manpower if you attack in several places at once. That's why I sent those other groups off as distractions. They've been lying to you for years. They need days to bring in more people to help. If we attack now we will succeed!"

A roar and the crowd carried them through the streets. Daniel linked arms with Talia, knowing that the first stumble would end up with them being walked over. Bay kept them close the entire way. Despite his obvious fear of Daniel, they were permanently surrounded by people watching them. Groups separated to harass other parts of the wall. Bay followed the railway tracks up the hill to the tunnel leading through the wall. Several trucks had been overturned, partially blocking the way in.

Bay turned to Daniel, "You gonna send a grey man up there for us?"

Daniel squared his shoulders, glared back and lied, "I can summon one, but I can't control it once it's here. You want it running riot through this lot?" He waved his hand at the crowd surrounding them and Talia squeezed his other tightly. What if he insisted? The only way to summon a grey man would be for Talia to open a rift. Could they both get through it without being torn apart? Talia stepped closer, tucking her arm through his.

Bay stared at him with narrow eyes. A stand-off, sweat ran down Daniel's face at the murmuring around them. He could see Bay calculating the pay off between having a grey man and the chaos it would cause in his own troops. He barely stopped himself from sagging in relief as Bay, sensing it wasn't the right time to insist, called for people to start up the tunnel.

Men armed themselves with wedges to keep the automatic doors from the trucks open and gathered in a group to start the long walk of death. Bay waited outside the tunnel, shouting his encouragements. Bolts flew down hitting those not covered, hot sand hissed through holes in the ceiling. Metal sheets and doors were used as makeshift shields. Daniel and Talia watched the workers staggering out, burnt, blinded and wounded. Daniel tried to blank out the screams, wondering if he'd ever forget this night, the torchlight flickering and the howling of the mob. Talia's hand gripped his hard and he tried his best to sink back into the peace of the morgue. He knew then that nothing he met there could ever faze him.

A roar from the tunnel, messengers raced back. The first people had got in. The gate keeper had taken one look and run – the coward. Daniel was jolted out of his fugue. They were moving, a door hoisted overhead for protection and they walked up the tunnel. Bodies lay all the way through and Daniel could barely see them in the torch lit, crowded tunnel. Groans and cries mixed in with shouts of triumph. He found himself apologising to every soft part he trod on, "I'm sorry, I'm so sorry…."

They were pushed along with the mob, no chance of getting away. Bay encouraged his troops, spit flying and his eyes wild as he righted all his perceived wrongs in one glorious night. Nothing lighting up the corridors this time, the electric had been cut off, everything was lit up by smoky torches. Daniel kept his battery torch in his pocket and accepted the brand given.

The situation in the tiny rooms and long corridors was horrendous and the muscular mill workers made mincemeat of any who got in their way. Daniel could see the so called nobs didn't live much better than those in the city, maybe a little more food, a little more sunlight but not much else.

No one was paying attention to them now, he pulled them both into a side room and was shoved out of the way by an excited worker. He shifted to protect Talia, despite her abilities, her small size was against her here.

"We need to get to Kenderick's rooms."

"I think we're going in the right direction. I don't think it's too far from the railway, do you remember?"

"I never saw the gates. Can't you take us there instead?" He mimed opening his hands.

Talia shook her head, "To much risk of a grey man coming through. Can you imagine what it would be like in here?"

"Let's start looking then." Daniel peered out of the doorway and they joined the stream of looters. The crowd was beginning to disperse, Bay was way out in front. Comments were passed back along the line of people, who they'd found hiding where, the riches discovered. It all seemed very little to Daniel, for the price paid. All the rooms and corridors looked the same to him and he glanced at Talia to see if she had any ideas. A louder murmur in the distance and abruptly the reports turned to panic and a knot of people began shoving their way backwards.

Daniel flattened himself and Talia out of the way against the wall. "What the hell's happening down there?"

He muttered a swear word as the torch licked flame against his hand and ground it out against the stonework. Talia tugged on his arm and mouthed something at him, fear in her face. She shoved at him, turning them around into the current.

"What is it?" He could still see nothing in the narrow corridors, hear very little above the echoes and cries. No one was paying attention to them, so he pulled out his electric torch to send a beam of light on the stampeding people.

"Grey man!" A shout rose above the din.

Panic filled him, so little space. People shoving and time slowed with the familiar lethargy. Daniel's only thought was to get Talia out of range. He could deal with a grey man, send it back into its component parts. Talia had to be kept safe. So tired, it must be close by, no room to get past people. No one had a care for their neighbours, the smell of fear and panic rose. An intersection and the corridor cleared, people stumbling away in different directions in the hope it would go another way.

Daniel's hope grew, they should be able to out run it, even at this pace until someone shoved Talia against the wall, half falling over her in his desperation to get away. Daniel saw her head connect with the stone and her eyes rolled. He grabbed for her as she slid, getting pushed aside by the same man. His knee twisted and he cried out as he stumbled, reaching out.

He looked up and saw himself. The grey man stood in the corridor, only a few paces away, a woman in front of it. The familiar desiccation, the clothes sagging and the thud of a body no longer filled with life. The lethargy, Daniel knew all he had to do was touch it, he didn't need to worry. These grey men didn't move fast, not like that one from the past.

It raised its head and looked in Talia's direction. Daniel groaned, his knee, the weight of his limbs, all he had to do was reach out… The grey man moved, faster than expected. Talia lay, half propped up against the wall, a dazed terror in her face at the nightmare of her friend coming towards her. Daniel coiled his good leg and flung himself in her direction. He gasped at the pain lancing through his knee and flopped across the floor. His finger brushed its leg and dust began to hiss, the lethargy lifting.

He closed his eyes in relief and was jarred by the sound of Talia's scream. The grey man's leg was dissolving but it had grabbed her arm. The dust was sweeping over her skin in the same way it had with her mother.

"No..." Daniel pulled himself up to bat at the figure, dust flying under his fingers, falling around them both. The dust seemed attracted to Talia, sticking to her. He swept his fingers over her wrist and found the dust moved away from him. The remains of the grey man lurched over Talia and engulfed her.

"Daniel..." Her hands clutched at him, gripping his shirt. Pale skin, shifting dust as he touched it. He couldn't stop it moving over her, covering every part. "No..." She stood awkwardly. "I don't want to go." Tears ran down her face and were absorbed. "Help me. It's taking me." Cracks appeared in the grey covering her and Daniel remembered the golden light when her mother had died – he had to keep her alive.

He stumbled to his feet, ignoring the pain in his knee. Daniel moved his hands to her face, keeping her mouth and nose clear. Talia began to walk away. He pulled at her arm and she screamed again. Most of her was covered now. He was barely aware of the people watching as he frantically moved his hands over her face as she walked stiff legged towards the door.

Daniel had thought it bad when Talia's mother had been taken, this was worse. She slid out of his fingers every time he touched her, the dust shifting. The only thing he could do was keep it away from her mouth, her eyes bulged as she gasped for breath between the waves attempting to cover her mouth and suffocate her.

The crowd parted at the sight of them, doors opened, people huddling out of the way in the narrow corridors. No one wanted to help, no one could help. Daniel, tears streaming down his face, ignored everyone. Hobbling along, his knee now an unnoticed inconvenience stopping him from helping his friend. Forget not being able to get out of this world without Talia, forget his family. All he could do was keep her mouth and nose clear of the infernal dust. Memories rose to blind him, making him stumble and trip. Playing with the dust on the floor, swirling patterns, raising men. The explosions of power, lust and hate…

He needed both hands free. He shoved the torch in Talia's hand, unpeeling her fingers and wrapping them around it in the hope she could keep hold. The beam lurched with her, waving through people's faces and dark doorways. He ignored everything and concentrated on keeping her breathing. The cool morning air hit him. At some point daybreak had begun. It pulled on Daniel's sense of unreality, a nightmare happening during the day. No time to switch the torch off. Talia's eyes were covered and he remembered the grey film that had covered everything. He babbled at her helplessly, "You'll be okay… I'll sort you out... You'll be okay," unsure who he was trying to reassure.

The familiar alleyway, the half blocked door. The beam flicking around the room with her unsteady walk.

He stumbled over the dry body causing more dust to puff up. Nearly too late with clearing her mouth, she sucked her breath in with the gurgle that heralded a coughing fit. Daniel froze at the sight of the figure in the middle of the room.

Himself. He was going to die. The memories rose, the shame of the anger, the wanting to hurt and feed and the sick pleasure of killing. A whimper choked out of him, was he doomed to repeat this over and over again? The figure raised its hands and Talia's came up to meet them.

"No!" Daniel threw himself forwards and grabbed her hands to stop them. Might as well stop a boulder falling. Their hands met with Talia's in the middle. A soundless explosion, his ears popped. He was pushed away hard and the world went black.

Chapter 20

The golden light, the warmth and the desire that makes me reach for it. A familiar shape in front of me, I raise my hands and the small part of me remaining, recognises Talia in the greyness. I fight to free myself and find I'm held in place, unable to stop. A silent scream breaks from my lips as the rest of me smiles in anticipation. The thought surfaces, the power residing in the slender figure is finally mine. Stronger than any other left, it is within reach, I will survive. Another figure is behind her, I ignore it, they are not important.

I stretch out trembling arms to touch the vessel's hands, waiting for the swelling to begin, the sweet amber of power. I twist inside fighting impotently, it's Talia – I don't want to kill her! The remains of what was once mine, what had once held me captive has been brought before me at last. My hands warm and I ready myself to take everything she has.

The shock wave slams through me, disturbing the very structure of my being. Cracks run down the fibres holding me to this worthless container. I am being pulled away from my chance of life, the being shrieks silently and I shriek with it. This shouldn't be happening, what could be destroying the ties holding me together? A tiny part of me laughs through the pain at the being's consternation and takes over the body.

The pull intensifies, dragging us away. The being coils and fights back with the last of its strength, desperate to escape. I catch the thought that the other figure would be a far more suitable container and he's touching me. They are the one and same, I can take over this new body and live to steal back the vessel's power. A tiny tendril reaches out and the rest tries to follow, like sand pouring out of a bottle. My will strengthens, I mustn't let it go to another person, even if it means keeping it inside me. My hand closes on a familiar cylinder and clings in my efforts to concentrate, cracking the housing. I hold onto it, refusing to let go. Weakened and denied the chance to escape into another body, it releases us both to be pushed through the latest opening and uses the explosion between us as kickback to send us both somewhere else.

The familiar sensation of nothing. I twist, caught in the void. The edges enclose me like rubber, and I swear at my inability to move. A wail deep inside, it can't cope with the void! Energy drains from it like a leaky bucket. The injured being curls up and nurses its wounds, broken. It knots itself into a kernel, hiding deep within me. Shocked by the sudden disappearance of its control, I try to inhale and nearly choke.

A determination fills me. I'm going to find a way through, I'll beat it and remain in control, stop it from taking over again. With the last of my strength I push where the lines are weakest. A glimmer or is it lack of oxygen playing tricks? I'm not going to give up. A brush of air against my fingertips and the void peels away and spits me into the street.

I stumble against the wall, gasping for breath. Dust pours from my skin and clothes. Where am I? Darkness surrounds me but the familiar darkness of night and a light shines against the wall. My eyes feast hungrily, it's real light, not the grey haze I'd known for what felt like centuries. My hand opens and I hear the clatter of something hit the ground, the light flicking out. My brain fumbles for the word. Torch. I reach for it and the darkness reaches back to swallow me up.

A spoon hovers at my lips and I taste a thin lentil soup. A voice says, "You've got a brand on you, but I don't recognise it. Done recently too. What's your name lad?"

I swallow with difficulty and the spoon pauses to let me speak. My brain whirs slowly, surfacing from under the cool waters of unconsciousness. "Dan."

"Hmm, and what were you doing in the streets Dan?" My eyes focus on the woman feeding me. She must be ten years older than me, looks more. Her robes cover a large boned figure and yet nothing is soft about her.

"I can't remember."

"Escaping someone?" The spoon dips and comes close, touching my lips, I open my mouth obediently. "The brand on your back suggests you might be." Escaping. Figures in a dark room flash before my eyes, seeing my face in front of me, mirroring my confusion then blackness covering everything. My own face must be showing my bewilderment. "Sleep now. It's the best healer."

"Who?" I manage to ask before my eyes begin to close.

"The name's Dodie. That means you're lucky. Most people finding you in the gutter would have stripped you for what you had and finished you off." She smiles, confident in her power. "I take my payment in loyalty, lad. You've the look of the ones up top. I'll get my price in my own time, when I decide."

Too tired to protest, I sleep. It brings the dreams of previous lives not my own, of being trapped underground in the stinking darkness. The centuries bringing boiling marshes and a warm shallow sea to cover my shattered grave. Half in the void, half in the corporal world, I fume, unable to extract my revenge.

Men with pickaxes arrive. Digging for riches, they break into my cage and the power holding me explodes outwards. I stay for years in the wreckage of my tomb, a shadow of my former self, incapable of raising more than a dust man. These aren't the smooth stone assassins I once controlled, feared by the strongest of warriors. These are wretched clumsy shadows defeated by the smallest pool of water. I sense the trackways opened by those who stole my strength and discover I can send my grey shadows down them. A touch from one retrieves my power and brings me life while taking theirs. Realising they are concentrated around the former mountain chain, a mile out from my lair, I plot my revenge.

Eventually when I have grown strong enough, I drag myself through a trackway, a singular achievement that I am never strong enough to replicate. The void hates me, dragging everything from me. The ground collapses catastrophically with my moving and the mountain I end up on, is surrounded by water. I am contained on an island, trapped again. Weak and helpless I fume in the cellar, frightened of the weaklings I once ruled. The water frustrates me, the one medium that can contain me, the haze blinding my eyes. The trackways diminish through the years and I become weaker, unable to send my shadows down them at will, unlike in the early days. So many died in the tsunami following my relocation. I have no pity for the people, just anger at the loss of what they contained. I can see those who stole from me as they blink out one by one over the years, becoming weaker through the generations. A few still blaze, I stalk them through the long nights.

I wake briefly, sweating and turn over to forget the dream, like I'd forgotten everything else. Visions of my former life rose to be swallowed in the grey haze, nightmares of being trapped in a cellar, unable to move in the dark made me cry out at night. Watching people crumble in front of my eyes and the warm jolt of power feeding me. The other dreams were worst, dreams of green trees and the falling white blossom not found here. A familiar silver moon, alien to this world and a small child playing.

Dodie visits, asking questions under the pretence of feeding me. I tell her nothing of my dreams, squirming under the shrewd gaze. She seems convinced she knows where I am from and I'm content to let her. The more mundane tasks to help my recovery, she leaves to others. I take several days to get out of bed, more to begin walking without becoming dizzy. I refuse to sleep in the dark, spending the small hours staring into the button lamp Dodie allows me, flipping the torch over and over in my hands. Dodie had given it back to me as a curiosity, it no longer works. I handle it like a talisman, part of a past I can't remember.

The unease grows as I become stronger, cutting through my passive state. I resist it for as long as I can but it remains an itch I'm unable to scratch. About a week after I'd got out of bed, I begin to roam the streets, searching for something I can't remember. I have periods of greyness falling in front of my eyes, and I'd not know where I'd been. The cold affects me and I have a desperate need not to be noticed in my different clothes. I keep a blanket wrapped around me, hiding from the shadows set to watch me by Dodie.

One night, having wandered for most of it in a haze, I feel a break and something squeeze through. A pop as it shuts. I stop and turn in the direction it had come from, my mouth open. Something stirs inside – the call of golden light – warmth. Without thinking, I start to run, ignoring the shout from my shadow behind me.

I lose the direction and stop feeling bereft in a way I can't articulate and feel another pop. More warmth, I begin to run faster, ducking down alleys, the weakness falling away as I lose Dodie's sneak. This is important, I must be alone. Memories flicker, distracting me, I push them aside in the effort to stop tripping over rubble. I can feel the greyness beginning to descend. I know I'm getting closer when another breakthrough happens. I know this thrill, I need to touch it, feel it, I need to… The warmth separates into different directions, which do I follow? The larger group is nearer, I decide to head for it.

I keep running until I reach the end of an alleyway and see three people outlined by the pre-dawn and the lights outside the building. I'm opposite Dodie's place, I run my fingers over the torch I still have in my pocket, my talisman. My eyes sharpen to peer, a child is held in a man's arms. She is important, I want her. I wipe my mouth, a touch should do it. I try to grasp the edges of a thought – what was it I wanted from the child? Hunger pulls at the tendrils of a seed inside, this is something I need.

One of the group, a small familiar figure, has disappeared through Dodie's door and I wonder if I can snatch the child. The door slams open and I instinctively flick my hood over my face – I don't want Dodie to know I'm here. A short conversation and the child is handed over. More men are coming out after Dodie, I need to move, I can get the child later. I know the men will deal with the adults, despite my self imposed isolation, I have heard of Dodie's methods. I will have no chance to get at the smaller of the two.

I stretch my mind to feel for the last bubble. It's moving away, I turn and begin to run after it. A grey haze descends over my eyes, filtering out the light. Chills shiver through me, I pull my hood down further and wrap my blanket tighter. Paranoia, I mustn't be recognised, people are starting to wake for the working day. I visual where that last bubble must be heading, I twist through the alleyways to cut it off, panting as I run. I stop, waiting. A grey figure turns the corner and heads down the alley towards me. I've done it!

The grey figure is small and I frown. This isn't right, it should be taller, a mirror of myself. Cracks appear as it walks, golden light spilling out in to the dark street and seeing them, I no longer care. My knees are weak in anticipation and I reach out to grasp a shoulder. One touch should do it. The words appear in my mind, saliva drools down my chin, unnoticed.

I try to touch it and it slips away, breaking into a run. The thought stuns me, it can't do this, I am its master. I trip over a brick, no longer agile and forget to break my fall. I recoil from the puddle I've landed in and lever myself up to stumble after it. Through the streets I give chase, no longer caring if I'm seen. The grey light fogs my brain and an endless hunger begs. I forget the other figures, the other bubbles. This grey man should be mine.

A siren call in the distance, a smell of a memory. I follow it and the streets become familiar although I can't remember walking them. I miss the feeling of a hand in mine and a mocking tone teasing me. I don't know where I'm walking to and yet my feet lead me without hesitation. Something uncoils within me and a waking dream fills my brain, the grey light expanding into a view of a cellar. My feet continue to walk, I'm like one of the grey men, unable to control my own limbs. I am the dead.

The slender grey figure stands before me in my mind's eye, it's a woman. She reminds me of someone. The name rises from the depths and her face flickers in front of my eyes for the first time in days. I come awake as though drenched in cold water. It's Talia, she's been taken. Despair fills me, I've failed. The golden light breaking through her skin doesn't light the room, it's as though it's only visible to my eyes. My mouth opens to croak her name and I see something move.

A hand, it reaches out as though it's my own and the figure kneels. We embrace and the golden light is sucked out. I groan at the feeding, from where I am it is an empty recollection of the satiation I should feel. Talia slowly disintegrates, leaving my hopes in the pile of dust with her. Hunger and its rage flash through me at being in this state and I feel the other part of me raise a hand to summon me.

I wake out the dream as I come to the expected opening. I clamber in and automatically try to switch the torch on. Nothing, I throw it onto the ground in disgust. It's only habit, I can see through the grey fine. A dead silence surrounds me, a presence and a slow horror rises. The memories tug, demanding my attention and dazed, I let them. I know who I am, I am Daniel. Talia is dead, taken by the being in this cellar. Hope dies inside me, I can never go home and I will never see my family again. I see the apple blossom falling in the orchard and Biggles' face turning to look at me and I can't even cry. The realisation empties me into a hollow shell.

I am an automation, the thing inside tugs me forwards. A being made of rags and bone crouches, its skin hanging off in flaps waiting for me. Even I can see it's not going to survive in that form, even with the power it's received from Talia, it's dying. The seed inside me responds, pulling my resisting legs towards it. It needs me, needs my body. I have nothing left inside, I am the walking dead.

Bulging eyes fix, a touch of its hands and it pours itself into me. The seed winding through me welcomes it. I want to vomit the sensation out and I can't. I am no longer in control of my body. I feel it's contempt. I am weak but more useful than the dying body it used to inhabit. The old body crumbles into the dust on the floor and my knees give way.

It sweeps through me, confident in its victory and a tiny spark of rebellion starts. I can't win, I know I have no escape and I'm going to kill myself in this cellar in years to come but maybe I can change something. I cling to a portion of myself, I can't allow myself to be lost otherwise I might as well be dead. I lost myself in a matter of days last time, this time I've got to last years. Talia will come for me, I have to trust in her. I make the terrible decision that I'm going to have to let it have my body in order to keep a small part of myself intact.

With the being's lust rising through me, I feel terribly alone. Power. Hunger. I feel a break happening and my hands raise to build a grey man in my new form. I will feed and grow. The semblance comes alive and walks out of the cellar to hunt, hood over its face, blanket over its shoulders like a cloak. I smile. Lord of Dust... I sit on the floor and play with it, swirling it through my fingers.

Chapter 21

Talia was on her hands and knees on the cellar floor, coughing her lungs out. The nightmare of not being in control of her limbs had ceased. Shivers ran over her skin, dislodging fine puffs of dust into the air. Tears and snot dripped as she retched, grey with the dirt that had covered her. Her thoughts were equally monochrome. The riot, the grey man taking her and the figure of her friend in the cellar, waiting to take her. She had survived somehow but Daniel had succumbed instead. He'd changed again and it was all her fault.

Eventually she sat back, wiping her sleeve across her face and stared into the dimness. The light barely penetrated the second room, all she could see were vague shapes. Talia slowly pulled herself upright and stood panting. She wiped the rest of the dust off the best she could and felt her lungs ache from coughing.

The pile of dust with Daniel in the middle stirred. She should get out, get away. The thoughts ran through her mind – she was too tired, she didn't want to run, where was the point? The pile rose, this time as a complete figure. It must be strong and she had no way to stop it.

Coated in dust the figure turned and smiled. "Talia." She stood, frozen in grief. A hand reached out to take hers and she waited passively for something to happen, for the dust to sweep over her and the nightmare to begin again. Her wrist was shaken gently. "Talia, it's me. I'm fine. It's gone."

For once she had no smart answer. He shook his shoulders off in a shower and wrapped his arms around her. They were solid and reassuring. She turned her head sideways so not to breathe in any more dust and could hear the steady thud of his heart. Her Daniel was alright. Talia found herself shaking into his shoulder, nothing left inside for tears. She squeezed her eyes tight and pulled away, smearing her face even more as she rubbed her hands over it. "What happened?"

"Do you remember we were in the wall? After Bay had succeeded in getting everyone inside?" She nodded. "That grey man you summoned was still in the building. I thought I'd got it but I was too late...I was trying to keep the dust away from your mouth... It was the only thing I could think of... I couldn't stop you walking..." he trailed off.

"I couldn't stop me," she whispered.

"I'm so sorry."

She tried to feel contempt for the way his eyes filled with tears and failed. "I could feel your hands keeping me alive." His arms came round her again. He rubbed her back, using the movement to reassure himself as much as her.

His chest swelled as he took a deep breath, "Anyway, I had hold of your hands as it tried to take you." A pause while he thought. "Something happened between us. I could feel my other self grabbing hold of it. It wanted to transfer to me. He wouldn't let it."

"Are you sure it's not there inside you?"

Daniel shrugged, "I think it's gone." Talia peered at him as if she could look inside and he shoved her away. "I know what it was like and I haven't got it." Daniel's stomach growled. He looked embarrassed, "I'm hungry."

"Well, I think that means you're all right." She looked at him straight faced until the absurdity of the noise made her giggle hysterically and he joined in, snorting. "Let's get out of here. I've got some food back home."

Daniel grabbed for her hand and shook his clothes out, "Sounds good." They walked through to the other room and they squinted in the daylight coming through the opening. His foot kicked something and it clattered against a piece of rubble.

"Look, it's your light, you must have dropped it." Talia picked it up.

"No, I gave it to you when you were covered. I made you carry it, I couldn't keep your mouth clear at the same time." He frowned, "But I'm sure you didn't drop it." He turned to look behind them. "That's strange, it couldn't have rolled that far either."

"Maybe it got thrown when that thing got done for?" They reached the opening and the new day. Talia turned the torch over in the light as she felt the roughness. "It's broken."

"The batteries have leaked, they've rotted the casing." He glanced about, the streets were quiet in the aftermath of the riots, a stillness after the orgy of violence. "Let's eat and think about this."

They sat outside after cooking, neither of them wanting to stay in the dark longer than they had to. Daniel hefted the torch thoughtfully, he'd been examining it all through the meal. "This has taken longer than a night to rot. These batteries are a mess, there's nothing left of them. I'm sure I felt him pushing away from me when we touched. Did you see him?"

She shook her head, "I couldn't see anything."

Daniel frowned in thought, "Those grey men it sent, they followed you through every time you opened a rift. What if it did the same?" He raised his head to look at Talia, "The last place we jumped to was to your mother, do you think he could be there?"

"You think he's in the past?" Talia's eyes were wide.

"That would explain why the batteries have rotted. You must have passed it over, the other me must have taken it with him and dropped it. That would explain why the grey men had my form. That's why I've had those nightmares of trains going round in circles, I must have been taken by the Dust Lord in the past." He paused, "Is it the past to me? The future? Should I even be here?"

Talia took his hand firmly, "You are here. I brought you here."

"I just wish I could remember how I'd got back into my world. I'd heard that when I was found, they were still looking for the perpetrator. Mrs Pickles had seen us, do you remember?"

"Perpet…?"

"They thought you'd hurt me, that you were responsible for me being in the state I was in."

"I was… you followed me through the rift." Talia tried to explain about seeing Daniel as a small boy.

Daniel frowned and then began to laugh, saw Talia begin to snarl and flapped his hands to hold back the tirade of abuse. "That was Dominic you saw. My nephew. They say he looks just like me at that age." He sobered, "I miss him."

"Still, it was my fault." Talia glowered from underneath her eyebrows, determined to hold on to her grievance.

"Yes, but you didn't beat me up or brand me." Daniel chuckled, "My parents weren't happy about that, but it does explain how I saw you the first time and why you didn't remember." They watched the tide begin its long slow creep up towards the docks, the oily waves lapping higher. Daniel thought about the nightmare moon dragging the water along with it and another question hauled itself into the light. "Can we stop him taking me?"

"We just did."

"No, I mean in the past. Let's face it, you can travel through time, maybe we could stop your mother being taken and all that."

Talia stared. "But that would mean going back to where the Dust Lord was. It's not here now, we're safe." She paused, "Aren't we?"

"Well, there's nothing left in that cellar but if what Kenderick said was correct, I had ten years of waiting with that thing inside me. It killed so many other people, it nearly killed me. Kenderick said to you it had nearly stopped sending out grey men, so maybe it was dying when your mother arrived." Daniel warmed in his enthusiasm. "Maybe your mother gave it that little bit of extra life so it could take me over."

"He had books on people from a long time ago, he told me." Talia was still doubtful.

"If it was that weak when it killed your mother then we might be able to stop it, we might be able to help me. Let's go see if we can find those books, they might give us some more information."

Talia and Daniel walked unchallenged through the wall, finding their way by guesswork. They peered at the view through the windows and followed the trail of desiccated bodies. The green of the plateau reminded Daniel of the rioters, he hoped they were happy now. The riot had come to a natural halt, there weren't enough people or treasure to keep the looters occupied. Every room they looked at had not just been looted but wreaked, the furniture broken and walls defaced. Daniel hoped that some of the nobs had escaped into the countryside inside the wall, there certainly weren't any sheep on the hills at the moment. He wondered what it would take for both sides to begin working together properly.

Another room, a dried up body lay on the floor and they both avoided it. Several doors led from the room. Daniel checked one – a study – the bookshelves half empty and a solid table pushed to the side. The remaining furnishings in both rooms were rich and colourful.

"Daniel!"

He stopped reaching for the books and ran into the room next door. A workroom and from Talia's description, this must have been Kenderick's. The heap of bones and papery flesh crumpled on the floor made him shiver. From the looks of it, it had been kicked several times, the robes barely hiding the decayed skeleton underneath. The place was a mess and not just of Talia's making. Tools had been thrown on the floor, benches over turned and Daniel winced at the books smeared in ashes close to the fireplace. Someone had obviously tried to start a fire and got bored throwing them on.

"My knife!" Talia pounced in glee. Daniel rolled his eyes to himself and picked up several books. He quickly realised he had the same problem as at the mill – the writing was incomprehensible.

"What does it say?" Talia peered over his arm.

He shrugged, "I can't understand it."

"You have books at your home."

"Yes, but it's written differently."

She looked puzzled. "This is the one I threw at him." Talia passed over a book, the cream binding now dirty from the floor.

"How can you tell?"

"It has the same cover."

Daniel sighed at Talia's logic and flipped through it. Dense writing surrounded hand drawn diagrams. He was reminded of the pictures he'd seen of Leonardo da Vinci's sketch books. "Nope, nothing in here."

Talia dumped several other ash smeared books on the workbench and went to inspect some tools she'd dragged out from underneath. The books Daniel looked through were a joy to handle with thick pages and a hefty weight to them, however he could read them as well as Talia. He muttered a swear word and thumped them down.

"What's the use of writing things down if you can't read them?" Talia rubbed her nose in boredom and disappeared to look under the workbench closest to the door. Daniel agreed and righted the chair Kenderick had been sitting in earlier. He slumped in it and leant onto his elbow, staring at the body.

"Hey!" She wriggled out with another book in her hand, the spine broken and torn in half, the edges were blackened and covered in soot. "This one's buggered." She flicked through and pointed. "Look! This must be it. That's the grey man who came through with Mamin." Daniel sprang up to peer over her shoulder. A line drawing showed a bulbous eyed nightmare as the Dust Lord.

Daniel shivered and took it from her. "I still can't read it, not that there's much left."

A noise from the other room, Talia whirled, knife in hand. Daniel tried to catch her and caught empty air. She was through the part open door and gone before he could tell her to stop. A scuffle from the study and Daniel threw open the door to find Talia holding a man with half a dozen books in his arms. He wriggled, trying to keep hold of the sliding books, despite Talia's knife under his chin.

His face was familiar and Daniel racked his brains trying to remember where from. The weaselly man nearly impaled himself as another book slid. Daniel took pity and caught the book, dumping it on the table. Close up, he recognised him, "You worked for Igren."

Talia's knife tightened as he nodded apologetically. "Only under contract, not anything else. I work for lots of people." He tried to wring his hands while holding the books and failed.

"Don't kill him! He might be useful." The scribe from the mill froze as Daniel took the rest of the books and tried to move Talia's knife away. She allowed him to, reluctantly. He asked, "Can you read this? It's not written in my language."

The scribe carefully took the remains of the book and smoothed its pages. "This is a bestiary, a book of mythical beings. I've seen them before, Lord Kenderick's collection of books was one of the finest. I came to save what I could."

Daniel snorted. He'd more likely come to steal what he could. The scribe stared at him with pleading eyes and Daniel remembered the way he'd tried not to drop the books even with a knife under his chin. Maybe he had been telling the truth. He said curtly, "Read what you can."

The scribe muttered to himself, coughed and began to read, "The Grey Lord... trapped in the void forever... grey men stalk us through the trackways under the light of the... defeated in water..." He looked up, "There are a lot of words and pages missing." He flicked to a previous page, less tattered. "There are more here on other beings. Doppelgänger, a being and his reflection cannot exist in the same world without consequences."

Talia made a sound of contempt, "Don't need to know about no doppelgänger. We need to know about the Lord of Dust."

"Wait, carry on. You could say that the grey men were my Doppelgänger. He made copies of me." Daniel waved the scribe to continue.

He bent his head, squinting in the uncertain light. "At a touch, one will push the other through the nearest weak point..."

Daniel cut him off and turned to Talia, "That's what happened, when the Grey Lord and I touched, I was right. One of us got pushed through the trackway – the weak spots in this world." His brain raced, "And maybe that's what happened when I touch a grey man. I feel the same explosion but maybe they can't take it and dissolve instead." He looked at her hopefully.

Talia's small face creased in thought. "It can send a grey man after me when I open a break, but I don't think it can do it itself, otherwise it would have done it before." The thoughts cascaded between them, barely allowing themselves to breathe in their excitement.

"Maybe us touching forced it through."

"Do you think he… you went to where Mamin was?"

"I don't know, I felt the power surge through me and nothing after that…" Daniel stopped as he remembered their audience. The scribe was sat watching with wide eyes, all confusion as he listened to them. Daniel turned to him, "Is that all that's written in there?"

He shrugged, "There are a few notes made in the margins, but this part of the book is too badly damaged." Despondent, Daniel thanked him, wondering how they could save his other self in the past. The scribe hesitated, clearly wanting to scoop the books up.

Talia said grandly, "Take any books you want." The scribe bowed low, and greedily began to pile the books back into his arms. "Where do I find you if I want you?" The question was casually asked. The scribe froze and stared at Talia. She smiled, "I might need a man who can read great works."

He straightened proudly, "Ask for Radnor. I am known hereabouts."

Talia nodded and smirked at Daniel's puzzled look, "I've got plans for later on."

He rolled his eyes as he watched the scribe leave – he was never going to be able to keep up with the twists in her mind – and asked, "What are we going to do about me? There isn't any more information in these books to help us."

Talia sobered, "We need to do something about Mamin too."

"I must be in the past, in the same time as her. You said you could feel a pathway leading back further last time. That must have been from your mother jumping. Can you get us to her time, before she came through? She might be able to tell us more if she came from an earlier time and if she doesn't jump then we might weaken the Grey Lord further." He quickly asked, "Well?" before he could talk himself out of it.

"You think we could?" Her face twisted, "Would I still be me?"

Daniel tried not to see the terrible hope in her eyes and felt sick. "I don't know but it might unpick all this in one move. We can only try."

She nodded and raised her hands. Daniel went to stand behind her and wrapped an arm around her waist, ignoring the churning of his stomach. Helping Talia's mother might help his other self, he just wished he could believe himself.

Chapter 22

They were half dead from lack of oxygen when they were spat out. They leant against the walls of the narrow alley and stared while they got their breath back. It was a very different Narith from the grey, tumbledown place Daniel was used to. The buildings were cleaner and in better repair, even the ever present mist felt lighter. He looked up at the walls, the windows were mostly intact, the frames still in one piece and holding glass.

He poked Talia, "Where shall we go?"

Talia was staring, her eyes unfocused. "I can feel the holes." Her voice was awed. "They're everywhere."

Daniel looked around, now nervous, "Can the grey men find us?"

"Only if we open one from this side." She shook herself like a dog, "Let's go down to the water."

They walked down the hill, each silent in their own thoughts, noticing the differences. Daniel saw the lack of tension, so obvious in Talia's time, there was still a sense of hope here. People were trying to keep their standards up, they had pride in themselves. There were still factories, he could tell by the vibrations and thumping, but they weren't as big and there wasn't the same sense of grinding misery.

The city continued its march out into the bay, still standing tall, unlike in Talia's time. No drop into the water, the street simply submerged at the tideline. Rope bridges swung from the shore to the sunken buildings, showing silhouettes of people crossing. There were very few boats, a couple of tiny coracles, nothing bigger. A market was being held in the square, people bustling through, talking and laughing at tables spread with goods. Daniel eyed them, noticing their clothes were brighter and with more colours rather than the uniform drabness of poverty in years to come.

"So, how do we find your mother?"

"Dunno." Talia was looking truculent and Daniel recognised the look from when she didn't want to admit she didn't know something. "What do you remember?" A cart rumbled by, pulled by two people. A far easier task on these roads than in later times. "Okay, let's sit here and get you to think." Daniel pulled Talia next to the wall, out of the way of the through route. Talia huffed and glared out across the water. He rubbed his head, "What was she called?"

"Mamin." She clicked her mouth shut, refusing to say anymore.

Daniel gritted his teeth and pulled himself up, determined to try despite being irritated at her shortness. A couple of ladies walked past. He tried a friendly smile and asked, "Excuse me, I'm looking for Mamin, do you know where she is?"

One laughed, "Sorry dear, I've no idea where your Mamin is." Daniel flushed as they walked off giving him amused sideways looks and cursed, his head tightening.

"Okay Talia, so Mamin was what you called your mother right?" She grunted, pushing her toes into a crack in the road. "What did other people call her?"

"How would I know?"

The urge to hit something rose and Daniel forced himself to breathe. "Maybe try closing your eyes and thinking of her."

"Why?"

"Bloody hell Talia, at least I'm trying. You might get an idea of where she is, like I did the Dust Lord."

"I can't remember anything." Heads turned at her wail and she lowered her voice. "I only remember Dodie looking after me, not Mamin." She sniffed, still staring at the road.

Daniel remembered the skinny bundle of child in his arms, far quieter than any child of that age should be and wondered what had happened. He wrapped an arm around her which she promptly shrugged off. "Please try for me."

She snorted but shut her eyes. "I remember her singing in the dark."

"How did that make you feel?"

"Safe." A rare smile crossed her face.

"Where were you?"

"I don't know."

"Try reaching for her, see if you can feel where she is."

Her eyes popped open. "Not here."

"No, I mean just get a general direction. It's better than nothing."

Talia stuck her lip out, "Can't feel anything."

Daniel sighed and suggested walking along the sea front. The high tide mark showed dark against cobbles, slime and seaweed decorated the slope. The sea lapped further down. Buildings were being demolished in what Daniel recognised as the bay in Talia's time.

One of the rope bridges swung close by and Daniel's stomach lurched at the figures swaying across it.

Talia stopped and pointed at the bridge, "I remember that." The supports had been hammered into the cobbles on the shore. A single line of wooden slats served as the flooring and rough hemp that didn't seem strong enough, was used as handrails. The bridge itself dipped in the middle and bounced alarmingly as people crossed.

"It's a one way system, I remember!" Talia's face had lit up. "Let's go round." She was on the bridge and several paces along when she stopped to look for him. Daniel gritted his teeth and stepped on before she had the chance to mock him. It was every bit as bad as he'd thought, only two feet above the ground and his stomach was protesting. No wonder Talia hadn't thought anything of digging in dangerous places if she'd been brought up doing things like this.

He concentrated on his feet and slowly walked out. He didn't notice she'd stopped moving until he bumped into her. "What's up? Lost your nerve?" The joke fell flat.

"Something's coming through."

"What?"

Her eyes widened, "I said something's coming through, we need to move. Not that way." She grabbed Daniel's shirt as he began to turn back. "Look!" He squinted, a rip in the air showed near the start of the bridge, a pair of hands holding it apart. Talia pulled at him, nearly making him lose his balance. "Move, we need to be above the water."

Daniel looked down and regretted it, they were still over the slime of the high tide line. The bridge shifted as Talia walked swiftly along, why couldn't it have been better secured? He looked back and saw the nightmare grey man appear. Men, women and children scattered in slow motion and he groaned as an arm flashed out to crumple a man. No slow disintegration, the man crumbled, his clothes falling into a pile on the floor. Daniel went cold as the figure turned to look in their direction.

Talia was well in front, he followed the best he could, fear prickling up and down his back as he tried not to look behind him. People were shouting from the shore, he could hear nothing over the roaring in his ears. A glance showed the grey man moved like a predator, stepping sure footed onto the bridge.

"Keep going." Talia's voice was thin. He'd reached the middle, grasping both ropes, the bridge swayed alarmingly. The water was oily underneath him, the shadows of more buildings reaching up from below. The figure behind walked with perfect balance, not holding on. Daniel felt the beginnings of the lethargy hitting. He had to keep Talia safe. He was on the upswing now, and he found it harder to walk uphill. He placed his feet carefully, trying to contain his panic over the monster behind.

A yell from in front of him and the bridge shivered. Talia. She'd thrown herself flat against the slats, hugging the planks with arms and legs. Her face was white as she turned to scream. What was she doing? Had she fallen? He kept moving, and glanced up at the people ahead. A flash of metal and his heart stopped.

They were cutting the handrails. The planks felt a million miles away by his feet. No time, his arms and legs felt like lead weights had been attached, the grey man couldn't be far away. The first rope tugged loose and he fell to his knees, frantically grasping for the edges through a cotton wool brain. The bridge twisted and he spread himself akimbo and wrapped himself around it as the whole bridge span upside down. Daniel's shriek was lost in the roar from the crowd at both ends. The grey figure fell past him, expressionless and hit the water like a stone.

Daniel hung on, his brain clearing – so close. He wiped his eyes against his upper arm as the bridge shivered and he looked up. Talia was pulling herself into the building and people reached out to help her. Others were waving to him. He looked up and down, only one way he could go. Slowly, he inched his way up, his arms and legs burning and remembered all the adventure movies he'd seen where the hero did this. He muttered to himself, he was never going to be able to watch a film again. The crowd were in party mood by the time he'd reached the top. He was dragged up and slapped on the back. He tried to return the smiles and failed.

"I forgot," Talia stood beside him. "That's what they did when a grey man tries to follow. They cut the ropes and toss them in the water."

"Did it dissolve?" Daniel peered down, expecting to see the scum of dust across the surface.

"Takes a while, but they do eventually." A gappy grin from another man. He pointed across the upturned bridge. "Look, they've got someone coming across already." A small figure had attached itself to the underneath of the bridge and whizzed down to the middle. A rope followed it out. A fiddling and the figure climbed nimbly up the other side towards them.

"There's a rope on the bottom of the planks. I remember attaching a clip to it and climbing across to reattach the handrails. It was fun." Talia's eyes glowed with her memories and she sniggered at Daniel's grunt. She poked him, "Come on, you're fine." She laughed again at his scowl.

"Up you come monkey."

The small figure had reached this side and was being hauled up. Daniel felt a shock go through him at meeting the bright eyes of a small child, he tapped Talia's shoulder. She turned and froze.

"Hang on while I tie the next rope." the man grumbled. The child was having her hair ruffled and trying to wriggle away.

Daniel stared. She was nothing like the child he'd carried to Dodie's and yet the clothes were right, it was definitely Talia. This child was bursting with life, desperate to slide back down the rope. They connected her up and let her go, chuckling.

"Who's that?" Daniel had to make sure.

"That's Talia. Little monkey she is. Climbs anything."

"Where's her mother?"

"Bronin? She'll be on the shore, looking for Talia. Right handful, she'll get a slap for this." The man sounded admiring.

Daniel sighed in relief, finally they had a name. "How long until we can get to the shore?"

The man waved behind them with a curious look. Daniel followed his glance and remembered Talia saying it was a one way system. People were already moving. He shrugged off the glance and dragged Talia towards the next bridge thinking that once he had his feet on solid ground, there was no way he was doing this again.

Talia had been gazing at herself swinging back towards the shore. "I remember now, I really copped it for doing that. Didn't care. It was fun."

"Maybe your mother was worried about the grey men," Daniel murmured in a low voice. "Still, I've got her name now, we can find her." He gritted his teeth as he stepped out onto the bridge, only one more until the shore. To distract himself he said, "I didn't see anyone come through before that grey man. Did you see?"

"No," she frowned. "There are lots of holes here, almost like trackways. There's nothing like this in my time."

He teased, "This is your time."

"Nob." She sniffed. The insult lacked its usual sting.

"What's happening over there?" The tide was at its lowest ebb, figures were busy on the shoreline breaking down buildings. Others pulled full carts down the slope to add to the piles between. Shouts carried from the distance.

"That's the fish traps or will be." She caught his puzzled look, "The tide carries the fish in. When the tide goes out, the fish get caught in the water trapped in the cup shape. The fishermen just wade in with nets. It's easy."

Fishing without boats. So many ways to get food without hard work. A crash of a wall hitting the ground and he amended his thought – once the trap was built.

"So, how much can you remember?"

"I keep remembering as I see things. It's all so familiar. It's weird."

"Can you remember where you lived?" She shook her head. "Okay, I'll ask."

When they asked for Bronin, a passer-by pointed out a half submerged tower further along in the bay. A rope spanned the distance from a nearby building across the water to it. They saw a slender figure working along the tideline, picking items up and inspecting them.

"The tide sweeps up all sorts. Mamin used to sell the things she found," Talia breathed. "I'd help, I was good at finding things."

A small coracle had been dragged up on the shoreline. The woman turned as they came closer and they both recognised Bronin. Daniel sighed, her stance was just like Talia's had been when he'd first met her, wary and on the defence.

"Are you Bronin?"

She stood and stared, her eyes narrow. "You want to buy something?" Daniel became aware of Talia hanging behind him, mute in the presence of her mother.

"No, we'd just like to talk."

"Not interested." She turned back to inspect the ground.

"We saw Talia back on the bridges." She grunted. "Bronin, we want to know about the grey men, about..." She had her knife out before he could finish his sentence.

"You leave me and mine alone. Do you hear? I don't want to see you snooping round." Bronin was actually snarling. The rest of his words died as she stalked to her boat and pushed it into the water, sliding into it with a practised swing.

Chapter 23

"So, what do we do now?"

They were walking back towards the market, neither feeling there was much point in staring at the lonely tower in the water. Bronin had sculled away and climbed up the side, disappearing in through a window at the top. Daniel had pointed at the rope stretching from building to tower, "Could you climb along that?"

"What, and have it cut? Not likely."

Daniel scrubbed his face in frustration and remembered Talia's comment from earlier. "What are you going to need Radnor for?"

Talia smirked, "I'm going to make me a clique."

"Is that the best you can think of?"

"What do you mean?"

"Just think, all the information in Kenderick's rooms. All those people who are going to need it. You've got lots of contacts. You could help bring the nobs and the workers together so it's fairer."

Talia gave him a funny look. "Me?"

"Why not? Someone's got to do it. Otherwise it'll go back to what it was, a few people having everything and a lot having nothing. Look at this place." Daniel waved his hand at the market, "You could bring this back, get people working together. They nearly had the right idea with the mills but make it so you have a choice, work for money rather than being branded. Somewhere it went wrong, you've got a chance to help make it right again."

She cocked her head, "I quite fancy having a lot."

"There's not enough of you to keep going in the same way. You need to work together, otherwise you'll all going to fail. Look!" Daniel interrupted himself, "There you are again."

They watched a darting figure go up to one of the food stalls and hand something over. A haggling ensued, the girl waving her arms and the stall holder joined in. The stall holder laughed at the child stamping her foot and bent to give her something off the stall. They watched her flit away and continued walking.

"I'm hungry, what food have we got?"

"Not enough." Talia was grumpy at the reminder. They'd not planned to go anywhere. Daniel stuck his hands in his pockets and ignored his stomach.

"Who are you?" The child stood to one side of them, her hands full of a thin bread wrapped around something that made Daniel's stomach rumble. She was dressed in a pair of cut off trousers that looked too small even for her skinny frame and a vest. Light shoes had enabled her to sneak up on them. Her bright eyes fixed on Daniel. Talia shrank back.

"I'm Daniel. Should you be talking to strangers?" He couldn't resist asking the question, ignoring the odd look Talia gave him.

"I'm Talia. We don't get many strangers here, I know everyone. Where are you from? Is that your girlfriend?" She sniggered, "You're holding her hand." Talia jerked her hand out of Daniel's and crossed her arms. Daniel was mesmerised, this Talia was nothing like the one he knew. She had a charm radiating from her, a confidence that nothing could go wrong in her world.

"I come from somewhere else. We want to speak to your Mamin."

"She doesn't like people trying to talk to her. You should try Estrella's food." She waved her full hands, "It's good. See ya." She darted away on almost silent feet.

Daniel moved to follow and was stopped by Talia muttering, "Bloody irritating, wasn't I."

He chuckled, "Still are." Talia glowered and feigned thumping him.

"So," she repeated his question. "What now?"

"I think we do as you suggested. Go and talk to Estrella."

Estrella was packing up as they arrived. "Not much left and it's going fast." A customer came up and she slid a flat bread out from her basket and scraped the last of something from the pot on her table. Daniel's stomach rumbled loudly and he flushed at Estrella's look. She pocketed the coin she'd been given and smiled kindly, "I have a couple left for a growing lad who'll help carry."

The contents at the bottom of the pot were thick and beginning to dry, Daniel didn't care. He passed a stuffed flatbread on to Talia and helped to collapse the table. Talia took the pot Estrella nodded at. He tucked the table under one arm and held the stuffed bread in the other, eyes watering on the spices.

"It's good," he managed at Estrella's laugh. Talia was nibbling at hers with a determination not to waste food, Daniel guessed she'd not tasted anything like it in a long time.

"You're from up over the wall aren't you? Don't need money up there, all done on favours isn't it? Well you'll need it here. Life doesn't work otherwise."

Daniel hesitated and thought about the amount of holes Talia had said she'd felt and the casual knowledge of the grey men in this time. He took a risk, "We're not from behind the wall. My friend can jump." He ignored Talia choking.

Estrella kept walking, her eyes fixed ahead, "That's not good knowledge to spread around. A lot still can, a fair few have family who could. The grey men hunt those people, take others who get in their way."

"Can you?"

"No and I'm thankful for it." Estrella's voice had gone flat, "but three of my cousins could. They were picked off one by one. My aunt died trying to shield Emilia. She was ten.

"I'm sorry. We want to stop them."

"You can't lad." They'd come to a door, Estrella pushed through and motioned them to go up the stairs. Washing hung from the windows higher up, people gossiped, blocking the landings.

"We tried to talk to Bronin. She wouldn't. We wanted ask about her past, we think she knows something."

Estrella smiled and shook her head, "Bronin's a funny one. I've known her for years, since Talia was born but I can tell you now, she keeps her mouth shut about her past. You'll get nothing from her."

"How old is Talia?" Daniel asked, remembering the fragility of her bundled in his arms.

"She's eight." He had no idea of how big a child was in relation to their age, still, she was older than he'd thought. They'd stopped on a landing and she motioned for him to put the table down.

Daniel tried one last time. "We really need to speak to her, it's important."

Estella gave him a searching look and reached over to touch the sleeve of his hoody. "I fancy that top of yours, it's a nice colour. I'll trade it for asking Bronin to talk to you. I can't guarantee that she will though."

"Please try." He shrugged it off and gave it to her.

"Meet me down by her tower in an hour, I've things I need to get done first."

Daniel checked his watch and they started back towards Bronin's tower. "Do you think she will talk to Bronin for us?"

Talia nodded, "I can remember Estrella now, she's solid and a good judge of character. You convinced her if she's said she'll try." It was strange seeing the gentle slope of the ground reaching into the water and not the drop from Talia's time. Daniel could see cobbles missing and the occasional hole where the sea had sucked soil out from underneath.

Two figures were sat on the slope further along, the coracle pulled up beside them. Dusk was beginning to creep over the sea, the shadows reaching out in fingers. Daniel shivered in the cool breeze and hoped his hoody was worth it.

Estrella came up to meet them, "She's agreed to talk. It's up to you." She patted his shoulder and waved off his thanks with a smile. Daniel and Talia exchanged nervous glances. Bronin stood, her back to the sea and watched them walk closer.

"Bronin, we need to talk to you about the grey men."

She stopped him with a sharp gesture, "Why do you think I know anything about the grey men." Her voice was low, her hand on her knife.

Daniel swallowed, "We saw you come through, saw a grey man following you. We're worried about Talia." Not quite the truth.

"You're lying." Her voice was flat.

"It was in the future. We came back. My friend can jump…"

"Tell me what it's like." Her eyes pinned Talia's.

She stared at her mother. "It's like being stuck. You can't move, can't breathe. Nothingness all around you, sucking you in and the grey men come afterwards." She hung her head.

"How did you find me?" Belligerence.

"I needed you." Talia's voice was nearly a whisper. Something caught in Bronin's face. Daniel saw it flicker and it was gone.

"Please, can we talk. We'll leave afterwards if you want."

Bronin snorted, sounding like Talia. "Yeah right. I'll take you first." She pointed at Talia. "Come on." Talia looked as though she was in a dream.

Daniel watched as they paddled the coracle out to the tower. Bronin held the boat steady while Talia climbed up the side and he hoped he wouldn't disgrace himself by falling into the water. The boat was barely big enough for them both, he froze as he was glared at for pulling his knees in. Powered by a swift figure of eight movement, they soon reached the building. Bronin held onto a metal spike to give him the chance to scramble up. They creaked as Daniel climbed slowly, hoping they wouldn't give under his weight. He nearly fell off as the child's head popped out of the window at him.

"You've come! She won't talk to me. You will, won't you?" His Talia was stood in the middle of the room looking miserable. Daniel raised his eyebrows at her and she nodded, she remembered this place. He allowed the child to sit him down and start showing him a complicated clapping game. The window darkened as Bronin climbed in.

"You hungry?" She started putting together ingredients without waiting for an answer.

"We don't want to leave you short."

She shrugged, "There's always the sea, it provides a lot for those that know where to find food. Your friend doesn't say much."

Daniel risked a glance at his Talia. She'd hunched herself up, hugging her knees and staring around. He got the impression she was drinking in the surroundings. "She was brought up in a similar place, it's a bit like home." He hoped Bronin wouldn't ask more, he wasn't sure he could keep that line going. He tried to change the subject, "How are things with the people on the hill? We have problems with them keeping goods." He missed a hand and the child shrieked with laughter.

"Things haven't improved in the last few years. There's always those that want more than the rest and can stop us by hoarding the best bits. I remember the green meadows up on the mountain being open to everyone. We'd go up to meet Father after his week's shift work. Now they're building their wall to keep us out."

The first hint of Bronin's past, Daniel breathed lightly, not wanting to disturb her train of thought. "How did you eat?"

"We grew most things. The marshes kept trade to a minimum, there weren't many ways through and people got lost in the mist if they strayed. Now there aren't many boats because there aren't enough trees. Wood's expensive." She gave a wry smile, "Yes, I'm not from this time."

"There are woods on the slopes in my time." Talia had her chin on her knees, staring into nothing.

"We're not from this time either." Daniel didn't like to say he wasn't even from this world.

"Where are you from?" He'd almost forgotten the younger Talia, tapping her hands automatically.

"A long way away." He smiled at her.

"Can I go there?"

"Not for the moment." Daniel hoped she wouldn't try, her bright eyes were far too interested.

Bronin changed the subject, handing out food and lighting a few candles as the dusk darkened into night. Daniel was surprised when her daughter curled up against him and closed her eyes after eating.

Talia hesitantly joined in the conversation as Bronin talked, asking for details about her mother's life, defined as it was by the shores of the ocean. She'd worked in the factories, cutting fish, doing everything she could to stay alive. She'd learnt to live off her wits – she was good at finding things and had been taken on by someone to do just that. The tower was her own place now and she mused on having her own eye on others she could train. No one bigger than herself, she didn't want to end up in the same place as her mentor.

"What place was that?"

Bronin smirked, "In the gutter with his guts hanging out. He didn't realise when I say no, I mean it." She tapped her knife and Daniel stared, horrified. Talia sniggered and then looked panicked at her mother's next comment. "You remind me of my man."

Daniel intervened, "Talia's actually related to you." He mentally crossed his fingers. "Your daughter jumped through to the future."

"I've wondered about jumping further ahead. There are so many trackways here, it's dangerous. If there are less people around who can jump then there's less chance of being surprised."

Daniel looked at his Talia, "The Grey Lord might be weaker too."

Bronin snorted. "Maybe. It would just be nice to relax and eat and trade without constantly looking over my shoulder. I can only stay close to the shoreline. My Talia doesn't help." As if hearing her name, the child flung an arm out in her sleep and Daniel tucked it back in against him. Bronin looked tired as she rubbed her face, "I keep her as safe as I can. She doesn't listen though. She doesn't understand how easy it is to die."

"You mean the grey men? They follow through the holes we make."

"They don't just follow, they use the trackways. They pop out when you're least expecting it, they don't need someone to come through first, they use existing ones. They've been hunting us for years. We've survived by staying away from everyone who can do this, by keeping to ourselves." Bronin sounded bitter. "They'll get us in the end."

"How do you know they've been hunting you?"

"Too many coincidences. They come through and fix on me or Talia. That's why we live here. It's an easy place to get away. The mud below holds them until they dissolve, all you have to do is tread water."

Talia asked, "How do you know they won't come through into this room?"

"We're safe, no trackways come through at this tower. I try to get my Talia to understand not to jump here. She's so young and she jumps naturally, it's hard." Jumps naturally, Daniel thought. Something had scared her into not jumping or even remembering.

It was full dark outside, the candles gave out a soft glow. The time seemed right to Daniel, so he asked, "What was it like where you lived, before you came here?"

"We were surrounded by marshes," Bronin's voice was dreamy. "Our lives were fixed by them and by our fathers working in the mines. They ran for miles in the rock under the marshes. Only certain families had access to the mines, others came to make use of our hard work. Traders would come for the gems and metals our families mined. Food was always grown on the plateau. Luxuries were brought in on the roads through the marshes, bridges built across the streams and rivers. We had everything we needed, the city was built off the miners backs and we lived in the large houses close to the plateau that are now in ruins." So much for Kenderick's underclass, thought Daniel.

She continued, "The marshes were treacherous if a person didn't know what to look for. There were mud holes where you could boil an egg, it stank like one too."

Daniel looked up at the plateau shrouded in mist and shuddered. That's why the sea was warm, even though the air was cold. All this land must be volcanic. The moon couldn't help either, it was probably pulling all sorts of tectonic plates about. He asked, "Did the sun shine then?"

"It was always misty down here. That was what the slopes were for, growing food and feeding animals. They got the sun up there." Her face turned sour, "That was before they scarpered."

"What do you mean, who scarpered?"

"What I mean is, before all this came. It was their fault. The nobles in charge." Bronin swung a hand at the black waters outside.

"How can anyone be responsible for this?" He had a vague twitch tickle his mind that she was wrong, it disappeared before he could analyse it.

She shrugged, "Dunno. They all disappeared though. Left us to deal with it. People were spreading rumours about them not coping with the grey bastards. The city came to a stop about a week before this happened."

"You were there?" Talia's voice was awed.

Bronin lent over to check on her daughter, Daniel moved away slightly to let her and the child disturbed, muttering. "I was out with Gian on the marshes. The city went down further in those days, the houses were smaller further out, the ground wasn't solid enough to take the weight of the factories. We'd been fishing for the day, a treat. We were on our way home when all of a sudden, there wasn't any water in the river. It was so quiet and we heard this rumble coming towards us. There was a wind, it blew the mist away." Bronin's voice carried on in its toneless way, reliving the horror. Daniel could see them running from the sight of the wave coming across the marshes, Bronin heavily pregnant. The watchtower on a strip of higher ground, people scrambling to get in when the wall of water hit. The debris of lighter buildings, trees, dead bodies carried with it.

She fell silent.

"You got into the tower?" Her head ducked. Daniel remembered the tower covered in seaweed, the gaping holes for windows and with no furniture apart from the home made stuff, crude and simple. "You jumped." Fear glazed her face. "You jumped to a safe place and ended up in this time didn't you. This," he waved his hand at the room, "this didn't happen eight years ago."

Bronin's face struggled between fear and anxiety. She buried her face in her hands, shaking her head, "It's gone. It's all gone and I can't go back." Daniel glanced at Talia, she was riveted, staring at her mother as though she was an alien being. Her mother was from that time in Kenderick's books.

"What actually happened?" He tried to sound as soothing as possible.

"We both jumped." Both? Bronin sniffed and wiped her cheeks. "He could too. Our fathers had been miners, years before I was born. They'd come off the shift before..." Her voice trailed off.

"Before they'd dug up the Grey Lord."

She nodded, "They were ill for weeks. I was told many of my father's friends didn't survive. The balance of power changed and the merchants took over. A new class, they called themselves nobles," Bronin snorted. "Mines were shut, many families didn't survive. It was a hard time. Some men went back to work and then there was another accident..."

"And they escaped by wishing for safety and coming through the void," Daniel finished the sentence for her.

The words came pouring out, a flood like the one she'd escaped herself. "People started to experiment and then the grey men came hunting. Rumours happened and my Mamin worked out that they were tracking people through the holes they made. She made us promise never to try and we hid by never being around those who jumped."

"But that day you had to jump, to save your life."

"We reached out together and ended up in water." Her face fell forwards into her hands, "A grey man came through as we were pulling ourselves through the window. Gian had just shoved me up, I was too heavy to help myself much and he was dragged under. It had climbed up the side of the tower behind him. I could see it. It coated him and walked away under the water, gold sparks showing under his skin… I couldn't save him." Tears ran down her cheeks again. "Then the tides came over the top of the tower I was on. I'd jumped in time, not space."

"Why didn't you jump again?"

"I was frightened." The snarl made him start. "I ended up trying to swim, hoping I'd get to dry land. I got swept out, the tides are strong here. I was lucky, a fisherman saw me as I went past the seaweed pontoons." Her voice was bitter.

"There's nothing past them but sea." Talia sounded awed.

"As I said, I was lucky. I'll have her now." She bent to pick her child up from Daniel's side and put her on the rugs in the corner and curled up, the conversation over.

Chapter 24

Daniel woke to the child Talia flicking water into his face. She giggled silently and put a finger to her lips. He leaned on an elbow and smiled as she drank the rest of the water from the cup and hopped onto the window ledge. She clipped herself onto the rope and disappeared with a wave.

"I'll need to get you to shore. I'm working on the pontoons today, it's a very low tide due to the moon and they'll need more people to clear things up out there." Daniel swung his head to see Bronin stretching. "She's gone?" She carried on at Daniel's nod, "She'll be fine, I keep that rope there so she doesn't need me to get in or out."

Daniel walked over to see the shore, a thick band of mud showed and very little water. "I can see the bottom. Doesn't it affect your safety in the tower?"

"No, it's still far enough out that they can't get through."

"Thank you for telling us some of your past." He saw a movement as Talia stood, Daniel guessed she'd been awake from the moment the child had moved.

"I miss the old days. Everyone had their place, it all worked. There was a man sorting things out for everyone here. He disappeared recently." Bronin snorted her opinion of this. "They're closing everything down and systems are breaking apart, people are trusting less than they used to."

Daniel raised his eyebrows and this was from a woman who didn't appear to trust anyone. "Can we talk more tonight?"

"Wait on the shore, I'll pick you up later." She took them back one by one and they watched the slender figure paddle back to the tower and climb up the wall.

"How do you feel?" Daniel asked.

Talia shrugged, "It's like I'm seeing things for the first time, but I'm remembering them as well. It's weird."

"How are we going to persuade your mother not to jump?"

"Dunno. The question is why did she jump in the first place? They're safe where they are."

Daniel felt curiously flat. They'd made contact with Bronin and yet they'd not really made progress in working out how to save her. How could they stop events that had already happened? Bronin's future – their past. They turned to walk up the hill and were stopped by a shriek floating across the water from the tower. Another scream and they stood rooted to the spot as they saw Bronin appear at the window, something in her arms. A string of swear words in their direction when she spotted them on the shore.

"What's happening?" Daniel swung his head wildly. The rope he'd seen Talia whizz across was far too slender for him but his Talia might make it…

"Mamin!" Talia's cry was anguished.

Daniel finally made sense of the load in Bronin's arms and saw the child's legs dangling as Bronin paused and threw herself out. His mind worked frantically, "She's holding you… but how?" They'd both seen Talia leave this morning.

Bronin tumbled towards the too shallow water and he felt his stomach lurch with her fall. A hand flicked out at the last moment and a rip appeared. Both woman and child disappeared into nothing. They were left gaping at the empty patch of water.

"Why?" Talia's voice was tiny.

In answer to her question, another figure appeared in the window. Daniel couldn't see properly at this distance but could imagine the nightmare face with bulging eyes. It stepped from the window and plummeted downwards. It landed in the shoulder deep water and stayed, raising its arms above its head.

"They've got into the tower, how did they do that? She said there weren't any holes."

"Shouldn't it be melting in the water?" Her hands were over her mouth.

"The Grey Lord's strong here, they don't..." Daniel's words dried up as another grey man appeared and stepped out of the window to land on the first. A slight crumpling of the figure in the water and they saw the rift opening again.

"It's gone to get Mamin… she's going to die."

"We could try..."

"We can't." Talia rounded on him, tears streaming down her face. "We tried, remember? It didn't work." Helpless, they watched open mouthed and within a few minutes, all that was left was a grey lump slowly dissolving.

"That's it. There's no one left here."

An emptiness filled him, they'd failed. Bronin would die and Talia would be raised by Dodie. Anger rose at the thought of those bright eyes wiped into blankness. He reached to touch Talia and she broke away, running hard from the shore and into the city. Daniel swore and ran after her, trying to keep her figure in sight and finding it harder with his larger size to dodge through the groups of people.

He stopped at an intersection having lost her and had the vague feeling of recognising the place. Daniel caught a someone's sympathetic eye and gave them a brief description. They waved him towards a small alleyway, the contrasting brickwork showing in bright patterns. He found Talia in front of a door, leaning against the wall and coughing. This time when he wrapped his arms around her, she leant against him.

"I'm sorry." He rested his head on top of hers until she pulled herself out of his arms.

"This was my home." Daniel looked around, not understanding until she pointed at the sturdy looking door, "My cellar." She linked her fingers into his and walked them away.

Daniel let her walk without speaking, allowing his own thoughts to run through his mind, no coherence to them. They couldn't beat the Grey Lord here. Estrella had been right, he was too strong, they'd been idiots to try. The viaduct marched overhead, deepening the shadows they walked through. They needed to go back to safety, there wasn't anything left for them here. Such a difference in the city, Bronin had jumped a long way forwards. Narith must have been a fabulous place in Bronin's original time. He imagined traders, miners, and smiths all rubbing shoulders in the wide streets. It was still magnificent, any damage from the flood waters was minimal in this part.

They came to a meeting place where two streets joined. The viaduct had pipes running down to provide water in barrels and people stopped to talk while filling containers.

Talia stopped dead. "Look." Daniel couldn't work out what she'd seen. "She's there. How?"

Daniel finally saw the small figure – it was Talia. The child caught his eye and waved. Horror struck him. "Your mother's not here. She doesn't know." Talia was looking glazed. He felt the same, time travel was beginning to do his head in. "We need to look after her." Daniel watched Talia skip towards them without a care in the world.

A distinct pop sounded in his ears and he froze. Talia hissed a swear word and tightened her grip on his hand. The people around began to move slower, anxiety clouding their faces. Where was it coming through? Bronin had said they'd fixated themselves on her and Talia. The child slowed, twisting her head. Daniel could see her trying to work out where the noise had come from. She still showed no fear, just curiosity.

The people shifted and Daniel saw it behind the child, several lengths away and the lethargy hit. She finally realised her danger and screamed, pinned into place by the nightmare coming towards her. His own Talia froze at the noise. He twisted her hand out of his grip, wrenching it painfully when she refused to let go. Daniel could barely move, he had to pull the child out of the way. The monster was close, so close. He threw himself across the ground, grunting at the ground bruising his shoulder and rolled, aware that if he'd got this wrong, then he would be the next pile of dust.

It reached down to grasp her shoulder and he hit her behind the back of the knees, making her fall out of reach and cradled her as they rolled. A muffled squeal burst from her at the impact. He was aware of his Talia moving back the way they'd come and he scrambled to his feet, pulling the child upright with him. So tired, he dragged himself back, swinging away from the grey man's swipes in a macabre game of blind man's buff.

"This way!"

A glance out of the corner of his eye showed Talia next to one of the barrels, rocking it back and forth, the water hitting the sides until it was ready to tip. They passed close to Talia and she shoved it over in the direction of the grey man. The heavy barrel struck the grey man making it stagger, then water slopped over in a wave and it paused, the fine details on it blurring. The lethargy lifted and taking the opportunity to get further away, Daniel scooped the child up and they ran.

Downhill, through a side street, Daniel followed Talia, cradling the child in his arms. Fear had dropped from her the minute they'd got out of range. She wrapped her arms around him, pulling herself up to peer over his shoulder. He hoicked her into an easier position and kept going.

She called, "There's another one coming!" A popping sound and yet another grey leg appeared out of a trackway, the body sliding out to stand in front. It stood, casting its bulging eyes around and fixed on them. Talia swore and swung in another direction. Trusting that Talia still knew her way around, he ignored everything but running.

Another pop to the side and she shifted them again. Talia's lungs gurgled and she spat on the ground. "We can't out run them."

"You mean we're being herded." The child in his arms was light but awkward and these grey men weren't slow. His mind raced through options, Bronin was no longer here, they'd have to take her with them. Where could they go with her? A mad thought that he could take her home, take care of her…

She twisted to touch his face, "I can get away, it's easy." He hushed her. Another pop and Daniel groaned, they couldn't run fast enough. Talia wriggled hard enough to slide out of his arms. He grasped for her and failed as she danced out of reach.

"We've not got time to play games," he snarled. He couldn't let her go, she had no one here.

"I'll see you in your place!" She spread her hands with a smile, pulled open a rift and was gone. Daniel stood in shock, utterly speechless.

"Come on." Daniel felt his muscles slow as the grey men rounded the corner. Nearly throwing up, he let Talia drag him away. Stumbling they ran faster without her in his arms. Pops began to happen all around them, grey men appearing to the left and right.

"Fuck. We're going to have to jump as well."

"Where?"

"Anywhere! Away from here."

Talia ripped open the void and Daniel grabbed for her, hearing the next pop happen close by. He shoved her through, desperate in the hope nothing would touch him.

Chapter 25

They came back to Narith in the future, which time Daniel didn't know or care. "We need to keep moving… something will come through…" But at least it's only the one something, he thought. The Grey Lord wasn't strong enough here.

"Mamin." Talia pulled in the other direction and stopped as the rift began to open again.

Daniel felt the cold run down his spine at the nightmare returning. "What do you mean? We've left her time."

"This is the time she came through to, where she died. I was thinking of her, I wanted to help..." Talia moaned, caught between her terror of the grey men and the fear for her mother. Daniel swore and pulled her backwards as the foot appeared and hit the ground. Two hands held the break apart and a body began to appear.

"We need to go."

The void snapped shut and the grey man stood, head swinging, searching and stopped, facing in their direction. They stumbled backwards, towards the mouth of the alleyway. The figure in the shadows seemed hesitant, it took a step and stopped again, turning in the other direction.

"Why is it doing that? It should be following you, we're not that far away."

"Mamin. She's in that direction." Talia's voice was anguished.

Realisation hit Daniel. "We're there too. It knows there are three people in that direction who can jump." They watched as it made up what little mind it had and turned away from them. He squeezed his eyes shut. "They won't be expecting another one. We need to distract it." Talia's eyes were huge and she whimpered and then stumbled into the alley towards it.

Daniel smothered a swear word as it turned to face them. They backed slowly away and it followed. Its steps were slow and deliberate, it wasn't moving as fast as it had in its own time. Still, the lethargy held its own terrors, the slow walk, trying not to get too far in front.

"The sea, Mamin said the mud holds them until the water can deal with them."

Daniel nodded, trying to keep an eye on both directions at once. Neither of them wanted to trip, despite the slow pace. Arms linked around each other's waists, they walked downhill towards the bay. After a while the grey man appeared not to be seeking anyone else and became more decisive in its stride. They backed into a larger thoroughfare and people scattered in slow motion, panic in their faces. Daniel and Talia kept walking, the sweat pouring off them in the chilly air.

A shout of rage startled Daniel as Talia gasped next to him. They'd backed into a man so transfixed by the sight of the approaching grey figure he'd not seen them. He'd grabbed hold of Talia, fear twisting his face and yelled unintelligibly as Daniel struggled to free her. He had hold of her knife hand, Daniel could see her scrabbling to reach her knife with the wrong hand. Terrified, Daniel punched him hard and swung him around so the man was between them and the figure striding towards them. He had to keep the grey man away from Talia, he couldn't stop it. Time slowed, each foot taking an age to hit the floor while he tried to free her. The skin of her wrist was pinched white between the man's fingers and he didn't seem to notice the punches Daniel frantically landed.

The grey man loomed in their vision, its hand rose to take his shoulder. Talia twisted and her captor finally let go with a gurgle. Daniel dragged them both backwards, fighting the impulse to stay rooted to the spot. The man's face etched itself in his mind, his mouth opening, pleading as he sank to his knees, the other grey hand reaching out for his shoulder.

Inch by inch they crept away, the man's face turning paper-like, the life sucked out. Dark red coated the front of his shirt in contrast to the drab clothes and the figure behind. It turned from crimson to brown. Daniel didn't understand until he glanced down and saw the knife held awkwardly in Talia's left hand.

She saw his look, "I had to…"

Choices – the man's life or Talia's. His stomach turned, if he'd had the knife he would have used it too. "Come on. Let's keep moving, slowly." The lethargy weakened as they moved further away. The figure straightened and turned back to them.

"It'll be faster, it knows we're here," Talia warned them both. They were coming down to the main street that ran along the water front. Daniel had a momentary worry of the tide being out, of a nightmare scramble over broken buildings covered by seaweed and sliding while the danger strode ever closer. One glance stopped his worries, the water lapped high, grey as the figure behind on the dull day.

"Can you swim?" he asked Talia.

She gave him a disgusted look, "Course I can. Mamin taught me before I could walk." The street cleared in the same unhurried fashion, people drifting to each side, stalls and transactions abandoned in mid-sentence.

No barrier between the street and water. Daniel gave an inward sigh of relief at the lack of health and safety, common sense was clearly expected to be enough, and jumped in feet first. Thoughts of raw sewage crossed his mind in the split second before he hit the water and he shut his eyes tight and grabbed for his nose. Beside him, Talia dove smoothly in.

The warmth of the water nearly made him gasp in shock. He surfaced and swam away from the docks, waiting for the figure to appear. The stride remained unaltered, a foot suspended in the air and then it plunged forwards, disappearing into the deep. A hotter stream of water engulfed them and pushed them further on, across the bay. A fine layer of grey dust spread towards them and not wanting to be near it, both he and Talia swam strongly away.

"Is that far enough?"

She managed to shrug as she trod water, drifting slowly. "Let's try landing further up." This current was harder to swim across, it wanted to push them towards the end of the bay and out to the open sea. "It's taking us towards the fish traps." Talia pointed at the curved structures and she cut across towards them.

"We saw these being built." Daniel couldn't stop himself from commenting. So many years ago, they looked nothing like buildings now, they were just a natural feature of the harbour. Nets were hung on the sides, waiting to be thrown when the tide had gone out. Daniel swung his head around as they were swept into it, high walls, slick with slime confronted them. Talia swam to the middle of the wall and found a series of grooves, the surface covered in barnacles. The chill air hit and steam poured off them as they pulled themselves up.

They scrambled over the stones to where the shore started. Daniel began to shiver, the air was far colder than the sea. Talia led him to a building with an awning over the windows and haggled with the person inside. He hopped from foot to foot, still dripping. A large blanket was thrown at him and he was nodded inside to see the brazier heating the room. The owner left them to dry off.

"So, do you think you'll be okay?" He qualified himself, "I don't remember seeing you as a child, do you get to me in my time?"

"Yes. I'd been jumping to get out of trouble a lot. They'd marked me last time, nearly got me. I remember seeing you now, you were standing in your garden." Her voice turned thoughtful, "I don't think the grey men can go through time on their own, it must take too much energy. They must need someone to open the rift for that, otherwise what would stop them from coming through at any point?"

"So you've let one of those things into my world?"

"You'll deal with it."

Her arrogance left him gaping. He pushed for more detail, anyone could get hurt by one of those things. "You remember me dealing with it?"

She shook her head, "My mind's blank after seeing you."

"How come they can come through without anyone opening up the trackways in your mother's time?"

"There are so many holes there, it's nothing like that in my time or even here." Her face was serious as she thought, "If it's stronger back then, it might be able to push them through."

He agreed, "I think it was dying when it got me. It hated me. I could feel its contempt all the way through my time with it but I was better than the alternative."

Talia nodded and then swore, "Mamin said they couldn't get through to the tower – no holes, I must have jumped back to her."

"But why and what was wrong with you when we saw you after she'd jumped?"

"I don't know." She squeezed her eyes shut, "All I remember is a noise and a smell."

"What sort of noise?"

She twisted, "Don't know." Daniel gave up as she moved towards the door. He'd stopped dripping by now although he was still damp. "Come on."

He shook his soggy jeans, "What?"

"We need to find Mamin. We might be able to help." Her face was tight. Daniel couldn't blame her for wanting to try, despite knowing it wouldn't help.

They ran through the streets, Talia pointing the way and stopping to catch her breath to cough. As they got closer to the underground room, Daniel felt something waking inside, a stain beginning to spread. He slowed in horror, he thought he'd got rid of it. He remembered the tendril brushing at the contact with himself in the cellar and the shove as his other self had gone through the rift. Somehow it had left a part of itself inside him and been waiting for the right moment to wake.

Talia tugged at his hand, not understanding. The opening to the cellar hadn't changed, a little less rubble in front, the doorway partially closed by a rotting door. Talia kicked the remains down and Daniel recognised the now tattered entrance from their first visit. They both hesitated at the thought of going down there without a light. They stopped in the entrance to let their eyes adjust.

The stain plucked at Daniel, calling to a part deep within him. "Talia, I don't think..."

She ignored him, sliding her hand in his to pull him down the rubble. He knew it was in there, in the second room, waiting for him. He pulled away, not wanting to go closer and turned to see a figure blocking the light through the door. Small, grey with the golden light appearing from cracks in its skin to shine onto the walls of the cellar. They were too late. Bronin's corpse walked steadily through, ignoring them.

"Mamin..." The cry came from deep within Talia. Daniel followed the figure as though attached by a string. He swayed like he was in a dream. The stain spread and darkened, it was inevitable he thought, to be consumed again. Years of hatred, years of waiting, a never ending madness. Doomed to repeat the circle.

The emaciated being in the room raised its arms in a parody of a child wanting to be picked up. Bronin knelt before it as Daniel held onto Talia's other arm. He was no longer sure if it was to stop her from rushing forwards or to stop himself from doing the same as her mother. He could feel the ecstasy of feeding and wanted to go to it. The sane part of him shrieked soundlessly and he forced the words out. "Talia, she's dead. We need to go… I can't stay… it's going to want me too…"

Talia reacted as though he'd slapped her. White faced and with eyes blazing, her hand snapped out and hit him across the face. It didn't help. He reeled backwards, hands over his face, dizzy from the emotions pouring through him. A hand grabbed his arm and shoved him towards the door. The pull grew stronger, it had nearly finished. Daniel held his head, helpless, he'd be finished if he stayed here. He took a step towards it and folded over as a hard fist slammed into his stomach. Unable to stop Talia, he let her pull him out, dry retching from the punch and the greasy feel in his mind.

Outside in the cold air and the daylight, his mind cleared a bit. Talia shoved him against the wall and peered closely. The dunking had done nothing to improve her looks.

"You'd better be worth this. You still there? You ain't going nowhere nob." She grabbed his hair and pulled until tears came into his eyes.

"I'm here." A movement caught his eye and he groaned again. "Talia, I'm here. You need to get me away."

"Come on." She moved to take his arm.

"No. I'm here, over there I mean."

Talia turned and saw the figure walking down the street, hood over his head and a blanket over his shoulders. Daniel watched himself as though in a dream. A strange sight, nobody expects to see a complete copy of themselves walking around.

She ordered, "Grab him."

"I can't." A glower from her and he explained, "That last rift you opened, he'll go back to your mother's time."

Understanding bloomed. Daniel looked at his own face and saw nothing he recognised in it. He recalled the nightmare of not remembering anything and felt dis-orientated. The pull came from both directions now. One from the being in the cellar, another, equally strong coming from the person in front of him. He wanted to embrace himself, to take away the pain and recognised the stain running through his previous self.

Daniel forced the words out, "Don't let him touch me..." He reached out to himself, in the same way the grey men did. Fear chilled him more than the air.

"Take hold of me then." She stretched out and grabbed the arm offered in front of her, swung the unresisting figure away and tore open the rift with ease. The mental howl from the cellar stunned him and Daniel saw his other self stagger. Joy coursed through him, it didn't have the strength to stop them getting away! Talia elbowed the rift open and dragged them all through.

Chapter 26

Talia twisted through the void, trying to find the correct route. None of the trackways before were quite right. She felt her way through carefully, it had to be the right time, they had to put Daniel back where he belonged. Her arms ached from keeping hold of the dead weight of one of the Daniels, the other held tight around her waist and pushed with her. Finally they were expelled to fall into the leaves.

The warm air of late spring hit Talia. The soft green of the leaves and the tall straight trunks of the woods. Birdsong and fresh green smells all around. She let go of the dead weight and flopped. Safe.

"We're home again. Who stays?" Daniel was sprawled on the leaves, feeling gingerly at his eye.

Talia jerked her head. "He does. I've got us back so you'll be in the right place for me to find you." The other Daniel sat, staring into space. "I'll get him back to your home while you recover. You'll need to find water in case anything comes through."

"There's some further along. I'll hide close by. Shout for me, but not too loud. You know they'll be looking for him. Can you find your way down?"

Talia nodded and pulled the other Daniel up. Different clothes and dirt were all that separated them. She looked closer, this Daniel was away with the fairies. The other looked fine, apart from the bruise forming around his eye. She squashed the guilty feeling, not her fault.

Daniel smiled and rubbed it, "Guess I asked for it, right?"

She snorted, "Nob." He got up as they started walking down the path and slowly began to make his way down the hill in a different direction. Talia fixed her own destination in mind and hurried her vacant charge along.

Several times she shoved him into the bushes on the side of the path as people climbed the hill. He was no longer as clean as he had been and people would notice in this world. She looked at herself, she wasn't exactly going to fit in either. She needed to get him back so they could look after him, make him better. She needed him to be better for later on. She shook her head, she had needed him… her past, his future.

Talia peered out and pulled Daniel along. She'd never seen this many people around here before. They were all paying attention to their surroundings too, sweeping the landscape. That wasn't right, most people, even in her own world only walked like that if they had a reason to. She looked at the papers nailed to the trees at intervals down the path. Daniel's picture was on all of them and she remembered he'd said they'd be looking for him.

She touched one, unable to read the writing, "See nob, that's you." This Daniel stared into space, lost in his own brain. There was another picture, smaller and closer to the bottom of the poster, looking as though it had been made up of sections. It took a few seconds to realise that it was meant to be herself. She swore and moved them along faster, she didn't want to be identified here.

Getting past the nosy old woman's cottage was hard. Daniel didn't bend easily and she didn't want to spend time creeping past with the amount of people around. She worried about grey men coming through, and if the other Daniel had been caught. Finally they got to the hole in the hedge. Coaxing Daniel over the fence was the last straw for Talia. She shoved him over and he fell with a thump into the scratchy plants below and lay there. She swore and was going to climb after him when she heard a thundering of paws in the grass and a deep woof. The dog, Biggles. She dropped off the fence and ran as the woof turned into a yodelling howl at a stranger.

She nearly cannoned into two people, they started at the sound of Biggles and shouted as she ran past the fussy garden. A loud conversation behind and another shout. She didn't stop her headlong race into the trees, Talia could feel her lungs wheezing going up the hill, she had to slow down. A glance back showed her that one of the couple, the man, had turned to follow her.

Almost blind with panic, she dove off the path and into the bushes. She skidded along the steep slope in the hope she'd lose him. Talia mentally reckoned Daniel's direction – uphill and to the side. Her lungs lost the battle for air. She stopped and spat out phlegm, gasping in between coughs. A crashing from a heavier body and she froze, trying to stifle the coughs and felt her face go red with the effort.

Her clothes blended in, even her blue trousers were grey and dusty from her world. All she had to do was stay quiet. Another wheeze threatened. She shut her eyes tight as the man above her shouted threats about calling authorities. He moved away, still shouting and Talia crept in the other direction. A thin wail came from down below in the valley. Peering through the trees, she could see a white vehicle with flashing lights appear in the lane. Hidden from view, she watched as tiny figures brought out a smaller four legged shape. Dogs! No way was she staying here, she had to get to her Daniel. She trotted up to the path and hoped she wouldn't bump back into the man. Reaching the spot where they come through, she worked her way downhill again.

Another shout, Daniel's voice this time. She broke into a run, ignoring her lungs aching and burst into a small clearing by another path. Grey mud spilled half in the stream and half out. Daniel was leaning against a tree further down, being harangued by a small, older woman with fussy grey hair. He was protesting, trying to stop her from moving him. Her voice became shriller when she turned to see Talia.

"You!" She shook Daniel's arm, "I saw her with you weeks ago. She's not from round here. One of those nasty travellers or whatever they call themselves nowadays. Leaving rubbish and the like everywhere they go, I saw that mess on the footpath..." The diatribe escalated as Mrs Pickles warmed to her subject. Daniel appeared mesmerised, unable to pull himself loose from the pinching arm. Talia watched with her mouth open, unable to understand how someone so small and with such little power could hold a grown man in one place.

A shout from further up the path, a figure flickered between the trees. She panicked – it was the man who'd been chasing her. Talia threw herself at the older woman to separate them and dragged Daniel behind her into the woods below. He tripped and nearly fell over his feet, barrelling into her. Mrs Pickles shrieked her outrage, making Talia flinch. The man seeing Talia's attack, bellowed and broke into a run.

They skidded down the hill and slid down a steep bank, barely missing an old fence.

"The quarry, it's below us. This way." Daniel had gathered his wits. Shouts came from the side and a dog barked. Flashes of dark clothing through the leaves. "Shit, it's the police. Come on."

Daniel was the one dragging her now, following the fence. She didn't know what this police was but a dog chasing with people following was never good. Trying not to lose their footing on the dry slope, they left a trail through the brown leaves. A gap appeared and they lurched away from the empty space of the quarry beyond the rotten woodwork. Wails from the old woman increased in volume as she realised that the man was ignoring her to chase after them.

Daniel muttered, "I'm not going to be able to show my face around here again."

"What?"

"Nothing. Careful here." He shoved a branch aside and began clambering down the rock face into the old quarry itself. Talia remembered the rocks soaking up the sun in the hot afternoon. No time to relax now. Not a difficult climb, she swiftly clambered past Daniel, her nimbleness making up for a lack of reach.

Dirt splattered down and Talia squinted upwards to see the man arrive at the top of the rocks. The swearing indicated he hadn't expected the drop. She grinned and carried on, close to the bottom. The bellowing from above made her jump.

"Shit, he's calling to the police."

Level ground at last, large blocks of stone littered the floor from when the quarry had last been used. The shouting continued, the man giving unseen people directions. The dog's barking came closer. Talia could feel her lungs gurgling as she drew breath and she tried to stop to clear her lungs.

Daniel nearly picked her up in order to keep them going. "No time for that, you need to take us through."

Blue clad figures burst through the trees fringing the stones, voices shouting out to give themselves up. A large dog on a lead, straining to get to them and a figure knelt to let it go.

Daniel ducked his head, trying not to show his face. "Inside."

One last sprint and they were in the cave. Talia ripped open the void, a smear in the darkness and heard the patter of clawed paws hitting the quarry floor. No hesitation from either of them as they pushed their way through and the seam slammed shut behind them.

Chapter 27

Talia pushed through the easiest way, no longer caring where they ended up, she only wanted to get home. Barrelling through, they barely missed braining themselves on the brick wall opposite to where they'd come out. They lent against the wall, panting and catching their breath.

"Fuck. When was the last time we just walked through a rift?"

Talia wheezed through her cough, "Nob."

"She's going to tell the police everything you know." Daniel grinned at Talia's puzzled look. "The men in blue uniforms. They're the authority in my world. I remember when I came round in hospital, they questioned me for ages." He chuckled, "Couldn't remember a bloody thing of course." He looked around, "Where are we, back in your proper time?"

"Yes." She didn't know how, the place just fitted even without looking. Evidence of the riots were shown in the fresh debris on the streets. Cobbles had been levered up, ready for use as missiles and yet more puddles and mud would appear when it next rained.

"Which one though? Is the Dust Lord still here? We did change time didn't we, by taking me back instead of letting it have me. Are we safe?"

Talia thought hard, trying to work her head around the jumping through time and space. "I don't know. Remember, I picked you up from your time later on. So did that happen before or not?" Thinking like this wasn't her forte, her head began to hurt.

Daniel rubbed his own in sympathy, "Should we check?" Talia hesitated and nodded, they both needed to know this world was safe. She took his hand and led the way through the quiet streets, stopping off on the way to pick up a bag of bits from her cellar. Daniel watched the mist swirling through the grey and black alleyways, a sense of loss filling him.

They both paused at the tumbledown entrance. A tiny plucking came at the edges of Daniel's perception, like a baby bird pecking, feeble and wanting feeding. Daniel shivered. "It's in there, I can feel it."

"Will it be you or the other thing?"

"How do I know? Does it matter?" He felt something slide into view, the stain was still there, waiting.

"If it's the other thing then you can't stop any grey men it raises."

"There's only one way to find out." They stared at each other, each daring the other one to make the first move. "Come on," Daniel spoke first. He could feel the stain gathering like a drip, waiting to fall into the waters of his soul, dispersing its many fingers to grasp his essence.

Talia nodded and rummaged through her bag to find a candle and lit it. Shielding it from the soft breeze, they ducked inside. Nothing in the first cellar, the old body still lying on the floor, half collapsed. A rustling came from the dark of the next room. He saw Talia squeeze her eyes shut, then she opened them again and marched herself to the doorway.

Daniel followed, peering over her shoulder. The stain spread, diffusing. It wasn't as strong, but the need was there to give himself up, he twisted his shoulders. The candle didn't give out a lot of light, despite their eyes having adjusted it was difficult to see. Daniel found himself quartering the room, looking for the source of the noise and the plucking in his mind.

A soft gasp from Talia, "There."

In the middle of the second cellar, it squatted. A pile of tumbledown bones, fingers scratching at the floor, dust swirling impotently. The reality matched his perception of a baby bird. It was helpless. The chill running down Daniel's spine stopped. Despite the stain inside, it wasn't strong enough to make him give himself up.

"It's dying." At his statement even its rage was febrile. The fingers stopped moving and it collapsed further inside itself.

"Is it dead?" Talia moved forwards and Daniel caught her hand.

"Not quite."

A spasm, the arms raised and Daniel could feel the last herculean effort as the dust built in front of them. The fight to survive even in the state it was in, struggling for every breath, for every second and hating the life that stood in front of it. Talia pulled away and casually walked to the end of the room, the shadows made by the candle looming large over the walls. Daniel watched the dust form, every ounce of energy poured into making something to capture more energy to keep it going. The stain stopped diffusing and darkened, the call becoming more urgent.

The form built until it was waist high. A pause, Daniel dragged his eyes away to see Talia knelt on the other side of the room, her head cocked, watching.

The start of the familiar lethargy began to drag at him and he felt himself take a step forwards, "Talia, we need to go." He concentrated, he had to resist this, had to stay away and give it chance to die. Despair filled him, even with it this weak, he still couldn't defeat it.

A chuckle startled him. "Nah," she said and a wave of the remaining water from the tilted bucket soaked the half built grey man, washing it across the cellar floor.

The backlash of energy caught Daniel by surprise and he was pushed hard against the wall. As he blacked out, he felt rather than heard the curdling death shriek and the stain inside burnt to ashes.

He came to with Talia's face in the light of the candle peering down at him. "You okay nob?" He nodded, not quite trusting himself to answer. "It's gone. Fell to dust after I soaked its toy."

Daniel jacked himself up on his elbows to peer at the pile on the floor. "It's gone, really gone this time." He smiled at her shadowed face in the candlelight. "Can you still jump?"

"I could last time, want to make sure?"

"Be nice to jump without something running after us." He rubbed his face, "Let's go past the wall, see what's happening there? We could find Bay. Maybe we can persuade him help the factory workers he got through the wall."

Talia snorted, "Doubt it."

They jumped into a room full of people. All eyes were on them as they emerged, weapons gripped in white knuckled hands and Daniel remembered that people had only seen the grey men coming through rifts before. A sense of angry arguments hung in the air and he looked around, trying to work out what was happening.

"Bay, what are you up to now?"

Daniel peered over Talia's shoulder, Bay was hunched in the corner. She swaggered over, lording it for all she was worth. The crowd parted for her, murmuring.

One was brave enough to shout, "He led us here. There's nothing for us. He promised us a better life, gold and riches." The speaker was aggressive and Bay shrank back.

Daniel recognised the man as one of his former room mates. "Garren, you could have a better life but it's not Bay's to give to you. Gold and riches? I can't promise you that either but you'd have to work for it."

"Who are you?" Another man, not one Daniel recognised.

"He's the Dust Lord." Bay announced with a smug expression on his face, trying to get any advantage he could.

"He's from Igren's mill. Name's Daniel. Decent lad." Garren vouched for him.

"Yes, I did work at the mill, with Garren, and Vihaan." A murmur. Vihaan was dead and Daniel saw the flicker in people's eyes as they now recognised him. "I was also the Dust Lord for a time. Not anymore. Talia vanquished him." All eyes turned to Talia. Her face was a picture as she tried to work out if he'd complimented her.

He continued, "Look, you can't keep doing this. You can't keep killing everyone who gets in your way. You need to learn how to work this land, same as you did the mills." Grumbling came from the crowd and Daniel raised his voice to speak over it. "Yes work but this time for yourselves, not for the mill owners or the nobs. If there are any farmers left, free them. Get them to teach you, because now," he lowered his voice and they strained to hear. "Now you have completely broken the system you need to rebuild it again, otherwise you will be the walking dead." He paused having deliberately used that term.

Talia jumped in. "I was from Dodie's clique. She picked me up and looked after me when I needed her and not just me either, lots of us. Nothing in it for her to begin with. I was a burden until I was old enough to help. I'm willing to learn this." She peered around the room and saw a familiar skinny figure. "Radnor, you'll help won't you? You can read the books and give us the knowledge."

Radnor shrank back at all the eyes on him. Ignoring his silence Talia carried on, not allowing any of the workers to shout her down. "We can do this for ourselves, all of us. None of us need to make ourselves slaves for anyone." She rounded on someone grumbling and snapped back, "You've seen the nobs here, they've got sunshine and freedom. I want that too." A murmur of agreement and her face turned sly, "There aren't many of them left though. Let's help them with their work in the sunshine, have what they have and work together."

The atmosphere in the room slowly changed, Talia was giving them new ideas and Daniel got the impression the tide was turning. The workers were fed up of fighting, they were used to a life of hard work and being told what to do. Some would make the leap and start new lives, others would go back to the jobs they knew. Either way, they had a chance to make this work.

Bay had also sensed the change, "My father's friends will want revenge. They won't let you stay here."

"More of a case to make the co-operation work then. We still need the factories and the sea. Others will join from further away if they see this working," Daniel argued back. "You said yourself there weren't enough people to defend the wall. Let's break it down. The Dust Lord has gone, there's no need for it." He gazed across at Radnor and raised his eyebrows. The scribe fiddled his fingers together and finally squeaked out his agreement to help.

"One man." Talia crowed, "Who else is for helping. I need men and women both here and in the city. Your children can choose where they want to work. No more brands. No more forced labour in the factories. Farms, mills or the sea. You choose and work for yourself or others."

Daniel smiled to himself, she wasn't above using his words. He quietly stood and watched Talia. She glowed, more like the bright little girl who'd caught hearts in her childhood than the sullen teenager he'd known when he'd first come here. The factory workers were charmed, plans were shouted out and ideas suggested. Talia countered them all, deferring to Radnor's whispered suggestions. She reached out to

Bay who'd shrunk into sullen silence, asking him questions that appealed to his knowledge.

Daniel slid out and left them to it. The people in the room let him go without comment, wrapped up in planning their future. He followed the track up to a lookout point high up over the city. Not realising it was the one where Talia had met Kenderick, he sat under the trees and stared out over the mist. Maybe they did finally have a chance here. A new system might work. It would be hard but worth it.

He chuckled, remembering his thought about heroes from long ago. He'd changed a world, vanquished an ancient evil and time travelled. What was he going to do next? Go back to paperwork? The office? His gaze transferred itself to his feet and he gradually fell asleep in the sunshine.

"Hey, nob!" A poking finger woke him and he wriggled away. The sun was beginning to set, turning the mists into an orange sea with the black islands of buildings sticking up. "I'm busy sorting the world out and you're here sleeping." She was laughing at him.

Daniel stretched, "How's it going?"

"Lots of people are joining. I'm going to be the leader of the biggest clique in the city." She waved her hands, her eyes enormous at the power she held.

"You'll have to look after them and make it work," Daniel warned. "Watch out for Bay too. He'll turn on you if you don't keep him on a short leash."

"That's easy. I'll just go back and get a grey man every so often. That'll keep them in line."

"Talia!"

She laughed, Daniel had never seen her so happy. She sobered, "You can't stay, can you?"

"No, I want to go home. You can come and ask me things if you need to." He tried not to sound hopeful.

The sound of people talking excitedly spilled out into the evening air. Talia held out her hand, "Let's get you home then."

"What about them?" He nodded at the noise.

"I can come back any time, remember?"

The beech trees of home, gold and bronze in the autumn. Talia had brought him back to a grey day, threatening rain. She looked up, curious.

"I don't think I've ever seen your sky like this."

"Best get down the hill before it starts."

They walked down still holding hands. Sneaking under Mrs Pickles' hedge, they giggled about what they would say if she saw them. Daniel jumped over the fence and grabbed Biggles, delighted to feel his strong body shoving against him. Biggles investigated Talia who petted him gingerly. Daniel took a deep breath, breathing in the smell of the apples and sighed – home.

Talia's eyes grew wistful, "Can I wash?"

"Aren't you going to offer to cut something off?" Daniel teased her and quickly agreed as her expression grew black. "I'll sort some more clothes for you too." Talia came out, glowing at the new clothes and Daniel offered to finish cutting the hair hanging in front of her eyes.

When he stepped back, his own eyes widened, "Hang on, was it you I saw in the woods, the day before I came through? You were on your own, dressed as you are now. You were laughing at me."

She shook her head, "I don't remember that."

A smile lit his face, "Maybe you haven't done it yet. Nothing to follow you through this time."

An answering smile came from her, "Best fill that one in then, hadn't I?"

Chapter 28

I'm still coming to terms with the fact that I've died or one of me has. I don't know what to call what I've done, I killed myself that day in the cellar but it's not called suicide or murder. All the jumping through different times and not quite remembering makes my head ache. I got a refund on the counselling sessions, it's not the sort of thing you can talk about.

It's funny, after having been in hospital and on sick leave for so long, Clive took my place in the office. They were a little embarrassed when I found out. I didn't want my old job back anyway and asked to work in the morgue instead. Mr Davies was delighted when I asked to become an apprentice undertaker and despite Clive taking the piss, I fit in far better. It's less money but I no longer care. Unsurprisingly, dead bodies don't bother me anymore – I've seen far worse.

We'd had the usual Sunday meal with the family today. I'd spent most of the day on my shed floor with Dominic, building the most enormous layout for his trains. Sarah had been her usual self, full of mocking comments until I'd stopped her in mid sentence by sniffing my hands and mentioning the difficulties of getting the stink of embalming fluid off. In fact, the whole conversation had stopped and Mum had actually snapped at Sarah. The general consensus is that I'm not to be upset. Sarah had eyeballed me and then carried on her conversation as if she hadn't noticed. I'd found it funny, she doesn't realise she's got nothing on Talia.

My smile grew wider and faded. I wonder if Talia is happy. It's been a few days since she said goodbye. Her dancers are waiting for her. I've painted them in pretty colours, knowing she'll like it and mended a few rods that have nearly broken. I miss her already and hope she will pop up at some point. I've been looking up books to help her world, simple things like seed drills and harvesters, anything to help the mill workers survive. Knowing they won't be able to read the books, I've drawn pictures showing the mechanics – someone will be able to work them out. I sigh and carry on watering the flower beds on the driveway. The threatened rain never came, it's been warm and humid ever since.

The cat had taken one look at the hosepipe and disappeared. It'd been a small ball of malevolence in the last few days but had stayed away from me. Biggles was shut in the shed, whining at the unfairness of not being allowed to play in the water spray.

The sound of Mrs Pickles revving her engine in the driveway beyond nearly stops me hearing a familiar ripping. I blink and my heart starts to race. Was it Talia? Was she having problems? My mind begins working overtime at the thought of talking through all my ideas with her. I scan the garden, going on tiptoes to peer over the hedge to where the footpath was. The water from the hosepipe dribbles onto the ground, forgotten.

A small figure moves lightly along the road, her feet almost skipping. Her hair is translucent in the light, she's dressed in cut offs and a vest, showing her skinny arms and legs. An ethereal child. She dances over to the hedge on the other side of the road to look at the leaves, her hand reaching up to touch and she jumps back at the cows in the field.

I stand, mesmerised, until the sound of the car coming down the lane intrudes. Panic forces its way through – Mrs Pickles always takes that corner too fast. I drop the hosepipe and shout. "Talia!"

She turns to smile, "Daniel! I made it!"

A wave and she begins to run towards me, delight in her face. The car rounds the corner. The sun comes through the clouds and shines onto the windscreen. Terror seizes me. I run, cursing the hedge in my way, knowing I'm going to be too late. Talia hears the car and stops in the middle of the road, staring. Her face twists at the machine flying towards her. Mrs Pickles sees her at the last moment and slams the brakes on, no time to stop.

I swear I hear the bang as the car hits. Is she thrown into the air or did she jump away in time? I hear the cry for her mother, hear Mrs Pickles' wail through the closed window and my heart dies.

All I knew is that Talia wasn't there when the car came to a standstill in the hedge. The engine has stalled and I am left staring at Mrs Pickles in the quiet. I walk over and open the car door. She's clutching the steering wheel, her face grey in shock.

"Did you see the child?"

I take a deep breath, "No. The sun came out. You were blinded." Something twists inside me, Mrs Pickles was responsible for Talia being like she was. If Talia had been well, she wouldn't have jumped back to her mother. There wouldn't have been a trackway to the tower, they'd have been safe. I force the anger down, Mrs Pickles wasn't to know what she'd done.

"There was a child," she insists.

"You must have been seeing things. Look, there's no one else here."

I help her out and show her. She's trembling. I wrap an arm around her and give her a hug. She clings to me and I'm surprised to find she's the same size as Talia, bird boned under the thin cardigan and bluster. I guide her onto our drive and pat her arm, "I'll deal with your car."

I start the car and reverse it out of the hedge. The steering drags on one side. The wheel's burst from a pot hole. I wonder if that was the bang I'd heard. I park the car on the drive and absently turn the hosepipe onto full as I pass.

Mrs Pickles is still standing next to the hosepipe, staring into the hedge, the water pooling into the grass at her feet. I'm feeling light headed, unsure if Talia's survived. I remember Talia's scared face the first time I'd followed her and the look of her being out of place. I wouldn't know if everything had happened as it should until she came back to see me – if she ever came back. I turn Mrs Pickles around to take her into the house.

"Here, let's take you inside."

The thread of lethargy spreads through me and I know I'm too late. I turn slowly, the dread fixing me to the ground. A shape is beyond the hedge, not ten feet away. The sun is still shining, a light wind rustles the leaves but I know it's there. Sweat drenches me, part of the hedge is darkening. The grey man from Talia's first ever jump in time.

Grey mud appears around the leaves and twigs, it's coming straight through the hedge at us. Mrs Pickles whimpers and I absently rub her arm. It moves slowly, I can actually see the chest and legs forming themselves around the leaves and twigs. The dread stays – something not of this world. The sunlight seems to dim in its presence as the bulging eyes turn to us and I notice the cracks across its chest aren't filling in. Another step and it's clear of the hedge. I carefully bend down and pick up the hosepipe.

As though from a vast distance I heard Mum call from inside the house and know she won't see anything from here. The last gap on the grey man's shoulder made by a branch stays. It raises its hand and points to me. My eyes wander in their own dream, noticing tiny details, the smears on the leaves, a grey stain marking footprints as it staggers towards us.

A whisper from beside me, "What is it?"

I look down at Mrs Pickles and say dreamily, "It's a grey man but it's okay, it only followed the child you didn't hit." She gapes at me, white faced and with tears in her eyes.

Slowly I pull the weight of my hands up and press my thumb over the end. Water spurts and soaks us. Mrs Pickles squeals and recoils. Another lurch and it's less than five feet away. Could it actually do anything now? Could it drag the liquid from me while it killed me? I fumble at the pipe, despite my preternatural calm, I curse my clumsy fingers. My thumb finds the end again and this time it goes in the right direction.

It hits the grey man square in the chest and goes through it, a hole showing the hedge behind. Water darkens the rest and my brain clears instantly. A joyful madness fills me and I blast the rest of it into the ground leaving a grey stain spreading over the pool of water. I spray the garden, arcing the water high. Finally I drop the hose, remembering the old lady stood beside me. "There, all gone."

Mrs Pickles moves her mouth a few times without speaking and eventually manages, "What was that thing?

"That was the last facsimile of the Grey Lord. You don't need to worry, I helped kill him. Shall we get you back to the house and have a cup of tea?"

"I'll...I'll..." Her brain isn't working properly.

"Say you knocked over a child that's no longer there and were stalked by a being that was vanquished by a hosepipe?" I wait, a tiny sadistic part of me enjoying her shocked bewilderment. A kinder emotion intrudes and I rub her arm, "Let's get you back."

I take Mrs Pickles back to our house to be looked after by Mum. She has no objection to my story that she was blinded by the sun and drove into the hedge. The dust I deal with, it soaks into the soil with the water. Afterwards I lean against a tree in the orchard and absently fuss Biggles. I have to trust that Talia will be fine. One day, she will be back.

***

More frog than princess, Erme Lander lives in Gloucestershire with her two children and a mad cat.

Other books by Erme Lander

The Vampire Duology

A Dark Inheritance
A Dark Infection

The Medici Chronicles

The Lion of Ackbarr
Blood Lore
Medici of Ackbarr
Blood Debt
War Lord of Ackbarr

Stand-alone books and short stories

Lord of Dust
Death's Touch
Sasha
Willow

www.ermelander.co.uk

www.ingramcontent.com/pod-product-compliance
Lightning Source LLC
Chambersburg PA
CBHW071555030726
47593CB00001BA/176